THE EDGE OF BEING

Also by James Brandon

Ziggy, Stardust & Me

THE EDGE OF BEING

JAMES BRANDON

 Nancy Paulsen Books

NANCY PAULSEN BOOKS
An imprint of Penguin Random House LLC, New York

First published in the United States of America by Nancy Paulsen Books,
an imprint of Penguin Random House LLC, 2022

Visit us online at penguinrandomhouse.com

Library of Congress Cataloging-in-Publication Data
Names: Brandon, James (Young adult author), author.
Title: The edge of being / James Brandon.
Description: New York: Nancy Paulsen Books, 2022. | Summary: Seventeen-year-old
Isaac Griffin sets out to find the father he has never met, only to discover that perhaps
the missing pieces of his life were never missing at all. Includes author's note.
Identifiers: LCCN 2022020941 (print) | LCCN 2022020942 (ebook)
ISBN 9780525517672 (hardcover) | ISBN 9780525517689 (ebook)
Subjects: CYAC: Fathers—Fiction. | LGBTQ+ people—Fiction.
Cutting (Self-mutilation)—Fiction. | San Francisco (Calif.)—Fiction.
Los Angeles (Calif.)—Fiction. | LCGFT: Fiction. | Novels.
Classification: LCC PZ7.1.B751516 Ed 2022 (print)
LCC PZ7.1.B751516 (ebook) | DDC [Fic]—dc23
LC record available at https://lccn.loc.gov/2022020941
LC ebook record available at https://lccn.loc.gov/2022020942

Manufactured in Canada
ISBN 9780525517672
1 3 5 7 9 10 8 6 4 2

FRI

Edited by Stacey Barney
Design by Nicole Rheingans
Text set in Adobe Caslon Pro

to the ones who
forged their path in the stars,
so we can be here now,
thank you for shining the way.

✦

Time is
Too Slow for those who Wait,
Too Swift for those who Fear,
Too Long for those who Grieve,
Too Short for those who Rejoice;
But for those who Love,
Time is not.

—HENRY VAN DYKE

1

IF BROKEN HEARTS ARE MAPS TO THE SOUL, WHY DO I KEEP GETTING LOST?

The billboard whizzes past me. I crane my neck to make sure I've read it correctly, before winding around the curve, watching the sign slowly disappear in my rearview mirror, taunting me. Rose Tyler sits on my lap, perched on the window, her white fur blowing wildly in the wind. I stick my head out to join her. A gust rushes through, a cacophony of white noise, freeing my thoughts, freeing me. I get it now, why dogs do this.

"Time is a sickness." The voice echoes amid the stillness. I sit back in the car.

"I didn't know anyone else was here," I say. I see them, but not really. A form of something: flowing hair, billowing clothes. Glowing so bright, I'm nearly blinded. And their voice is melodic, otherworldly. Maybe they're my guardian angel. Or maybe . . .

"Dad? Is that you?"

"Pull over. I have something to tell you." So I do.

We're sitting in an orange tree orchard on the edge of a cliff, sweet white blossoms snowing down on us. Below, waves thunder against jagged rocks. The sun scorches the sky, melting away the world's colors.

"We are the mapmakers of our own destiny. It's time for us to go," they say.

"Where to?"

"Home."

I want to reach out. To feel their hand in mine. But I can't move.

They turn to face me. I squint trying to see . . . anything . . . like where I got the freckles on my nose, or why my eyes are an azure blue, or why my hair's a surfer blond—anything to see more of me—when they place their palm on my forehead and . . .

My eyes spring open.

That dream again. Sweat covers my face, the pillow. Breaths shudder through my chest, the sheets. I turn to see Rose Tyler lift her broken ear, before snuggling back in the nape of my neck. I click my phone on—1:37 a.m.—and lay it on my chest, watching it rise and fall as I try to steady my breaths. Darkness pervades the room, my being. I can't see the stars I painted on my ceiling, but I know they're there. So I trace them with my mind's eye, to help bring me back:

The Cepheus constellation has seven main stars: Alderamin is blazing blue, Alfirk is the second brightest, Errai the third, Delta Cephei is a yellow supergiant, and the Mu Cephei a deep garnet . . .

I'm back.

I close my eyes.

If broken hearts are maps to the soul, why do I keep getting lost?

I see that question everywhere in my dreams. Last time it was written in smoke clouds left behind from a crashing plane. Once, it was etched in the sand, and when I tried to brush the words away, or waves swept across the shore, they'd return as if nothing had touched them. I don't need to be Freud to know what it means. I only wish I could find the answer. But I've been searching for so long now, I'm beginning to wonder if I'll ever find it.

If broken hearts are maps to the soul . . .

There have been several rips in my heart over the years. Fissures that have mended over time. Like when I was five and watched my first dog, Two Spots, get run over by a car. I'll always hear my scream from that morning. Or a year later, when I told my mom I hated her for killing Dad (she didn't really); the crushed look on her face is permanently tattooed on my brain. Or when I called Lorelei Jenkins a four-eyed stupid head. I'm seventeen now and still feel guilt for being a playground bully.

But I slowly stitched those pieces back together.

Why do I keep getting lost?

Because one tear refuses to be healed, one I've tried over and over again to restore: Dad. Or the imaginative being I call Dad, since we've never met.

In kindergarten, Mrs. Holtmeyer asked us to draw a family tree. I drew mine with Mom and me dancing under a weeping willow. Some kid made fun of it because there wasn't a dad in the picture—which never even occurred to me until then—and I replied by punching him in the nose. That night, after a good scolding, Mom said my dad was Alex, Frozen Sperm Person #4781, an unknown donor, and she demonstrated how it all works with a sock puppet show.

My face flamed. Out of fear or rage, embarrassment or shame, I'm still not sure. All I wanted to do was become so small I could crawl inside that sock and live a puppet life forever. Because I felt like a horrible science experiment gone wrong, a half-person. I didn't want to believe her, told her I hated her for killing the one person I'd ever love. She was so angry, she said we were never to speak of it again. So we haven't. Until recently. (More on that soon.) But in that moment, the break happened. And it's been expanding ever since.

Now it's 1:48. Great, another long sleepless night.

I like this time actually. It's quiet here, still. Easier for me to escape to another tomorrow. One where I've shared my life with a dad who teaches me to ride a bike for the first time in Beachwood Canyon. Where we go to baseball games together and eat foot-long Dodger Dogs. Where we hold each other after my first heartbreak.

Where I feel whole.

Instead, I taught *myself* to ride a bike because Mom didn't know how. I go to baseball games with my best friend, Charlie, and their dad because Mom hates sports. And I cried myself to sleep when Jamie Jones broke up with me under the oak tree, because Mom said she *could never hold on to love.*

My world has always had a gaping black hole in it, one that consumes the space a dad would fill. And without knowing who my father is, I'm lost in its inescapable darkness.

The thoughts begin to suffocate me again.

I close my eyes, feeling the room close in on me, wipe sweat from my face. Breathe. My heart pounds in my ears. I count Rose Tyler's soft snores. Tree branches tickle the windows. A light drizzle patters the roof. (Charlie taught me that trick: *Focus on every noise you hear,* they said, *to bring you back to the present.*) It usually works.

Was that really Dad in my dream? And what was said again? I've already forgotten. Charlie says I should keep my journal by my bed so I can write my dreams down as soon as I wake. But I left it in my backpack on the floor and I don't want to disturb Rose Tyler. She snores softly in my ear, lulling me into a space of calm.

I carefully reach over to my nightstand drawer and pull out a small wooden box with my initials carved into it. Huh. I just now realize Christopher's not lying next to me. Didn't even know he'd left. His pillow's cold, no *Sweet dreams, Fig* love note left in his place. He must've snuck out again without me knowing. He does that a lot these days, takes long walks around the neighborhood, or in his head, disappearing for hours. Like me, I guess.

Alone again.

Something I better get used to, as Christopher and Charlie head off to college in a few months, leaving me stuck in bed staring at the stars on my ceiling. Somehow, they easily found their new paths in life, while mine's come to a dead end.

I shine my phone's flashlight on the box, following the words scrawled across the top: *"Never cruel, nor cowardly. Never give up. Never give in."* Inside, I pull out my lucky talismans, clutching each one as I do. A deflated yellow balloon from the time my mom threw me a Cotillion Coming-Out Party when I was ten. A dried four-leaf clover from the night Charlie and I saw Grace Jones at the Hollywood Bowl. A heart-shaped piece of serpentine sea glass, found at Venice Beach on my first date with Christopher two years ago. Trinkets of joy I hold on to, threads that keep me tethered to this world when I'm feeling this pervasive dread strangle my heart and all I want to do is float away.

I dig a little more. There's that folded-up family tree (which I refuse to open), and a bundle of letters still tied together with scratchy twine, forever sealed shut. My handwriting bleeds through one of the envelopes: *Dear Daddy, I lost my first tooth today. Here's a picture of it . . .* Recorded moments in time I never wanted to forget, ones I'd hoped to share when we'd finally meet.

I shove a tear away.

Buried underneath the envelopes, I find what I'd been looking for. A love letter from Dad to Mom.

On Christmas Eve, I was rummaging through Mom's office, trying to find a picture of us from my coming-out party so I could frame it as a gift. Shuffling through her drawers, I found it stashed under a stack of old screenplays she'd never sold. *My Magical Meredith . . . Yours forever, Alex Griffin,* it said.

I knew it was Dad.

And in that moment, everything turned upside down. Joy became sorrow, truths became lies, sadness became ecstasy. Lost became found. And for a split second I felt the emptiness inside me fill with hope.

When I asked Mom on Christmas morning if she'd told me everything about Test Tube Alex, she was so taken aback she started crying, and proceeded to tell a long story about how I was never meant to be conceived, that I was a miracle baby, that it hurts her too much to talk about. The end. (I waited for the sock puppets, but they never showed.) Maybe she'd had too much wine the night before, or maybe my timing was off, it being Christmas morning and all, but how could I wait another second? I'd been waiting for a sign from the universe since kindergarten.

And a part of me knew she was lying, but I didn't know why.

Four months later, I still study the letter like an ancient artifact—seeking answers I'd been waiting my whole life to excavate. I analyze each line for the bazillionth time, trying to find any new clue I might've missed to finally give me a sense of purpose, a connection to knowing a piece of me I thought was lost forever.

There's not much to go on, but questions swarm, keeping me up every night: Why did Dad really leave Mom if they were so in love? Why didn't Dad write me love letters or, hell, just send me a Christmas card every few years? Didn't Dad want to know *me*? I still don't know. But I'm determined to find out.

On that kindergarten morning, I became unglued, shattered pieces of a person I'm still trying to fit together. And as the days have gone by, as each year comes to an end, as everyone else around me has mapped out a clear path for their future, I've been paralyzed in place, wondering who I am.

But now, I might finally have the thread to mend that tear in my heart, a hole I thought would never be filled. This is the map I'd been searching my whole life for. Because I've always wondered if I find Dad, maybe I will finally find me.

part one

THE LETTER FROM ANOTHER TIME

December 18, 2001

My Magical Meredith,

Enclosed, I leave a piece of me with you. I hope this bit of history gives you some solace. The world is falling apart all around us, but our love remains. I will always be grateful for the life we shared and the truest meaning of unconditional love you taught me. I am forever with you. And I can't wait to see how it all turns out. Remember: Life is a series of choices that can make our hearts sing. Choose wisely. After all this time, I finally am.

Yours forever,
Alex Griffin ;)

P.S. Should you want to find me one day, follow the trail I've left behind.

"Not everything that is faced can be changed, but nothing can be changed until it is faced."

2

My heart rattles me awake. Literally. No, my phone's buzzing on my chest. What time is it? Pink sunbeams tease my blackout curtains, desperately trying to break through. I lift my phone to see a picture of Christopher and me staring back, our wild laughter escaping the screen. It was taken at the LA County Fair two years ago, capping off our first summer together. We thought it was the best picture ever, until Charlie noticed some white lady dressed as a cow had photobombed us in the back. We still giggle about it. The clock says 7:01. He's right on time.

"You left me last night," I say, answering the phone. "Again."

"You sound like you're eighty-seven years old," Christopher says. "What's wrong with your voice?"

"Couldn't sleep. Don't answer my question with another question."

"You passed out at nine, and I was bored, so—"

"Where'd you go?"

"Here and there," he says.

"Always so mysterious," I say. "I hate waking up and you're not with me." I turn to face Rose Tyler, my white fluffy terrier of love. She cocks her head back and forth, eagerly awaiting my next move. One ear flops down because it was injured at birth, the other perks up. I open my mouth to blow on her face, and she instantly starts licking my neck. A game we play every morning.

"I went for a little walk around your neighborhood, then drove home," he says. "I didn't want to bother you. I just—"

"Needed to be alone. I know. You shouldn't walk at night. It's not safe." I lift my chin to avoid Rose Tyler's kisses on my mouth.

"You sound like my dad. He was pretty pissed I came home so late. Reminded me that cops are always following Black boys, that I should've stayed with you. I think you two are in cahoots."

"He's not wrong." I inch up my pillow. "You're lucky you have a dad who cares about you." He sighs. I know he's tired of me saying that, but it's true. Maybe we only appreciate something we've lost.

Rose Tyler pounces on my chest and stares me down. Above me, the night sky springs to life. When I was seven, Mom took me to Griffith Observatory for the first time; I was so overwhelmed seeing that many stars in the universe, I've been painting constellations on my ceiling ever since. Well, I used to anyway. It's been months since I've felt the urge to grab a brush. I've been working on Cepheus for over a year now. He's the robed king who went on a quest in search of the Golden Fleece and chose to become a cluster of stars at his death, a reverent fate.

"Hello?" Christopher says.

"Huh?"

"And you complain that I disappear too much. I asked if you're ready for the morning quote." Christopher loves to search for inspirational sayings to motivate us each day.

"Hit me."

"'When you change the way you look at things, the things you look at change.' Max Planck."

"Who's that?" I ask.

"Some old white physics dude." We're silent, then he whispers, "I wish I knew how to do that. Change the way I look at things."

"Yeah," I whisper back. "Me too."

"Shit," he says.

"What?"

"My agent's calling."

"Now? It's, like, seven in the morning."

"I know. But I have this audition next week. Fuck . . . I gotta go. See you at school?"

"Love—" But he hangs up before I can finish.

Replacing our picture on my phone is a photo of a Black man, cheeks puffed out like a blowfish with a wiry beard, playing trumpet. A jazz musician in New Orleans, stuck in place from last night's search. Out of 1,784,523 Alex Griffins on Google, he's number 543,765. And he's definitely not Dad. After all these years, it never occurred to me Test Tube Alex would share our last name, and since Mom refuses to talk, I've been on my own obsessive quest since. But with each passing day, it feels like I'm getting farther and farther away.

When you change the way you look at things, the things you look at change. It reminds me of the James Baldwin quote at the bottom of Dad's love letter to Mom. Charlie helped me with that one. Still not sure why it's there or what it means, and there was nothing else "enclosed." Believe me, I ransacked Mom's office for weeks—when she wasn't around, of course—and found nothing. Were they married? Maybe they'd had some secret love affair that eventually broke her in pieces, too?

Rose Tyler stretches her paw toward me, tapping my lips. "Go downstairs, girl. Go pee-pee," I say. She leaps down and disappears.

If only it were that easy for me to get out of bed. The warm blankets swallow me, the darkness in my room seduces me. Loneliness feels safe here. Out there, it tightens my throat, punches me in the gut.

I think of Christopher's quote. I think of Dad's love letter, how each moment is a choice that can make our hearts sing.

I slowly climb out of bed.

After showering and shaving, I slink into my black skinny jeans and the white T-shirt I folded over my desk chair last night and fling my backpack over my shoulder, before looking in the mirror one last time. I don't recognize this person. He looks . . . lost.

I wonder if he'll ever find his way.

3

Downstairs, Mom's sitting at the kitchen table reading the newspaper slash doing a crossword.

"Morning, honey," she says, looking up. "Sleep okay?" Her thick Ray-Bans teeter on the edge of her nose, eyes smudged in black kohl mascara, like maybe she didn't sleep okay. Her eyes were a sparkling aquamarine once, but these days, they're dull and lifeless, like I can see her own broken-heart map plainly visible on her face.

She takes a drag from a skinny cigarette. This is new.

"I guess." I kiss the top of her head. Smells like peroxide and tea tree oil. Newly bleached and blown out by Umberto on Rodeo. She lifts a smile. Sort of.

"Interesting dreams?" she asks.

"Not really."

I drink a glass of freshly squeezed orange juice and eat a plain bagel from Canter's.

We say nothing more.

Mom and I used to spend mornings catching up on crosswords or sharing the previous night's dreams or making plans together for the day. It's April now, mere months after that Christmas morning, and words feel forced, like when you're stuck on a plane sitting next to a chatty stranger. I hate it.

She studies the cabinets; I look out the window.

Rose Tyler's going nuts at the far end of the yard, bouncing up and down in circles under the blossoming orange trees that lead to a pathway up the hill. Haven't been up there in years.

Usually, the Hollywood Hills are a Technicolor dreamscape, dotted with purple jacarandas and magenta azalea bushes, spidered with jasmine vines. Lately, they've been a setting in an old Western, or the Dust Bowl: parched and barren. But today's a different palette altogether: Monochrome. A film noir. Like we might actually see some spring showers.

"I didn't get any writing done last night," Mom says. I turn back. She eyes the cabinets, addressing them. "I don't know how I'm ever going to make this deadline. I can see it in *Variety* now: 'Fifty-Four-Year-Old Academy Award Winner Meredith Griffin Can't Write to Save Her Life.'" She laughs. Sort of. "They always put women's ages in headlines," she mutters.

She hasn't written much of anything lately. She did before. In fact, in 2007 she won the Oscar for Best Screenplay for *The First Tomorrow*. (Kate Winslet played Barbara Gittings, one of the first out lesbians who was a force to be reckoned with in the queer movement. In the seventies, she helped convince the American Psychiatric Association to drop homosexuality as a mental illness, while simultaneously working with the gay caucus in the American Library Association to create a space for positive books about homosexuality. Among a thousand other things.)

"Oh," I say.

Our eyes meet for the first time this morning. And instead of joy, concern seeps through. Without makeup, you can see where she's had some work done, her face pulled in a perpetual state of awake.

"I have something for you," she says.

From underneath the newspaper, she slides a few college brochures toward me.

"What are those for?" I ask.

"I just thought, you know, if you were considering—"

"I'm not."

"Let me finish. All of these colleges have rolling admissions, they're nearby, and you can—"

"I told you. I don't know what I want to do."

"You have such a gift for writing and art, and I'm not trying to force you to—"

"Or where I want to go, or who I want to be, or whatever you're supposed to know a few months before graduating like every other normal teenager in the world apparently, so drop it."

"I want to help, Isaac."

"Well, you're not."

She sighs, defeated. Stares down at the crossword. I turn away, glare at the morning fog that's slowly dissipating over the Hollywood sign in the far distance, holding in the rage.

"What's a five-letter word for toxic berries? *Brun*—something?"

"I'm late for school," I say, walking past her.

"Okay," she whispers. "Well . . ." She takes another inhale from her cigarette, her voice trailing off.

Before I leave, I turn back. She looks down at the tiled floor, unblinking. A still life. Like that one Hopper painting.

When you change the way you look at things, the things you look at change.

For a moment, I remember the bliss she used to bring me, the effervescent smile on her face that would take over a room before she even walked into it, the way she'd look me deep in the eyes and say, "You remind me so much of me." And I believed her.

But it's hard to believe anything she says anymore.

4

My car horn sounds like a dying sea otter playing a slide whistle.

Fleeeewwwweeeppp. Fleeeewwwweeeppp.

And it only makes the person in front of me—who, by the way, is texting at a light that's been green for four seconds—look to her side like maybe she's just heard a clown fart.

Fleeeewwwweeeppp. Fleeeewwwweeeppp. STILL. TEXTING.

Only when a few other horns join me does she look up and speed off, flipping everyone the bird. The nerve. If I drove Oscar more than forty-five miles per hour, I would follow and *fleeeewwwweeeppp* her the rest of the day, but (1) I am 1,000 percent against tailgating, (2) I have a paralyzing fear of driving any faster than that speed, and (3) huge Los Angeles news flash: It's raining. So I keep my hands securely plastered at ten and two and drive steadily onward, hunched over the steering wheel. The windshield wipers skid across the glass, smearing my view so it looks like a preschooler fingerpainted the city. I lean forward, straining my eyes.

Franklin Avenue. Below the hills of Hollywood. Tucked between hipster hangouts and celebrity Scientologists. Thousands of pastel-colored apartment buildings invade the few remaining fairy-tale bungalows that once dominated the city streets, the only trace of Hollywood history left in the city. Well, except for Oscar. My 1977 cherry-red station wagon with wood trim, aptly named because he looks like the Oscar Mayer Weinermobile. Mom was gifted the car from the set of *The First Tomorrow* back in the day and saved it for me when I turned sixteen. We had big plans for Oscar. Road-trip adventures to undiscovered small towns, desert excursions to Joshua Tree, camping in the Redwoods. Big plans.

The wipers clunk across the windshield. I clean the window with my palm, smearing the fog. Clench the steering wheel. Why would Mom mock me with those college brochures? She might as well have poured a bucket of salt on the huge gash in my heart instead. And all those swirling neon colors that popped through the YOUR NEXT ADVENTURE STARTS HERE slogans made me nauseous. She knows I have no plans, no purpose.

At the start of senior year, I realized we'd all been walking this preset obstacle course our entire lives, a game we didn't even know we were playing. And suddenly we're being asked to create our own.

I'm still trying to figure out the rules.

Twenty-seven minutes later, I'm sitting outside Charlie's home in Silverlake, forcing a smile. And here they come running out, holding a denim jacket over their head as a makeshift umbrella.

"Doing the Debbie Harry–slash–Billy Idol thing today," they yell, opening the door. "You like?"

No idea what they just said. They model a frayed neon T-shirt. A kilt of some kind. Black army boots. "You never cease to amaze," I say.

"That's my job. And you know I love me some eighties vintage rock. Anyway, this rain feels so *gooood.*" Now they're spinning, arms outstretched, screaming to the heavens. "It's like God's laughing so hard she's crying, you know?"

"Right. But can we go? Traffic's gnarly and we're supremely late."

"Sorry, sorry." They jump in, slam the door, and dab themselves with a towel, throwing it in the back seat. Then they pull the visor down to look in the mirror. "Whoa. Okay, yikes. But never fear, MAC is here. First—" They grab my hand, which is still Velcroed to the steering wheel. "How are you, Fig?"

"Fine," I say. "You smell like a forest."

"It's sandalwood." They put their wrist up to my nose. I sneeze. "Thanks, and gross." They study my face a little longer. "You sure you're okay? You look a little tense."

"It's nothing. Just Mom."

"What'd she do this time?"

"She's . . . *Mom* . . . you know—well, you don't know because your parents are perfect." I try to mask the bitterness in my voice. I don't think it works.

"Far from it, but still. I'm sorry, Fig. Really." Glitter streams down their cheeks. I know it's from the rain, but it adds an exclamation to their concern. "Any more news on the father front?"

"Not yet." I look away, as my face flushes. I pretend there's a spot on my jeans I'm trying to rub out, along with my feelings. After all this time, even with Charlie, shame and embarrassment still creep in. Because I'm the fatherless kid who was left behind. I know the love letter's not much, but at least it's something I can hold on to, to try to make sense of my story.

My eyes begin to sting, my throat strains. Breaths clutch my chest. "Fig?"

"I'm fine," I mumble. "Buckle up, let's go."

The click of their seat belt. Rain gently tapping the windshield. Charlie's soft voice humming some eighties tune. The sounds bring me back. Sort of.

I check my mirrors and pull off.

We sit in quiet for a while as I inch my way through traffic. The easy stillness between us begins to calm me.

Charlie reapplies gold-glitter streaks over their eyes, dusts pale white powder everywhere to matte their cheeks, spikes their bleached hair. Their phone buzzes for the thousandth time since they've buckled up. They're Internet Famous—*Time* magazine called them the Gen Z Enby Guru, but they're affectionately known to their followers as the Zenigma of YouTube—after posting these motivational videos that have inspired tens of millions of people.

They reply to comments in between makeup retouches.

I turn down Highland as the rain eases.

"Seriously," they say, looking at their phone. "The world is a dumpster fire. Literally burning up all around us. And these fools have nothing better to do with their time than to call me names? To what end? Make themselves feel better? Mask their shame and guilt for some secret attraction to me they can't contain?"

"You are pretty irresistible."

They show me their screen, and I quickly glance over before turning my eyes back to the road. "So now I'm a 'Fat Faggot Freak' who should stay away from children. Kids are literally being killed by guns, and I'm the threat? And this is from a white mom in the Midwest whose bio line, by the way, is a Bible quote."

"Damn." They type a message back. "Does it ever hurt your feelings?" I ask.

"Sometimes," they say, clicking off their phone. "I'll cry in bed wondering how humans can be so hateful to each other. Then I think of you and my parents and a bunch of other folks who love me, and it's like my flashlight through the darkness. So, I let their hate bring me closer to love!"

"You always were *ahead of the curve.*"

They finish with their eyeliner and clap the visor closed. "Which was the exact theme of my award-winning NYU application, thank you."

"I know."

"Come with me," they say, facing me. "I don't want to do this without you."

"To New York? I can't. I never applied, and anyway—"

"We'll find a tiny apartment—"

"I'm not even sure that's—"

"—and sleep on a piece of foam—"

"—what I want to—"

"—and eat ramen soup for every meal. Come on, we do everything together. It'll be so much fun!"

"I can't keep following you the rest of my life, Charlie!"

We've reached Sunset and Highland. Stopped in traffic, surrounded by a kaleidoscope of taillights.

"Sorry," they say softly. "I didn't mean—"

"That came out wrong." I turn toward them. They lean against the passenger door, their jade eyes twinkling through gold dust, smiling, always smiling, like they're the actual embodiment of The Force. "I didn't sleep again last night and I'm feeling . . . I don't know. I need to find my own way is all." I only wish I knew how.

"You're right," they say, squeezing my arm. "I'm being selfish. I'll just miss the fuck out of you, Fig."

"Me too. But that's months away, so can we not talk about it right now?" The stoplight flashes green, but only a few cars get through before it turns red again.

Their eyes narrow. "What were your dreams?"

"My dreams?"

"Last night. You said you couldn't sleep."

"Oh. Can't remember much. I was driving along the edge of a cliff as usual, but someone was with me this time. A person, maybe, but more like an entity or angel. And they said something about being a mapmaker. Maybe it was my dad, or—"

"You."

"Hmm?"

"Maybe it was you. Dreams are more than for sleeping, Fig." They lean toward me, excitement flaming their face. This close, I can smell their strawberry lip gloss. "Remember when our counselor Dr. What's-Her-Puss said, 'Dreams are the gateway to your truth.' Well, maybe it's time, Fig. Maybe you're telling yourself to go on a pilgrimage to find your truth!" They're holding my hands so tight I can't help but feel their joy seeping through.

"Maybe," I say. Or maybe I'm closer to finding Dad than I think. And when I do, maybe then I can start writing my next chapter.

A car honks behind us. We both jump. The light's turned green again. Oscar jolts forward. And dies in the middle of the intersection.

"Oh God, oh no, oh God." I turn the ignition. Again. And again. And again.

"It's okay. He'll start up."

A chorus of honks sounds from every direction.

"Oh God, Oh God, Oh God."

"Hey now, hey now!" Charlie pops their head out the passenger window, lifting their arms. "Chill, my friends. You are only in a hurry because you think you're late. Time's a social construct—"

"Fuck you, freak! MOVE!" an angry driver screams.

"Well." Charlie plops back down, buckling up. "Best be getting on then, Fig." And with that, Oscar putters to life, thrusting forward and slapping our heads against the backs of our seats. "There. See? We're good as new."

Charlie goes on about some party tomorrow night and how they wish I'd stop dressing like a mime, wearing black and white all the time, and on and on, but I can only think of what they said about dreams, and how I remembered something else that was whispered in mine last night: *Time is a sickness.*

I wonder what it means.

And if it's true what Charlie said, that I was sitting next to *me* in the car. Then I wonder why I'd say that to myself.

5

Seventeen minutes later, I'm weaving through the halls of Hollywoodland High School. It's extra frenetic today. People buzzing about their upcoming spring break plans and Garrett Davenport's party tomorrow night and college dreams coming true, but I try to ignore it. Walls are plastered with posters that say, GET YOUR PROM TICKETS BEFORE IT'S TOO LATE! or SENIORS, HAVE YOU ORDERED YOUR GRADUATION GOWNS YET? or LOOKING FOR WHAT'S NEXT AFTER HIGH SCHOOL? ASK YOUR GUIDANCE COUNSELOR, which I also try not to see. It's like my dream's sprung to life and every tiny thing is determined to taunt me wherever I go.

What I'm looking for: An instruction manual on how to survive as a half-person. A sign from the universe to show me what to do with my life. Directions to Dad's house.

Christopher's leaning against the locker next to mine as I approach, wearing black jeans perfectly ripped at the knee and a loose yellow shirt covered with daisies. A tank top underneath sculpts his chest. He acts like he's lost in his phone, but really he's fixated on the linoleum. This is new. If he's not wandering the streets at night, he's wandering through the thoughts in his head.

Something changed in him after Christmas, too. Before, he knew all the answers in his life. Now, he always has a distant look in his eyes like he's trying to solve an impossible riddle. And like me, no matter how many times I've asked, I know he's never told the full story.

"Hey, you," I say. He jumps, as if I'd just teleported in front of him.

"Hey, babes."

"You good?"

"Fine, fine." He peers around the nearly empty hall before quickly kissing the top of my head and wrapping his muscles around me. (Those are also new. Last year, he was as thin as me. But after signing with his dad's agent over winter break, he's been at the gym every day since, leaving me behind in Skinny Twerpsville.)

"Sexy T-shirt," he whispers, licking my ear. A waft of mint aftershave and lavender laundry detergent. Smells like home.

"You're ridiculous," I say.

He props up a foot, leaning his back against the locker. I watch him through my mirror, face furrowed, lost again. It's hard not to stare, because by the way, total model here: tall, with big saucer eyes, a jawbone for days, perfectly crooked teeth, skin that always seems to glow.

Used to be all my thoughts evaporated when I'd see him. When we first met, we shook hands to introduce ourselves and I felt *it*. Whatever that "it" is. I'd been with boys before, but this was something different, inexplicable. He's from St. Louis; I'm from LA; but we found each other at a party in the Valley.

I think we were destined, he said.

I thought so, too.

Sometimes I wish I still felt the electric spark in that handshake. Maybe time really is a sickness.

"It's Decades Day tomorrow," he says to the floor.

"What's that?" I empty my backpack, stacking my books on the shelf.

"The last day before spring break? Where everyone dresses up as their favorite decade?"

"Oh. Right."

"I want to be someone from the seventies."

"Okay?"

"It's a cool time. Studio 54. Hip-hop was born—"

"And you get to wear tight clothes to show off your body?"

"Ha ha. Doesn't your mom have some stuff? From that movie she did?"

"She took a few costumes and things. They're up in the attic, I think. Although I've never been up there."

"Can I dig through them after rehearsal tonight?"

"I have to work. Meet me there first. My coworker wants to show me some meteor shower or something."

"Cool."

This entire exchange, he's been talking to the linoleum, eyes glazed over as if on autopilot.

I drop my backpack and lean into him. "What do I get in return?" I whisper in his ear.

"What are you doing?"

What *am* I doing? I'm not exactly sure. Maybe I want to forget the unanswerable questions in my own head for a moment. Maybe I want to forget who we've become and remember who we were. "Any ideas?"

He pockets his phone, glances around before peeking down at me. He lifts a smirk. "Not here, Fig."

"Come on . . . tell me."

Damn, his eyes are hypnotizing: Golden rings of light crackle through his pupils. Tiger's-eye, a stone used for resilience and courage and to gather self-confidence. (In a faraway time, Mom and I used to collect gemstones, and she'd tell me how they each held a different spiritual quality.)

"Tell me."

He inches closer. "Fig . . ."

I miss this: the flirting. It's been so long since we've—

A slight, curly-haired blond boy steps up. Christopher pushes me off. I stumble slightly, catch myself by grabbing the locker door. He stands up straight, clearing his throat. Did that just happen? No, I must've imagined it.

"Hey, Christopher," the boy says, with an adorable lisp. "I know this is, like, literally the weirdest thing to ask, but can I get your autograph? I thought you were, like, so totally amazing in *Rent* last week." He hands Christopher a red Sharpie and a poster from the senior year musical, blushing.

"Of course, dude. What's your name?"

"Eric. I mean, for real, I just thought you were, like, everything. I hope I can be as good as you one day."

"You're sweet."

I peer over Christopher's shoulder. He scoots away from me. Okay, definitely did not imagine it. I act like I'm rummaging through my backpack to find a pencil or protractor or something, my head scrambling.

"I watched your dad on his cop show last night," the kid says. "He's so good in it."

"Yes, he is." Christopher hands him the signed poster.

"Anyone ever tell you that you look exactly like Chadwick—"

"Boseman. My agent seems to think so," he says, winking.

"Thank you *so* much." Eric squeezes the poster to his chest before floating away.

I eye Christopher through my locker mirror.

"What?" he asks.

"What the hell was that?"

"He wanted my autograph."

"You pushed me away."

"Jesus, Fig. Come on. Don't start."

"Start with what?"

He whispers, "You know I can't be out. We've talked about this a million times."

"In, like, the film world, maybe, but at *school*?"

I slam my locker to face him. A few people stroll by, gawking, but I don't care.

"Don't do this," he says through gritted teeth, lifting an awkward grin. He waits until they round the corner. "And I didn't push you away."

"You literally just did, Christopher. Twice. Why'd you—"

"I'm sorry, okay . . . my agent—"

"Is an asshole. What's your point?"

"Fig. Please. It's more complicated than that."

"Not really, it's not."

"Yes. It is."

We were at some Hollywood bigwig party a couple months ago, where I was introduced to his agent as his "best friend." Because apparently Christopher will never be an international movie star as long as the world knows he's gay. It took a bit of adjusting, but since it was important to him, I surrendered, refusing to squelch his happiness. But this is new.

"God, I just . . ." He rubs his face, probably trying to erase the pain that's often piercing his eyes. Sometimes the hardest part of looking at him is that I'm always seeing me.

"What's going on, Christopher? What are you so afraid of? Who are we becoming if we can't—"

The bell rings.

"I'm sorry, Fig."

"I just—" I look down, shake my head. "It's fine." I reach for his hand. This time, he takes it. "Meet me at work tonight?"

He nods, and we walk down the hall in opposite directions.

6

Something else I'm looking for: to understand the difference between being alone and feeling lonely.

7

_____

Later that night, I'm standing on the precipice of everything: the rooftop walkway of Griffith Observatory, an hour after my shift at the ticket booth ended, lost in the twinkling cityscape far below me. The thick cloud cover glows an iridescent orange from the light pollution. No stars tonight. Or any night for that matter. The city looks stuck.

Christopher pulls into the parking lot, and as he steps out of the car, I text him: _Look up._ When he does, I wave.

Besides him, the lot is empty.

When he finally reaches me on the rooftop deck, we might be the only two people in the universe. The city noise is muted up here, the world still. He pulls me into him, locking his lips to mine. Soft, cushioned kisses that taste like the ocean, infinite and free.

"Hi," he whispers, holding my face in his hands.

"Hi," I whisper back.

We stand like this for a moment, lost in each other.

I can't shake what happened this morning. I've replayed that push over and over again, the memory permanently bruising my heart. And although I've tried to ignore it, our relationship has felt off to me for some time now. Uncomfortable even. Like an itchy sweater that doesn't fit anymore. And I have no idea why.

"Come on," I say. "Let's go see some meteors."

He follows me up a steel staircase that winds around the east-end dome of the Observatory. The second we enter, we both gasp.

Inside, a spectacular telescope commands the room. With a sixteen-foot-long tube that stretches to the opened copper roof, and levers and refractors and mirrors and I-don't-even-know-whats attached to its core, it's hard not to feel like a specimen swimming under a microscope, insignificant and small.

"You think that's something, wait'll you peek through it," says Dr. Wheeler. I've only ever seen her in a white lab coat, so when she steps out from behind a desk, I'm slightly taken aback. Like she's a paper doll cutout standing there in a simple white V-neck and blue jeans.

"Oh, hi, Dr. Wheeler."

"Please, call me Deedee. And you must be the famous Christopher I've heard about."

"Hope it's all good," he says, after clearing his throat.

"Nothing but." The kajillion freckles on her cheeks and hair the size of a stormy cumulonimbus seem fitting for a doctor of astronomy. Up close, thin lines on her forehead connect the dots, and there's a look in her eyes I don't recognize, like she exists in a constant state of wonder. I'd like to live there.

I say, "I can't believe I've worked here for a year and have never seen this before."

"The first time's always the best," she says. "You've seemed . . . distant lately. I thought this might help."

"What?"

"We can all use a little reminder of what's really important." She gestures toward the large lens. "Take a look."

For some reason, my heart starts racing. Maybe it knows something I don't.

I bend over, peer through. And at once, my breath catches in my throat. I step back, turn to her. A grin spreads across her face. Christopher grabs my arm and furrows his brow, concerned. What must I look like right now? I gaze up at the opened roof to see only the orange dust of city lights, nothing like what I just witnessed through the telescope lens.

I peek again, my heart galloping now, and I let myself sink into the wonder. She's homed in on a star, I think. But it's not like any star I've ever seen. Radioactive hues of every kind spread across a luminous ocean-blue center that seems to have its own heartbeat, pulsating colors I couldn't begin to name because words wouldn't do them justice. I don't know what to feel.

"Amazing, isn't it?" Dr. Wheeler whispers. "When Griffith J. Griffith opened the Observatory—and yes, that's his real name—he said, 'If all mankind could look through this telescope, it would revolutionize the world.'"

"What is it?" I somehow ask.

"The Ring Nebula. Part of the Lyra constellation, where I'm hoping you'll see a few meteors fly by. Not as clear tonight as I'd like it to be. It's near one of my favorite stars in the sky."

"I feel like I'm inside it."

"In some ways, you are," she says.

I step back for Christopher to see, and the second he bends down he grabs his chest.

We're silent for a few minutes before he says above a breath, "It's so beautiful." Then he squeezes my hand and says, "I want to look at this with you," so I join him.

We stare, awestruck, cheeks suctioned together, as if we're one being. I feel his breath tremble, his hand gripping mine like we're about to free-fall from the edge of a bluff. Maybe we are. It's so close,

I feel like I could reach out and pull it through the lens and be tele-ported to another tomorrow, even though I know it's light-years away. But I wish for it anyway.

"I had no idea what you meant when you said we were going to look at meteors," he whispers.

I didn't either.

In that moment, a brilliant white light flashes across the sky, scaring us both. We scream. Then for some reason, we both start giggling.

"That's a good omen," Dr. Wheeler says. "In ancient times, seeing a meteor meant change was afoot, forcing those to look within their own shadows for guidance."

We steady our breaths as we let the nebula wash over us, swimming through the light, still glued together, still softly giggling.

"You said this was near your favorite star?" I ask her.

"Yes," she says. "Andrew. Want to see him?"

"Andrew?" I ask. "I don't know that one." Another meteor streams across the sky and Christopher grips my hand even tighter, if that were possible.

Dr. Wheeler clicks coordinates on the computer and the telescope shifts position, landing on a gleaming cerulean star with a golden halo. "That's because I named it," she says.

"You can name stars?" Christopher asks.

"Oh yes. There are too many up there to scientifically label. Did you know there are more stars in the sky than every word that's ever been uttered by every human who's lived."

I believe that now. Words seem inconsequential to the feeling I have looking through this lens, and yet we always work so hard to fill space with them.

"Why Andrew?" I ask.

"After my son," she says flatly. "He died several years ago. Suicide."

We both stand, turning to her. But instead of sadness in her eyes, a wise curiosity swims through them, a reverence. And they're the color of a crystal I can't name, like they're their own radioactive nebulas.

"I'm so sorry," I say.

She glances through the scope. "This way he lives for lifetimes, eternally shining. And I always know where to find him, especially when I feel lost."

We're speechless, taking it all in.

"This is here for you, anytime you want to remember," she says.

"Remember what?" I ask.

She's still gazing upon Andrew. This time, a small tear falls down her cheek. "Where you came from, where you're going . . . where you'll always be."

✦

When we step back outside, I realize for the first time that I've been distracted from my thoughts. From "what if" questions and "what next" possibilities. From finding Dad. My body tingles, my heart flutters like a freed caged bird. Something has shifted inside me, cracked open. But I'm not sure what.

We scan the sky. The city lights hide the stars, but the Ring Nebula and the Lyrid meteors and Andrew still gleam in our minds.

"I feel so small," Christopher says. "Like nothing really matters down here anymore."

"Yeah," I say, though I disagree.

Because for me, everything matters even more now.

8

An hour later, we're in my bed.

I grip Christopher's back, digging deeper into his skin, to become him. To disappear. Our sweat, sticky and sweet, caresses our chests. Soft moans in my ears. Heavy breaths synchronize. Kisses on my neck.

I pull him closer still, ignoring the memory that echoes through my mind, of him pushing me off this morning. I'm lost in my ceiling behind him, absorbed in the fake stars. Dreaming of distant nebulas that are actually inside me. Of exploding meteors and destined journeys. Of naming galaxies to live in for lifetimes.

"Fig?"

Christopher looks down at me, holding my chin in place.

"Huh?"

"Where are you?" he asks, panting slightly.

"Here. I'm here."

"No. You're not." Our eyes lock. "I've been trying to tell you—"

"What?"

We don't blink. This close, I notice the light pollution has cleared from his mind and he can see clearly again, even if just for this moment.

And it's here he begins to cry.

"Christopher?"

He lies next to me on the bed. I sit up, cover his heart with my hand on instinct. I don't want him to feel any more pain. "What's wrong?" I whisper.

"Just . . . looking up at that star . . . did something to me, I think. I can't stop thinking about . . ." The rest of his words garble together, so I tell him to take a few deep breaths.

He wipes his eyes and holds his hand over mine.

"I'm sorry for hurting your feelings today," he says.

"Christopher—"

"I hate this." He turns to me, face shattered and damp with regret. "I hate hiding like this."

"Then don't. It isn't worth—"

Rose Tyler leaps onto the bed. She licks Christopher's cheeks, his ears. He chuckles. "Hey, baby girl."

"Why do you let them decide who you are?" I ask.

"Because this is all I've ever wanted, to be an actor like my dad, follow in his footsteps but . . . it's so much more than that, and I don't know how to change any of it."

"You let your agent go and find a new one."

"It's not that simple, Fig. He's my dad's agent, too. He creates stars and makes them disappear just as fast."

"Tell your dad, then. He's the most understanding human I know."

"I told you, I can't tell my dad!" He says this with such force, Rose Tyler backs away. He inhales deeply, glaring at the ceiling. "I've always wanted to use my voice for good . . . But I didn't know it would come with a price."

"And that's more important than your soul?"

"Geez, Fig. Dramatic much? Don't make me sound so shallow."

"That's not what I—"

"You don't understand." Another tear falls, and I wipe it away.

"Then help me to—"

"It's embarrassing. There are more . . . things I haven't shared, with anyone." Then, quietly he says, "Sometimes I feel so alone."

"You can trust me. I'm here."

He looks at me. "Are you?"

I open my mouth to answer, but words get caught between us.

Because he's right, I'm not.

I lie back down next to him. Hold his hand, but I can't feel it. As if I can suddenly see our broken-heart maps have built a wall between us over the years, without either of us knowing it. Because as much as I haven't been there for him, I also know he hasn't been there for me. But it's not his fault. It's mine. He barely knows anything about my search for Dad these days, how finding Dad might help me find my own voice to bring good to the world. How alone I've become in the journey.

Like him, I don't know how to talk about it.

I'm not sure how much time passes.

The silence is thick and black.

"Want to go look in the attic for those costumes?" he asks at some point.

"Sure," I say.

9

It's after midnight and Mom has long gone to bed, so we tip-toe up the attic stairs. When we reach the landing, the moon casting shadows on the floorboards through the small round window is our only source of light. My eyes try adjusting to the darkness, but after some time I give up. I scan the wall for a switch, when Christopher, from somewhere in the middle of the room, whispers, "Here," and flips on a lamp.

It's a sparse and tiny space. Cobwebs and a thick layer of dust and old memories blanket the loft. Boxes of tax forms and old scripts are stacked high in the corner. Bins of Christmas decorations with silver tinsel streaming out. A plastic Santa as tall as me when I was four years old waves. I haven't seen that in years.

"I found them," Christopher whispers. He creaks over to the other side of the attic and opens the few boxes labeled THE FIRST TOMORROW. Soon, he's trying on tight polyester pants and satin shirts covered in flowered prints and saying, "Far-out, man," flashing peace signs. I can't help but smile.

I walk over to the once-towering Santa. The colors have faded, muted and dull like me. I blow away dust. Sneeze. Grandma gave this to us when I was little. I used to sit in the corner and share secrets and wishes with them as if Santa were my dad, just as mythical and magical.

Santa knew how scared and excited I was after my first kiss with Bobby Jones on the jungle gym, how it felt like I was climbing a never-ending hill on a roller coaster. And a few years later, when Jamie Jones and I made out under the school's big oak tree—the same one she broke up with me under—Santa knew the tingle in my tummy was just as exhilarating. I didn't know it was possible to love girls the same way I loved boys, but Santa did.

And Santa always smiled, too, when I told them what I wanted to be when I grew up: first a teacher, then a cartoonist, then a writer like Mom. Every step of the way Santa would say, *You can be anything you want to be, Isaac, if you set your mind and heart to it.*

And each year I'd wish for my plastic friend to come to life so I could finally feel their embrace.

I lift them up to say hello, and that's when I see it: a small box tucked deep in the alcove behind them. I pull it toward me.

My heart stops.

Breath stunts.

Sitting in front of me is a cardboard box labeled ALEX.

Is this real? How is this even—

"What'd you find?" Christopher peeks over my shoulder. "Who's Alex?"

"My dad," I whisper, my voice trembling.

"What?"

"At least I think it is. Remember that letter I found?"

"At Christmas, you mean?"

"Yeah, and I've been looking for Dad ever since and—"

"What do you mean? I thought you said you gave up."

"I didn't want to tell you."

"Why?"

"I felt embarrassed—"

"Why?"

"Because . . . I don't know! You wouldn't understand!"

"Okay. Sorry."

We don't move.

"I can't believe . . ." How long has this been here? If I hadn't moved Santa, I would never have seen it. That's how far back in the shadows it was hidden. Like Mom shoved it into the darkness to completely forget.

Christopher whispers, "Open it, Fig."

I slowly lift the lid. It takes me a minute to realize the moisture on my cheeks is from my tears. I push them away.

Staring back at me is a framed black-and-white picture of a vintage version of me. Alex Griffin stands among a group of drag queens or trans folks—it's hard to see—their fists in the air, screaming through the glass, holding a broom and protest signs that read 1966 VANGUARD CLEANUP.

"Fig, what is this?"

"I don't know."

Underneath the picture, some folded-up clothes: A green turtleneck cashmere sweater. A silver chain with a dangling Gemini pendant. A yellowed copy of James Baldwin's *Giovanni's Room*. A black leather jacket.

I hold the coat to my nose. After all these years, it still smells like clove cigarettes. I wrap it around my shoulders. The crinkle and scent of old leather embraces me. I close my eyes. And feel Dad hugging me for the first time in my life.

"Fig," Christopher whispers.

I catch myself. Tears again. Shove them off.

"There's something in here," I say.

I unzip the inside pocket and pull out a thick envelope. Scrawled on the front is written: *A piece of my history. Follow me.*

Over the years, I began to lose faith in signs from the universe, but if this isn't one, I don't know what is. The envelope is still sealed. Maybe it was meant for Mom, but I don't care. I rip it open.

Inside, a stack of folded notebook pages. Dad's handwriting. I recognize it from the love letter.

I unfold them and begin to read.

May 17, 1966

I stepped off the Greyhound bus in some part of town called the Tenderloin. I immediately thought, You're not in Kansas anymore, then laughed and thought, Being a friend of Dorothy and all. I hated myself for thinking that. Groovy. One foot on San Francisco soil and I'm already becoming one of them. But I guess that's why I'm here.

Too bad I smelled like one big, unwashed sweat stain, mixed with whatever powdered soap they use in those bus toilets. Too scared to get off along the way. Scared they'd find me, cart me away.

I had a duffel bag thrown over my shoulder. Filled with whatever I could shove in there before running. It all feels like a dream. One minute I'm putting on Momma's lipstick and heels and Maidenform bra, singing, "Tammy, Tammy, Tammy's in love . . ." and the next minute Momma's beating me with her hairbrush. When she left to get Daddy, I ran all the way to the bus station and didn't look back. Didn't think it would happen when it did. So fast. So sudden. But I always knew I had to get out of there one day. My only chance to become a real writer. My only chance for survival. My only chance to be me.

And the minute I stepped off the bus, someone yelled, "There you are!"

I looked up and saw this old lady, in her forties maybe, wearing a brown pin-striped skirt-suit. Form-fitting. Businesswoman type, I thought. Her hair looked like these burnt wheat fields back home.

She waved in my direction, but it couldn't be for me. I knew no one here. So I kept walking.

"Where you going?" she yelled again in a thick Hispanic accent. I looked up.

"Yes, you! I'm here!" she shouted, running toward me. "I'm so glad you made it back home!" She looked over her shoulder a few times before finally reaching me. Then she kissed each one of my cheeks and whispered, "Just act like you know me, for Chrissakes. Give me a hug." So I did. When I looked behind her, I saw a few cops walking toward us and pushed myself off to run.

She clutched my arm. "They're not after you, honey. Not yet. They're after me. About to arrest me for loitering, and I ain't going back to the hole. Just act like you know me and smile." So I do. She talked gibberish about sales at Woolworth's or something; I couldn't catch a word because it was all happening so fast. The cops were coming closer. Through a gritted smile, she said, "Laugh," which I did, until they slowly walked past us.

When they rounded the corner, we both exhaled at the same time.

"Don't worry," she said. "They mostly leave white kids alone, especially when you're new. Follow me." She dragged me down the street with her. "Keep looking forward. Act like you got purpose. First rule: You get arrested for obstructing the sidewalk here, so don't." Then she stopped and said, "You can trust me." Her eyes oozed kindness, melting over me, and for some reason, looking in them, I believed her.

Up close her makeup was caked on, more forced than natural, revealing a relief map of wrinkles. And she smelled like menthol cigarettes masked with Chanel No. 5.

"How old are you?" she asked.

"Sixteen."

"Where'd you come from?"

"Oklahoma City," I said.

"Figured as much. You saved my life back there. Now it's my turn. First: your name."

"Alex." Guess that's my name now. I made it up in that second. I didn't want any part of the old me in this new land.

"Honey, you're gonna have to use your voice around here, or they will eat you alive. That's rule two." So I said it louder. "Better. I'm Esmeralda. Esmeralda Esperanza." She rolled her r's and held out her gloved hand for me to kiss. I did. "First time meeting a transsexual woman, I presume?" She winked.

"First for everything," I mumble.

She hurried on. "Well, now that we're friends—hey, keep up, or you'll end up getting caught. We can't dawdle in the streets."

I skipped up to her. It felt like I'd entered some alien land that was covered in a layer of soot and smelled like a burning landfill. Had to step over piles of trash and used needles and unspeakable other things more than once. Flashing neon lights. Cable cars clanging. And the people. Oh man, the people. A few kids my age caught my eye as I walked past: crouched in the caves of glass storefronts, leaning, smoking, smiling.

"You're fresh meat to them," Esmeralda said. "And competition. But not if I can help it. Keep going."

Some people sat under tents muttering to themselves. Some offered me every colored pill imaginable. Some said, "Hey, girl," to Esmeralda as we passed. "Feds are thick tonight. Be careful."

We walked into a hotel where everyone knew her, treating her like the Queen Mother. Men were draped over each other like clothes on a line. Waving free. I'd never seen anything like it. We took the elevator to the fourth floor. Inside her room, dresses hung like a Penney's catalog, a vanity covered in powders and paints. And a white man, smoking, sitting hunched over a desk.

He looked up. "Hello there."

"This is my Tommy," Esmeralda said, kissing him on the cheek. She sat on his lap and slipped a pair of glasses on that were slung around her neck, paging through some paperwork on the desk.

"Newbie, eh?" Tommy said. I shrugged. "Welcome aboard the Cuckoo Train. Choo! Choo!" They laughed. I didn't. "You must be pretty damn lucky to have this one find you." He squeezed Esmeralda around the waist. She giggled and cooed.

"Tommy's my husband," she said to me. "Well, in spirit. He's a beautiful man, isn't he?" She grabbed his cheeks, kissing him on the lips again. Then she turned to me. "First things first. You need to shower. Back there. Towels are in the first drawer."

✻

I stepped back into the room after my shower and Esmeralda was smoking, sitting on a love seat shaped like a pair of big red lips. "Much better," she said. "Tommy left. He's meeting us at the cafeteria. But first, come here and sit. Let me break it all down for you."

I questioned nothing and did everything she said.

"You heard all the rules, right?" I nodded. "Good. Because those aren't rules like some board game. They're for your survival. This may be 1966 with all that peace and love bullshit. But for us, mess one of them up and you're pretty much dead. Even here." She wasn't kidding. Not even for a millisecond. "I'm not going to have another one of you killing yourselves on the streets. And I know this is the first stop in town from that bus, but you aren't staying here. I have a place I'm going to send you, okay? Just met this sweet hippie chick who's opening her house up to help

us out. She's lovely. I'm sending you there." I nodded again.
"So, let's be clear: You're homosexual, right?"

Hearing those words, so blunt, so strong, I almost burst
into tears right in front of her. Never heard them said back
to me before. "I'm not sure . . . exactly."

"Well, either way. Welcome home. You made it." She
winked and smoked. "So, now that you're here, you gotta
keep it to yourself, okay? You're not going to find work even
in this town if people know who you really are. And you
especially aren't going to find work in this part of town.
I'm not letting you. All clear so far?"

"What's wrong with this part?"

She laughed, showing half of her back teeth were
missing. "Nothing at all, honey. It's my home. But we're
the outcasts of the outcasts here. This isn't where you start
out, it's where you end up. Now, I'm a respectable woman.
I run this hotel with my beautiful husband, make a decent-
enough living. But I'm lucky. I've done my time, trying to
spare you from doing yours."

"Why me?"

"You can still make something of yourself. That's why I
wait at the bus station. I don't want you kids getting lost
before you even have a chance to be found." She lifted my
chin. "You got this one chance, you hear me? I just gave you
your Get Out of Jail Free card. That's it. Your only one. Don't
you waste it, now. And don't you forget who gave it to you."

I nodded again.

"Good. Now let's go grab you a bite and send you on
your way."

We walked down the street another block to Compton's Cafeteria, with a sign over the front door that said ENTER AT YOUR OWN RISK. Well, we sure did.

A bell dinged. And life on the other side whiplashed me: a menagerie of wigs and crinoline skirts and intoxicating perfume and angora sweaters and hairspray and a sea of laughter and chatter swirling in smoke.

"Welcome to Wonderland," Esmeralda said. I followed her to a corner booth by the front window, where a gaggle of girls sat with Tommy.

"What'll it be, sugar?" the waitress asked. She looked like an ironed white linen napkin, crisp and clean, with plastic butterfly barrettes bouncing through her hair. She pulled a pen attached to a long chain out of her pocket.

"Adam and Eve on a raft. Stretch me a redhead and hold the ice," Esmeralda said. This made sense to the waitress: She nodded, scribbled, and walked away.

I spent the rest of the night devouring eggs on toast and Cokes with cherry juice and no ice, listening to the girls gossip as they paid me no attention. From the latest word on the street: "Did you hear Louise ended up in the hole?" to Vietnam drafts: "Honey, I just said I was as queer as a three-dollar bill and they x'd me out right there," to secret woman tips: "You can fill nylons with birdseed to make boobies."

This is where I sit now, listening and writing in my spiral notebook (my only safe place), because I don't want *to forget anything Esmeralda told me. And I especially don't want to forget Esmeralda before she sends me off to Aunt Luna's.*

CALL AUNT LUNA

421-7070

JERSEY AND CASTRO

XOXO ESMERALDA ESPERANZA

10

The world has been a hologram since I read Dad's letter last night. Everything continues to flicker in and out of focus. Colors I've never seen before vibrate around me, like I've been consumed by that nebula we almost touched in the sky.

Christopher held me for a few minutes, before I asked him to leave. He wanted to stay with me, but I needed to be alone. Not because I felt weighed down with darkness, but because I couldn't feel. Anything. Couldn't even form words. Thoughts flew into my head and just as quickly out.

I felt as if I was living inside the wonder of that star.

I read Dad's words over and over again, possessed by dreams and questions I recognized as my own. I studied the photo for hours, searching for any more clues. I didn't take it out of the frame, afraid of erasing any piece of history I could hold on to. Alex Griffin, surrounded by friends, filled the picture with an infectious smile. Even with the dark flowing hair and a taller frame, the eyes were mirrors of my own. And the stubby nose and cleft chin I always hated, I now loved. Because they were Dad's. They were ours.

As I sat there, lost in a history I'd never known, morning sunlight filtered through the attic window. I crept downstairs, before Mom woke, and slid into my bed after locking my bedroom door. Rose Tyler cuddled into me as I once again stared at my ceiling. This time, I was no longer lost in thought, but filled with questions.

I texted Mom, said I had a stomach bug and was staying home from school. She softly knocked on my door thirty minutes later, but I ignored it. She texted back saying if I needed anything at all to call her and she'd come home, that she was in meetings all day and having drinks with studio heads later tonight. I didn't reply. Because what I *need* is for Mom to stop lying to me, to finally tell me the truth once and for all: why she's hiding Alex Griffin from my life.

So I spent the day and night alone, watching the sun fall over the ocean.

I didn't let myself think about why Alex Griffin disappeared. Or whether Dad ran off to start a new family, leaving us behind. Or if Dad's ashes are scattered over the Big Sur cliffs, and that's why Mom cries every time I ask. No, I pushed those feelings down with the sunset, and let the brilliant pinks and oranges left behind wash over me. Where I'm choosing to live in hope instead.

This is when I call Charlie and Christopher to help me figure out a plan I'd begun to devise, which is where we are now. It's sometime after nine and they both rushed over from Garrett Davenport's last spring break party as soon as I texted.

"Whoa. I mean, whoa, whoa, whoa." Charlie's pacing my bedroom, pages in hand. They look like a faded version of themselves: no makeup, no wig, just a plain white tee and jeans. They flip their Dodgers cap backward to think. "Okay. What we know in this moment: Your dad's living in San Francisco. Maybe. And is an exceptional storyteller—"

"Like Fig!" Christopher says. Sort of. We've propped him up with pillows on my bed and he's slouched over his phone, wearing only his plaid boxers and Radiohead T-shirt, drunk out of his gourd. (The second he came into my room, he thrashed his jeans and Adidas off, yelling, "Clothes are so fucking restrictive!" to no one at all.) Rose Tyler's splayed out on his belly. "You know who else wrote letters like that? Oscar Wilde. And d'you know where he wrote them? In pissin—prison, I mean. Considered the greatest love letters of all time. Learned that today."

Charlie and I look at each other as he continues, enunciating each word to make sure they fall out properly. "And you know who else went to prison because they were gay? Bayard Rustin. Know who he was?" He's still staring at his phone, so we don't answer. "The Black wizard behind the curtain, that's who! He had to hide in the quiet queer shadows his whole life, while he organized only *the most iconic* March on Washington with Martin Luther King that ever happened! That's . . . who he was," he says.

Charlie and I study the pages.

"And you want to know something else?" Christopher throws his phone on the bed. Rose Tyler jumps down, snuggling into his wadded-up jeans on the floor.

"Christopher," I say, "we really have to—"

"Rumor has it, while in prison, he read Oscar's letters." He gapes at the ceiling. "Couldn't really confirm those rumors," he says softly. He appears to be having a dialogue with himself. "But that inspired him to keep going, to know he'd be okay. Imagine that. If Oscar hadn't been taken to prison because he was gay, he would've never written those letters, and who knows, maybe Bayard would've just given up! Thrown in the towel! Maybe he would've never organized that march and who knows what else . . . Been thinking about that one all day. Yuppity yup. Trappity trap." He giggles.

And now he's opening the wooden box with my initials carved on it!

"Hey! No! What are you doing?" I yell. "Don't touch that!"

"Why not?"

"You know why not. Put it down."

"You don't want to look at all the *scary* letters inside."

"You're being an asshole now," I say, grabbing the box away from him and stashing it safely back inside my nightstand drawer.

"What's he talking about?" Charlie says. "The pages in my hand?"

"It's nothing."

"No. These are letters he wrote to his *dad*," he says.

"I should've never told you."

"I'm glad you fid, Dig," Christopher says. "Did. Fig. Finally let me in on something." He flops over on the bed, pulling me toward him. "Come here."

"Not now, we—"

"Oh, just come here for a sec." He yanks me down, our faces inches apart. Lifts a screwy smile. He smells like a brewery. "Gotdamn. You're so pretty, Fig. You know that? Isn't he pretty, Charlie?"

"He's damn fine, Christopher." Charlie walks over to the open window and sits, still scouring the pages.

"Where'd you go, Fig?"

"I'm right here."

"No, you're not. You've been missing for a while." He attempts to caress my cheek but hits my head instead. "Whoops. Sorry, I mean. That's what I meant to say. I'm sorry, Fig. I didn't know how . . . important all this"—he flings his arms in the air—"was to you. I mean, I *knew*, but you didn't tell me everything and I don't understand why."

"It's not you, it's hard to explain."

"Do you ever feel like you're in prison, Fig?"

"What?"

Except he's not really asking me. He gazes past me, lost in the ceiling again. "I do," he whispers. But just barely, so only I can hear.

"You have to go to San Francisco," Charlie says. I turn to them as they glance up from the letters.

"And do what? Walk the streets asking strangers if they've seen my dad? Where do I even start?"

"San Francisco?" Christopher fumbles forward. "Let me see those pages."

"Be careful," I say, handing them over.

"I'd start with the name and number on that last page," Charlie says, pirouetting down on the bed next to us. "Who was it?"

"Aunt Luna," Christopher says.

"These pages are over fifty years old," I say. "I bet that phone number doesn't even work. And that woman's probably dead."

"Your dad might be, too," Christopher mumbles, now typing on his phone.

"Christopher!" Charlie says, punching his knee.

"No. He's right. I've thought of that. According to those pages, Alex would be around seventy now. Mom said I wasn't planned, that she had me late in life. I was a *miracle baby* or some shit."

"Suzanne Pressley's dad is, like, seventy-five," Charlie says. "And he's still running the LA Marathon."

"Either way, if I go, how do I get away? And when? And where do we go if Aunt Luna isn't the starting point?"

"Not so fast, dear Watson," Christopher says, in a weird English accent. "Just did a quick ol' search-a-roonie on this here durn finagled contraption—"

"Why are you talking like—"

"And BOOM!" Christopher flips over his phone to show us his screen.

It's an article from the *San Francisco Chronicle*, dated August of last year: "Meet the City's Adopted Aunt: Luna, the Woman Who Saved the Streets!" And underneath, a picture of a round woman, covered in layers of shawls and wrinkles, surrounded by a People-Rainbow and smiling so bright it looks like she just swallowed the sun.

"Oh," I say.

"Wow," Charlie says.

"Yup," Christopher says.

We read. About how she's been saving people on the streets since the sixties. About how she's saved thousands of LGBTQ+ homeless kids' lives. About how anyone's welcome to stay with her, anytime. And on and on and on. In short: She's the Mother Teresa of San Francisco.

"I mean," I say.

"Yeah," Christopher says.

"There it is," Charlie says.

"We're leaving tomorrow," Christopher says.

"What? No, we can't."

"And I'm going with you," he says. "Never been to San Francisco."

"Christopher, I meant someday, not—"

"If not now, Fig, when?"

"He's right," Charlie says.

"But how? I work and—"

"Get your shifts covered," Charlie says.

"And it's spring freaking break," says Christopher.

"You always said you were looking for a sign. To figure out what's next in your life. Well, Fig. Here it is."

"But I—don't know. What about Mom?" I ask. "She'd never let me go, even if I could tell her."

"I'll stay here," Charlie says. "You can both tell your folks you're sleeping over this weekend."

"You like to feel all alone in this cuckoo world, Fig," says Christopher. "But we won't let you."

Look at them. All wild and wonderful, covered in whacked-out smiles, radiating love. Maybe they're right. This is my chance. The actual map I've been waiting for. I felt it the minute I read the letter, too: I had to go to San Francisco. It's the first tangible answer to the question I've been asking since I was five years old. But I didn't think I would actually *go*.

Their faces blur as I feel the tears brimming my eyes. I walk to the window, stare out into the sea of orange blossoms in our backyard. My heart flutters, the same way it did when I thought I could hold the nebula in my palm.

I don't know what will come of it, or who I'll find along the way, but Charlie's right: Something's pulling me to San Francisco and I can't ignore it. Maybe this is exactly how Dad felt.

"Okay," I say, feeling more and more alive with each word. "Let's figure this out."

So we do.

We spend the rest of the night coming up with the ultimate plan to maybe, *finally*, find my dad.

part two

THE QUEST
FOR YESTERDAY

11

One hundred and eight.

That's how many miles we've driven so far this morning, and it's been exactly three hours and twenty-two minutes. What with the combination of Satan's Treadmill to Nowhere, aka Los Angeles traffic (yes, even on a Saturday), and the fact that I don't drive Oscar more than sixty miles per hour on the freeway—which is making Christopher slowly go bonkers—I've done the calculation and realized we will get to San Francisco in approximately eleven days.

I slept all of twelve minutes last night, anticipation fizzing through my veins, hoping our plan would work. I left Mom a note saying I was staying at Charlie's house for the weekend and taking Rose Tyler with me. Charlie called Aunt Luna this morning to reserve a room and reassured me, after a lengthy discussion with her, that she distinctly remembered Alex Griffin and was the kindest woman they'd ever talked to. So I pocketed my lucky talismans for good measure and Charlie waved us off, saying, "You'll find what you've been looking for, Fig."

I hope they're right.

Christopher's leaning his head against the passenger window, going in and out of consciousness. He woke up grumpy, hungover, and remembering very little of last night, but for the fact we were going to

San Francisco. He's been mostly quiet since we left, leaving me alone with my thoughts.

I wonder what Alex Griffin looks like today, whether Dad will recognize me as instantly as I did them in the photo. I wonder if we'll run into each other's arms and never let go, or run away from each other and never look back. If we'll catch up on lost dreams and create new ones together. If we'll even care . . .

I even started rehearsing what I'd say, all the questions I could finally ask. Beginning with: *Where have you been?*

But now I can't stop thinking this may all be for nothing. Maybe Dad left the city years ago. Maybe Dad died. Or maybe Dad never wanted me in the first place. I was an accident, after all.

I can't decide what's worse, finding all the answers or never knowing the truth.

Christopher's up again. He's snuggled in his green bomber jacket, wearing the same ripped skinny jeans from last night. I let him borrow one of my T-shirts because his was extra-ripe; it's so tight on him I'm convinced his muscles might burst through. Rose Tyler's curled on his lap sound asleep.

We haven't talked about what happened the other night, how we left my bedroom choked with unspoken feelings and thoughts. How I realized he's been pushing me away for a few months now, without the actual shove. How it's been so long since I've seen him cry.

And we haven't taken a road trip together for over a year. So now that he's awake, and we're driving safely through a long stretch of flattened fields, I tell him.

"Huh?" He glances over, his usual sparkly gold eyes muted and dull.

"I said I'm happy we're doing this together. Thanks for coming with me."

"Oh, babes, totally." He lifts a strained smile and looks back out the window.

"I mean, we haven't done something like this in forever." I laugh. "Remember when we went to the LA County Fair and took a picture together in front of the blue-ribbon jam and that woman in a cow costume photobombed us?"

"Oh yeah." He chuckles.

"That's still on my phone when you call me. Good times." And they were. For some reason, they feel so far away now. "Anyway, I'm glad we're doing this because, I don't know, I guess I've felt this distance between us for a while and I didn't even realize—"

"Huh?"

"Distance."

"Oh." He checks his phone. "We have about . . . two hundred and seventy-five more miles to go. Oh boy."

"No. I mean between us."

"What?"

Why do I feel like I'm talking to myself here? "You okay?"

"I'm just tired, is all. I have a headache." He pulls up his shirt, exposing the hairy trail down his stomach. "First thing when we get to San Francisco—if we ever do—I'm getting a bigger shirt somewhere."

"Okay . . ."

He squirms in his seat, sighs. "What were you saying, Fig?"

"I don't know . . . Like, we've been together for almost two years now, right? And a lot's happened between us, I know. And I guess, well, you ever think about that first time we met? I mean, it was wild. For both of us. Remember?"

"Yeah, it was."

"All those feelings we had inside, you remember? Like we were free-falling in space and—"

"Why are you talking about the first time we met?" He leans his head against the window again. Rose Tyler stretches out and he rubs her belly.

"I mean, look. The point I'm trying to make is this: I'm sorry for getting mad at you at school the other day."

"When?"

"When that kid asked for your autograph."

"You're still thinking about that?"

"Well, yeah. I can't stop thinking about what a supreme asshole I was, and I'm sorry for what I—"

"We both were. It's okay."

"But what I said was . . . stupid. I was pissed, I guess, and a mess of other things."

"It's okay, Isaac."

"I know you can't be out—"

"Fig. Not now."

"It's not my place to say when or how or to whom you should come out because—"

"Babes—"

"That's none of my business and it's a very personal decision, obviously, and you need to know I'm sorry."

"Fig."

"What?"

"Can we drop this now? Please? I don't want to talk about it."

"Sorry. It's just—"

"You really have no idea what it's like. None."

"I know."

He shifts in his seat, facing me. "And you for sure don't know what it means to be Black and gay. Hollywood acts like it's woke, but it's not. Far from it."

"I thought things had changed."

"Not according to my agent. So, can we move on? Please? I just want to have a relaxing time away from everything." His phone vibrates, but he doesn't look at it. Instead, he looks out the passenger window, muttering something to himself.

"I'm sorry. You're right."

"And please quit saying sorry."

"Sorry, I—"

"Isaac!"

To stop myself from saying sorry again, I turn on the radio. Static fills the space between us.

Exactly seventeen miles later, I ask softly, "Ever think we'll have what we once had?" A tear trickles down my cheek, surprising me. I wipe it away without him noticing.

"What'd you say?" he asks, shifting up.

"Never mind."

"Can we pull over? I have to pee."

"I think there's a rest area up ahead, or a McDonald's."

"I have to go now. I also have to get out of this car for a minute or I'm going to rip my eyeballs out."

"Oh. Okay. Sorry if I—"

"Fig. Seriously. Quit saying sorry. I'm not pissed, okay? Just—why do you always hold on to stuff for so long? It's not good for you."

"I don't."

"I've moved on from that morning. You should, too. That's what you wanted to do here, right?"

"It's bigger than that, though. It's not as simple as—"

"It is actually. And the way we do that is if we stop talking about things that happened in the past."

"Fine." So I shut up and pull over. He starts to open the door and I quick-grab Rose Tyler's collar. "Christopher!"

"What?"

"She could've . . . never mind. Can you take her out with you?"

"Sure." He snaps her leash on, and I watch them trot down the shoulder, disappearing behind some rocks.

I stare forward, waiting. Only now realizing how tight I'm gripping the steering wheel. My knuckles throb and pinch together. I shake them loose.

Maybe it's because we've left the safety of home. Maybe we've been living on two separate continents in our heads for longer than I thought. Maybe I've been so blinded by my search for Dad, I haven't let myself see what's been happening in front of me. But it's clear now that Christopher's become another fissure in my heart. And I wonder if I'm one of his.

Rose Tyler's bouncing on the seat again, smiling, panting. Christopher jumps in, closing the door.

"Much better. I needed air," he says. "Look, I didn't mean to— It's all just so—*argh*—you know?" He tugs his shirt down, pulls up his jeans. "I mean, with school ending and this being our last summer together before college and—"

"You're going to USC. It's not that far."

"I know, but they say things change." He leans over, kisses my cheek.

"Things don't have to change that much," I say under my breath. But he doesn't hear.

"I was thinking we should go out tonight." He buckles up. "I found all these amazing bars that sound so—"

"Reminder: We're not headed to San Francisco to go barhopping."

"I know. But we're not allowed to have some *fun*? We need to go to at least one gay bar in San Francisco, Fig. It's like sacrilege if we don't."

"Maybe." What he seemingly fails to understand is that this journey to find my dad, in and of itself, is fun for me. Well, it was, anyway.

"There's this place called the Oasis," he says, "which is, like, super famous with these awesome drag shows and has been around a while. And, also, I wonder how far that Aunt Loon lady lives from the Castro—that's the gay mecca of the world, basically." And on and on he goes, as I pull back onto the highway.

Two hours later, Christopher says, "I gotta pee again."

"Seriously? We haven't even gone that far."

"It hurts."

"Fine." So I pull over in front of what appears to be a cow farm factory—because there are literally thousands of cows mooing and feeding into cow-infinity. "Please hurry, this smell is melting my insides."

He laughs, opening the door, and all my thoughts come crashing down from the clouds as I watch Rose Tyler dash into the field.

12

This next moment in history is sponsored by Shout, Panic, and Unrelenting Terror.

Everything is a Technicolor blur. And I am screaming. Oh, am I screaming. The wailing pounds me back into my body, and I am scrambling through (what I hope is) mud, my vocal cords stretched so taut I think a few pluck loose.

I see Rose Tyler disappear like a cartoon cloud and Christopher bolt after her, stumbling a few times as he zigzags through a maze of cows. And he's gone.

I'm still screaming, my arms flailing through the air, when suddenly the ground is too close to my face and the world spins. I'm rolling down a hill and land face-first in a pile of please-God-let-it-be-mud (it is) splatted into the earth.

That's when I look up to see a cow tongue that is way too big for this planet. And I shriek. Loud. Really loud. So loud, the cow runs off, slopping more mud in my face. This makes me yell louder.

I scramble up when I hear Christopher shout something at me. I can't see him. Can't see anything. I wipe my eyes and follow his voice, waving my arms in all directions.

And in that second, I see a flash of blue. Like a crystalline streak that shoots down from the sky and lands in the form of a person, all wobbly and disoriented, several yards ahead of me.

I run after her/him/huh, still flailing, darting in and out of a stunned cow obstacle course. My brain feels like it's full of exploding meteorites, my heart might be experiencing a cataclysmic attack, and my legs noodle under me. Until I turn a corner and see a blue-haired person and Christopher crouched down, huddled over something. I stop. I cover my mouth. Then I yell, *"Is she dead?"*

They both turn.

That's when I see Rose Tyler's little pink tongue kissing the stranger, and it may be the first time I actually believe in a Jesus Christ.

I dash over, grabbing the muddy Rose Tyler blob. I can barely make out the blacks of her eyes peeping through, her heart pitter-pattering in my palms. And damned if she's not smiling, currently the happiest pup on the planet. I squeeze her to my chest. She licks my face in between supersonic pants.

Christopher rubs my back, saying, "I'm so sorry, I'm so sorry," ad infinitum.

The blue-haired person gazes up at the sky, inhaling deep breaths, like she/he/they need to suck up the clouds to stay alive or something, and says, "Man, that's some gnarly smell."

That's when my senses return, and a putrid stench overtakes me. "Holy God, let's go" fumbles out of my mouth.

"Agreed. This girl needs to change her shoes," says the stranger, who I can now see is a white girl with long, blue-tinted hair floating down her back. She leads the way.

Christopher still holds me, apologizing profusely.

I clutch Rose Tyler and glance at Christopher for the first time. His face is streaked in mud, shirt's torn in a few places. His jeans might officially be destroyed. He wheezes, shakes. I nudge him and say, "Quit sayin' sorry. You're driving me nuts."

And we look at each other. And smile. And that's when I finally exhale.

13

We've stopped time.

Or something's happening.

Because we're standing, the three of us, on the side of the road, not moving, not talking, as cars whiz by behind us.

This is when I'm able to slowly take in the blue-haired girl, who's around our age and whose sudden appearance I'm still questioning. One thing is certain, though, there's a serious amount of blue happening: blue long-sleeved flouncing shirt; blue jeans that hug her thighs; blue Converse splotched with mud. Not to mention her thick strands of electric-blue hair, like little flames flickering on a gas burner. She's beautiful.

"Isaac?"

"Huh?"

"You want a towel?"

"What?"

"Towel? She asked if you wanted a towel?" Christopher's somehow smothering his face with the one from my back seat, like Time edited out the boring parts, and Blue Girl is no longer standing in front of me but hunkered down in the trunk of her Jeep—also blue, by the way.

"Well . . . uh."

"Here ya go," she says, throwing it to me.

"Thank you." I mop Rose Tyler's face.

"Thanks for your help back there," Christopher says, sitting on the edge of Oscar's passenger seat, now using the towel to clean his hair. "I couldn't have caught her without you."

"Be glad I used to be on varsity track," she says. "It was the weirdest thing . . ." She's still tucked in her trunk, changing her shoes, I think. "I was behind you and saw you pull over, and then you start barreling into the cow fields, and you—" She peeks up, pointing at me. As she does, her blouse billows away from her chest and she is most definitely not wearing a bra. My eyes bounce back. "You basically looked like a Baby Yeti running after him, so how could I not stop to see what was happening?"

Christopher laughs at this.

She mutters something to her car, then looks up at me and says, "Come here."

"Oh. Uh—" I glance over to Christopher, who's now stripped his shirt off and is fishing through a bag to find another. At the same time, Rose Tyler starts squirming in my arms.

And I swear Blue Girl reads the thought bubble that pops from my head: *You should really thank her for helping.* Because the next thing she says is: "You're welcome. Now come here." So I do.

She reaches toward me; I flinch back. "You have a—"

"What?"

"Something on your—"

"Huh?"

"Right on your—"

"Who?"

"Stop fidgeting, you fool!" She grabs my cheeks with one hand, squishing my lips together, and starts cleaning my face.

Up close, her sea-green eyes shimmer like two pieces of emerald. Wish I could remember what that stone is used for; I think it's the heart. And she has impossibly long lashes.

"I'm Max, by the way," she says. She grabs my hand to shake it, and sparks fly. I'm not kidding. A literal shock rips through us.

"Ow," I say, at the same time she exclaims, "Well, would you look at that!"

But we don't let go. We're still shaking.

"Maximillian, actually," she says finally, "but Max is fine. Mad Max even. Totally works. And to answer your question, yup, every kid called me Maxi Pad. Some still do. But for the love of the gods, do not call me Maxine. It does something to me I cannot explain."

"Ah. Oh. 'Kay."

"Well?"

"What?"

"Your name?"

"Oh, right. Fig—Isaac, I mean."

"Which is it?"

"I go by both—Isaac."

"Cool. Nice to meet ya, Fig Isaac."

"Heh . . ."

We're still shaking. This may be getting weird, but her hand's supremely soft. And warm. Like it just came out of the dryer. And looking into her eyes feels, I don't know, safe. Familiar even.

"Guess we should head on out," Christopher says, grabbing my waist from behind.

"Right," I say. "Thanks again."

"Sure thing." She makes her voice all babyish. "And don't you be running out in those fields again, you hear me?"

"Ha, I won't," I say.

"I was talking to your dog."

"Right."

I peek inside her trunk just before she slams it shut. Trash bags full of clothes. Two boxes of groceries. And a collage of bumper stickers: I BRAKE FOR SCIENCE GEEKS and YOU ARE THE PERIODIC CHART OF MY HEART. But the one that sticks out to me, peeling and faded, reads: THIS CAR IS ACTUALLY A TARDIS, which is indeed a dark blue boxy Jeep.

"So, lemme guess, you boys are running north," she says. "Spring break?"

"Oh yeah."

"I feel ya. Doing the same. Just goin' where the wind blows me. Which is north, so—" She points her fingers in the shape of two guns and *pows*.

We stare.

"So, anyway," she says, "have a good life!" She climbs into her Jeep. Seconds later, jazz music croons through her speakers. We both jump. "Just need to check some directions on my phone before I go," she yells.

We wave goodbye and slide into Oscar. As soon as Christopher's closed the door and buckled in, I hand him Rose Tyler. "Don't let her go," I say. I see Maximillian in my rearview mirror bouncing her head, typing on her phone.

"I like her," I say.

"Yeah, she's cool."

Well, have a good life, I think, and off we go.

Nope. No, we do not.

"Oh no," I say.

"What? What is it?"

"Oh no no no no no."

"What?"

I turn the ignition again. Nothing. And again. Nope. Again. "NO."

"Fig, it's okay. Just let it rest for a second, then try again."

I wait.

Then I turn it again. Nothing. I slam my hands on the steering wheel.

"Okay, okay," Christopher says. "Let me see." He starts scrolling on his phone.

Max honks and shrugs her shoulders. I give her two thumbs-up.

"Turn it over again," he says, looking at a YouTube video.

"What?!"

"The ignition. Turn it again."

I do.

Nothing.

"Huh," he says.

"What huh?"

"Think he's dead."

"I know that! What do we do?!"

"I don't—"

And somehow Max has teleported because she's now knocking on the passenger window. We jump again. Christopher rolls the window down. "He won't start."

"Oh no," Max says. "Turn it over. Lemme hear."

I do.

She bends down, peering in. "Mm-hmm. It's your starter."

"My what-er?"

"Starter. You'll likely need a new one. Trust me, I know these things. Had to change a couple myself." She nods back to her Jeep and laughs. "Happy to give you a lift up north if you—"

"That's nice of you, but—"

"Can you give us a minute?" Christopher asks her.

"Sure thing." Max walks away, covering her nose from the cow stench.

Sweat streams down my face. This is not part of the plan.

"Babes? You okay?"

I nod.

"We really don't have a choice here."

"Meaning?"

"We go with her."

"And just leave Oscar here to rot and rust? Great plan, Christopher." I wipe my face with my shirt, which I only now realize I'd forgotten to change and is covered in mud and cow shit and—"GOD!"

"Fig. Listen to me. We get in her car; she drops us off at Aunt Luna's; we call a tow company; we have Oscar taken to the nearest station to get him fixed; we spend two nights in San Francisco as planned; we pick up Oscar; we're home the same night *as planned*. Just a little hiccup, but still on track." He smiles.

"I don't know."

"Look, it's either that or we get towed now and waste a day trying to figure out what to do next. And anyway, she's *right here*, Fig, she totally saved Rose Tyler, and you just said you liked her."

"I did. I do. But—she's a *stranger*? And just leave Oscar?"

"We're in the middle of nothing but cows. He'll be fine. Trust me. And if we got a cab, we'd be with a stranger then, too. Only it would cost a ton more."

I glance back up in the rearview mirror. Max waves, points her fingers into guns, and mouths, *"Pow,"* laughing, which for some inexplicable reason makes me feel at ease.

"Just . . . let me think a minute." I close my eyes as everything flits in and out of focus. I breathe—sharp, fluttering, staccato breaths, like a bird's trapped in my rib cage. Okay. So, Oscar is dead. Max is here. And Christopher's right. We're already way behind schedule, and losing a day is not an option.

I open my eyes. Max is now leaning against her car staring at us.

"Let's go," I say. "But I'm writing a note to leave on the dash."

"Great," Christopher says. He waits until I have Rose Tyler securely tucked in my arms before opening the door, grabbing our bags, and jogging back to tell Max the plan.

After securing my note under the windshield wiper, I clutch RT and lock Oscar up, conjuring some incantation protective spell like Mom might use. As I walk toward the Jeep, Christopher's already buckled up in the back.

I hop in the passenger seat. The door creaks shut, and I know Max is saying something, but I barely get my hand on the seat belt before she revs the engine and takes off.

14

We don't speak for a few miles, unsure of what to say to each other.

Soon, the dark, muddy cow farm turn into endless rows of blossoming trees, all perfectly aligned between patches of light green grass and dirt paths. The sun hits the pink blooms and gives them an extra shine, as if they're radiating from the branches. With no breeze, they sit motionless. Like a painter ran through the fields to create a landscape you'd only see in your dreams. All I want to do is run naked through their perfection.

"What kind of trees are those?" I finally ask.

"Almond," Max says, glancing over. "You've never seen them?"

"We have orange trees with white flowers, but I've never seen anything so pink before."

"They don't look real, do they?"

"No, they don't."

Max starts petting Rose Tyler, who strangely stops trembling in my arms when she does. "She is so adorable. What's her name?"

"Rose Tyler." But anyway, *Max is not looking at the road anymore.* "And, you know, uh, the road." I'm trying to be nice to her, for saving our lives and all, but this is not how I want to die.

She turns back and screams, "Wait, what?!"

"It's just . . . the road . . . you weren't looking and—"

"No. *No.* Hold up. You mean like the greatest most awesome *Doctor Who* companion, season one and season two Rose Tyler?"

"Oh. Well. Precisely."

"You know who that is?" Christopher asks from the back seat.

"Do I ever," Max says, lifting an incredible grin. This time I see her teeth—they are not blue, they are newly-braces-free perfect. "Well, ain't that something else." And she laughs so hard it punches a hole in the roof of her car.

First of all: excellent laugh. Second of all: *Who is she?* I've never met a single soul who knows *Doctor Who* by choice. Okay, she's mesmerizing.

As is her car, by the way, which is another serious work of art. The dash is covered in twisting plastic vines, and the roof is spattered with artifacts: tarot cards and bird feathers, clipped headlines and ripped-out book pages with highlighted passages, and dried flowers, to name a few. Like she collects trinkets along her alien travels.

She sips from her Big Gulp, then talks into it like a microphone. "Welcome aboard the TARDIS Express, fellow travelers. Our estimated time of arrival is approximately three hours and twenty-two minutes. Now we ask you to sit back, relax, and enjoy the ride. And try to ignore the cow poop emanating from the passengers." She slurps. Turns up the jazz music. Takes a deep breath. And smiles.

I laugh, settling into my seat, and finally relax for the first time since we left.

15

The sun has shifted closer to the mountains, the shadows lengthening against their ridges.

A thundering breeze flies in through the open windows, to help mask the stench that now seems to be infused in our pores. It's impossible to talk without us yelling at each other, so we eventually give up. I hold Rose Tyler as she perches on the door, her fluffy fur blowing wildly in the wind, free. The dashboard trinkets chime around her, like how you might imagine stars would sound if you could hear them twinkle.

Outside, the painted almond trees have morphed into lines of strawberry fields that stretch to the horizon. Towering farmhand figures carved out of wood wave back as we drive by. Underneath them, actual workers hunched over rows of vines dot the fields. They wear sun hats with long canvas flaps and add bundles of strawberries to their baskets.

But soon, even they disappear, leaving the flattened countryside once again barren.

"We're pulling over there," Max suddenly says. "That feels right."

"Huh?" I ask.

"What'd you say?" Christopher yells from the back.

"It smells like Satan's butt in here and I can't take it anymore," she says. "We're going to that farmhouse to see if we can rinse off or something."

"Can't we just wait till we get to San Francisco?" Christopher yells.

"Sorry, kids."

"Uh . . . is this a good idea?" I ask as she exits the freeway. "It looks abandoned." A lone, ramshackle house sits in the middle of nothing, miles away from any farmworkers we've last seen. In another story, this is the perfect backdrop for a *Texas Chainsaw* sequel. I hope it's not that story.

"Where's your sense of adventure, you two? You'll thank me, I promise."

There's a difference between adventure and meeting serial killers who have a garage filled with meat hooks, but never mind. We have no choice but to surrender here.

"We really do smell," Christopher says as we pull onto the dirt road, the breeze subsided.

"Damn," I say. "You're right."

"Told you," Max says. "Look, there's a hose over there."

She drives to the side of the house where a long hose snakes on the ground. I see no cars in the makeshift driveway, no gigantic men with leather faces peering through the window. In fact, no movement at all. The house is empty of any signs of life.

We step outside, stretch. Rose Tyler, securely fastened to her leash, immediately pees.

I inhale deeply.

The quiet of the open land, even with the cars rushing by behind us, is comforting.

Christopher and Max walk toward the house. I catch myself in the passenger mirror for the first time. Dried clumps of mud—and I refuse to think what else—splotch my face. Christopher, ahead of me, is similarly flecked. Max's blue hair has turned into strips of clay.

"You think it'll work?" Christopher says, his hands on his hips, watching Max bend over the hose.

"Only one way to find out," she says. Max squeaks it on, and soon water pours from the spigot. "Eureka!"

"Excellent call, Max," Christopher says. He's stripped out of his shirt and jeans and stands in his boxers, letting the water fall over him. "Oh man, this feels nice."

Rose Tyler pulls me toward them, panting heavily. She starts lapping furiously at the stream of water.

"Aww, you must've been parched. Sorry, RT."

"Damn, I really needed that," Christopher says. "Go rinse off." He kisses my cheek and runs back to the car to change.

I turn to Max, who now holds the hose, the water drenching her clothed body. As the mud washes away, colors spring back to life in her hair, her eyes, her pale moon face. Like the water is painting her.

I wonder if she's happy. There's a sadness inside her smile I recognize from my own. I wonder if she feels the same in me, if there's an unspoken thread that connects people in pain. I wonder where she's going, what happened to her. Maybe this is what she does: drives with a directionless map, stopping whenever it *feels right*.

I wish I could be more like that.

"Thanks, Max," I say.

"For what?" She flings her head from side to side, sprinkling the air. Rose Tyler bites the air, trying to catch the drops.

"Stopping here. That was a good—" She points the hose at me, splashing me from head to toe. "You did not just do that."

"Oh, I did," she says, giggling.

"Okay. Funny. Can you not—"

And she does it again.

"Really?"

Christopher laughs behind me. Rose Tyler keeps bouncing up to grab the spraying water. Max giggles uncontrollably.

"Your face," she says. "Good to be surprised once in a while, isn't it? That feeling is so underrated."

"Give it to me," I say.

"As long as you don't spray me back."

"It's no fun when you know what's coming," I say.

"Truer words were never spoken," she says, and hands me the hose. I rinse off as she takes RT for a short walk.

It's refreshing, cleansing even. Like I'm removing years of built-up mud from my body. The thought catches me. Because maybe it's true. Maybe I'm starting to do just that.

Max is right. It does feel good to be surprised.

Soon, we're all changed and sitting back in the Jeep. And although we didn't clean every inch of mud from our bodies, the smell at least has mercifully diminished.

I exhale slowly, gazing out the window.

As we drive away from the farmhouse, pulling up the ramp onto the freeway, a feeling begins to settle inside me I haven't felt in a long time. Lightness.

16

Somehow, two hours and eighteen minutes have passed.

The sun's fallen behind the mountains now, spattering the sky with fluorescent pink and apricot clouds. It's breathtaking.

Max has been humming to the jazz music, every so often chewing on a Snickers bar or something, perfectly content.

Like Rose Tyler, Christopher fell asleep not too long after we settled back into the drive. His head is propped against the slightly open window.

In this moment, all is well.

And because we're no longer competing with the blaring wind, I decide now's a good time to talk to Max.

"Cool music," I say.

"What's that?" She turns to me, suddenly alert and energized, like I've just plopped a coin in a slot.

"The music. I like it."

"Ah. Miles Davis. Ultimate classic jazz trumpeter. My dad's favorite. Grew up listening to him. He made this mix, actually." She's still dewy and glowing and adjusts the vent to blow more cool air on her.

"Never heard him before."

"You don't know what you're missing, Fig. Oh, hey, can I call ya Fig, or is that like a cutesy boyfriend-only name?"

"What? Oh. *Him?* No! I mean—no idea why I just said it like that—heh. My friend Charlie gave me that nickname years ago because all I ever ate growing up were those cookies and my name's Isaac, so yeah."

"And the common denominator is Newton. Clever kid, your friend!"

"Yeah."

"How does it feel to be named after a famous mathematician?"

"Eh. It's a curse actually."

"Oh? Tell me more." She turns down the music. Rose Tyler flops over in my lap. I stroke her belly. She opens her eyes slightly, then falls right back to sleep.

"I don't know. Pretty much every famous Isaac in history died with some lonely secret, like there's something jinxed about that name." Max says nothing, still staring at the road. "It's silly. Never mind."

"No, it's not. But I think you're wrong." She drums her fingers on the steering wheel.

"I'm not actually, but—"

"Newton? What was his thing?"

"Died a virgin. Never found love."

"How awful. Asimov?"

"Died of HIV. Couldn't tell anyone."

"Really?"

"Yup."

"Wow. 'K. I know you're wrong here, but I don't know how just yet and need to get back to you."

"I'm not. But whatever, I love your name."

"I do too. My dad gave it to me. Although the only famous Maximillians I know are all dead white dudes." I laugh. She swipes a blue strand of hair behind her ear to look at me. "It was my grandpa's name."

"Cool."

She grabs a bag of jelly beans from her cup holder. "Want some?"

"Sure, thanks." I pour a few into my palm, replacing the black licorice ones, because: *blech*.

"I'm staying in San Francisco for the night, too," she says. "Who are you staying with?"

"Oh, this Aunt Luna woman who isn't technically my aunt . . . it's a weird long story."

"We've got time."

"Well, I guess she lets people stay with her, like a boardinghouse or something, and uh, yeah, incredibly long story short: I'm looking for my dad."

"What? No way! That's some serious *Star Wars* shit right there."

"But it's my actual life, so."

"Right."

"What about you? Where are you staying?"

"Oh . . . my aunt's, too," she says.

Which is oddly coincidental, but that's when I notice the tattoo on her forearm peeking out from under her shirt. The start of some thorny rose vine twirling up her arm. "Cool tattoo," I say.

"What?"

I nod at her exposed wrist. "What kind of rose is—"

"Oh shit," she says, and quickly pushes her sleeve back down. "It's nothing."

"It looked pretty. Why'd you—"

"It's nothing!" Rose Tyler snaps up. Christopher stirs in the back seat.

"Sorry," I say.

Her smile has caved, so I rub RT's belly and watch the world outside slowly fade to black. The sky begins to turn a violet color I've never seen before, disappearing into the darkness. A few lonely stars peek through.

"Funny, isn't it?" she asks after a while.

"What?"

"Us meeting like this. I mean, I don't know if you figured it out, but I'm kinda into *Doctor Who*."

"I wondered."

"Well, full disclosure: I wasn't a huge fan. My dad used to make me watch it all the time, but it grew on me. He liked the classic vintage episodes. I'm more into the revamped version."

"Same."

"That's who I'm headed to see, actually."

"Your dad? He's with your aunt?"

"Not exactly. He's near the Northern Lights. And he always told me to 'Follow the patterns and pay attention to the signs,' so I can't help but wonder what all this means." She waves her hands in my direction.

"Yeah. I almost gave up on that philosophy. Until recently," I say, looking out the window. Mountains painted with deep magenta tips whiz by.

"What changed?"

I look over. Her eyes have softened and there's something familiar in them, but I can't tell what it is.

"It's . . . another long story, but I've never met my dad. Didn't think I ever would. Then, out of the blue, I find this letter. And now here we are in your car, going to San Francisco to maybe meet the person I've been missing my whole life. If Dad's even there, or alive."

"Following the signs," she says, sending a soft laugh to the heavens. Rose Tyler lifts her head, starts to crawl out of my lap toward her.

17

An hour later, the sun has long disappeared, and in its place San Francisco city life shines all around us. Neon glows from tattoo parlors and vintage clothing stores. Fluorescent glares from corner bodegas. Rows of Victorian homes built impossibly close together stack the hills like a line of brightly colored dominoes.

Above us, electric lines string in every direction between buildings. Every so often a bus drives by, sparking a few volts along the path from an outstretched pole on its roof. And each time, it sends a surge of energy to my heart. I imagine Alex Griffin sitting in a bus seat looking down on me. Or walking into a bohemian bookstore, waving back at me. Or eating pasta at a candlelit booth, inviting me in. Being here, I already feel that much closer to Dad.

"There it is," Christopher says. We look up to realize we're across the street from Aunt Luna's home. I recognize it immediately from the article. Like looking at a postcard labeled SUMMER OF LOVE. It's a two-story Victorian slabbed with brick-red siding that's been patched up in places over the years, smothered in a front garden of thick vines, twinkling trees, and torn Tibetan flags.

"I guess this is us," Christopher says, opening the door. "Thanks again, Max. You're a true lifesaver. Is the back open?" He jumps out.

I wipe my palms on my jeans. "So, yeah. Thank you . . . for all this." I extend a hand, clutching Rose Tyler in the other.

"Sorry, Fig. I only hug." So we do. She smells like earth and cinnamon. "Good luck," she whispers. "I hope you find everything you're looking for."

"Thanks. Thank you. You too. Good luck."

We hold each other. And not like two people who only just met a few hours ago on the side of a freeway.

"Let's go," Christopher says, opening my door.

"Right. Take care of yourself, Max."

"You too, Fig."

Christopher is already carrying our bags up the street. I run to catch up to him, holding Rose Tyler tight in my arms. As we near the house, chatter and music and laughter hidden behind the gates waft through the sweet air.

I turn to wave to Max, but she's already gone, two brake lights vanishing around the corner.

18

We've stepped into another time.

Beyond the wooden gates, characters from a Woodstock documentary mill about the garden, artsy hipsters underneath a canopy of white lights. Up close, the house looks rickety and Old Woman in the Shoe-ish rather than postcard perfect-ish, but either way we've entered a drug-infused Aesop's Fables.

Some people sit cross-legged under a tree of dangling trumpet flowers, holding hands and *om*-ing. Others sit at a picnic table passing a smoking pipe and talking about purply-blue auras, laughing madly. Some play bongos and a tambourine, while a few swathed in see-through fabric twirl in circles. Someone stands next to me, staring at the tree.

We charge ahead, weaving through them. A fog of different-flavored smoke fills the air, and a sweetness from night blooms drifts through. It's intoxicating. In Disneyland, they pump smells throughout the park so you'll buy their food, like buttered popcorn or churros. It's like that. Or I could be getting a contact high.

Everyone we pass smiles and waves and says, "Hey, hey, welcome," as if we've been expected.

"See? I bet this party's for us," Christopher says, grabbing a bottle of beer from a cooler and cracking it open. He starts to guzzle it down, then stops to ask a twirling hipster where we might find Aunt Luna. She's naked as a jaybird.

"Oh, you sweet things," she says, cocooning us under her arms. "We're so happy you're here. Welcome." She starts crying.

"Oh—" Christopher.

"Uh—" Me.

"Luna's inside," she says. "I'm so glad you made it." Then she whirls away like we were figments of her imagination.

"Well, that was a first," Christopher says to me.

"Come on."

We walk in through an open door on the lower level and find ourselves standing in the middle of a real-life curiosity shop. Murmurs and mumbles and soft classical music twinkle through the room. Shelves are covered with dusty old books, lanterns drip with layers of rainbow-colored wax, walls billow with a kaleidoscope of tapestries. Look close enough and I'd swear the house is breathing.

We round a corner into another room and see her. She's hard to miss. Aunt Luna lounges on a leather chaise wearing a shimmering green muumuu, her long gray hair splashing all around her like tangled spiderwebs. She inhales from a cloth-covered hose attached to a hookah and blows three perfectly round rings. Two folks a little older than us sit beside her talking politics.

"Democracy's literally crumbling," the guy with the thick beard and a FUCK THE PATRIARCHY shirt says. His pink-haired friend agrees.

I step forward, clearing my throat. "Aunt Luna?"

She looks up. She's so luminescent, it's blinding. "My darlin's, welcome! Come give Aunt Luna a hug." We do just that and I am instantly at peace.

I don't want to let go.

Christopher pulls me back. "Thank you for having us," he says. "We're happy to meet you."

"That's why I'm here." She inhales again, blows a few more rings.

We don't move.

Her friends nod.

Aunt Luna stares.

She may be hypnotizing us?

"So, how long you sweet boys been on the streets?" she finally asks.

"What?" Christopher says.

"Were you kicked out? Parents can be so cruel," Aunt Luna says. "People think there's all these loving liberals out there these days, but have mercy, I think I've seen more kids in the past couple of years than ever before."

"Mm-hmm. It's a damn shame," her friends agree.

"Uh, we—"

"Don't you worry your pretty little heads. We'll get you a nice hot shower and some good home-cooked food, and you can stay here as long as you need."

"Uh—what are you—OH!" Everyone jumps. It hits me: We look like extras from *Oliver Twist*! "Oh, ha ha ha, running fields, cows, dog, mud—" (It made sense in my head.)

Christopher gets it, too. "Oh! Right, right, right." And suddenly we're in a two-man stand-up routine:

"There was this cow farm—" I say.

"And we pulled over so I could pee and—"

"When he opened the door, Rose Tyler—she's my dog—" I lift her body so she dangles loosely in front of us; they *awww*.

"She ran into the field."

"And we ran out after her."

95

"That's why we're still covered in a little mud."

"Or it might be poop."

"So, a shower would be great."

"But we're not homeless."

"No no no. We called you, remember?"

"Well, our friend Charlie called you."

"I'm Christopher. This is Isaac?"

"Hello," I say.

"And we're looking for his dad. Alex Griffin."

We're panting.

They blink. I'm not even sure they realize we're still standing here.

"My sweet darlin's," Aunt Luna says finally. "I can barely remember what you just said, let alone who came tumblin' through these doors yesterday."

Her friends laugh.

Oh no.

"Uh . . ." Christopher says, snatching the thought from my head.

I unzip my backpack and pull the notebook pages out of the plastic bag, pointing to the last paragraph. "That's you. And my dad was here, I guess . . . or maybe not. We thought you knew . . . where . . . or something . . . so we came here looking." I clasp Christopher's hand.

"Show her the picture," he whispers.

I pull out the framed photo, the one I found in the attic with the rest of Dad's belongings.

"Maybe this will help?" I ask, handing it to her.

Aunt Luna scans the pages, then the photo, then back to the pages again, the cloth-covered hookah resting on her lips. She looks up, pulls the pipe away. The distant gaze in her eyes tells me everything I need to know.

"We'll go," I say, near tears.

"Go where?" Christopher says through gritted teeth.

"Well, you sure do give up easy, don't you?" Aunt Luna says. "You aren't going anywhere, darlin'. Except upstairs to take a hot shower with this strapping young fellow standing next to you. And then you'll come down to eat some supper. And meanwhile, Lenny here'll bring out my scrapbooks." The bearded guy—Lenny, I guess—walks over to a small door tucked underneath the stairs.

"What?" I ask.

"I may not remember who this Alex is, but anyone who stays with me ends up in one of my scrapbooks somewhere. I make all my kids sign a page before they go. They leave me a tiny piece of themselves to protect." She winks, starts wiggling up the chaise lounge. Her pink-haired friend wearing strings of malas stands to help her. "Oh, what fun. Haven't dug through those in years. Julie, honey, take them upstairs to the little guest bedroom with the stained-glass window, you know the one. And, Lenny, dear—" He looks up, crouched now in a small closet of books. "Grab that sweet little dog, will you? My gracious, she's a matted muss of poo-poo, isn't she? Guess you all are." She stands now, filling the room with a soft guffaw, like a worn-out version of Max's.

"I'll take good care of her," Lenny says, somehow smuggling Rose Tyler free from my arms.

"There's only three rules here," Aunt Luna says. She pats our hands and starts waddling away. "Do your own dishes. Keep your room clean. And make yourselves right at home." She mumbles to a few ferns hanging in the window and disappears into the kitchen.

"Follow me," Julie says. "I'll show you the way."

"Told ya she'd know what to do," Christopher whispers, after downing his beer.

We follow Julie up a winding staircase and down a narrow hall-way. The floorboards wheeze beneath us and framed pictures plaster the wall. Not an empty space to be found. In each photo, Aunt Luna hugs another smiling someone, spanning every decade since the six-ties. Like we're walking through a history book.

We reach a small room in the far corner of the house. Two twin beds, neatly made, with a nightstand in between, sit tucked against an exposed brick wall. A framed psychedelic poster of a moon—that looks like it's been ripped to smithereens and taped together again—hangs on one wall, and there's a circular stained-glass window with a violet om symbol on the other.

"You can scoot those two beds together if you want," Julie says, her voice soft and careful. She switches on the light in the bathroom. "Fresh towels are under the sink there. Take your time and enjoy. See you in a bit." She clicks the door closed.

"So, I was thinking," Christopher says, immediately stripping out of his clothes. "After showering, and before we do anything else, we should go out. You know, explore the city. We haven't—"

"Not a chance." I turn on my phone to text Charlie.

"Why?" Dried mud still covers his skin in places.

"Because we're not here to party, we're here to find my dad, re-member?"

"Come on, Fig. It'll be good for us." He pulls me up and wraps my arms around his waist.

"What are you doing?"

"What does it look like?" He kisses my neck. *Because we're alone now,* I think. But I say nothing. Instead, the memory of him pushing me off stings my heart.

"When's the last time we went out and danced?" he asks. His lips caress my ears, my cheeks. "Or made out on the dance floor?"

"Ages," I say, throwing my head back. Damn, he feels good. "Okay, okay. Maybe after we look through some scrapbooks first. Maybe."

"I'm gonna shower," he coos in my ear. "Wanna join me?"

"You go. I'm going to text Charlie and Mom."

He nods. "Don't worry, okay?" And he shimmies out of his boxers, wiggling his butt at me before closing the bathroom door.

The shower squeaks on. Water drizzles. Christopher sings Bob Marley. *"Don't worry 'bout a thing . . ."* Dulcet sounds to bring me back to the present. Because as I sit on the edge of the bed clutching my phone, I suddenly do exactly that: worry. If I start thinking about where I am, where Oscar is, how Rose Tyler's in some strange man's arms, how we're locked up in the attic of an old Victorian murder mystery mansion—

No. Instead I focus on the torn-up poster in front of me and breathe. The first footprint on the moon: I think it used to glow, but it's so faded it almost looks like a mirage. The bottom corner's been burned.

I text Charlie: *holy shit we're here!!!*

I reply to a text from Mom checking in to make sure I'm doing okay: *all is well. love you.* Best not to make her second-guess anything right now.

I'm still waiting to hear from Charlie when Christopher comes barging out of the bathroom, looking like a shiny new statue. "That was seriously everything," he says, toweling off. "You okay?"

"Yeah. Just a little overwhelmed."

"Take a shower. It'll help." He snaps me with his towel, pushing me toward the bathroom. "Trust me."

Soon, the water's trickling over my body, and I slink back into my skin again. I'm able to finally piece together what Aunt Luna said. There's a feeling tingling through me. Like each word she spoke was made of helium, pumping through my veins. *Hope.* Because the more

I think about it, the more certain I am there's something in one of those scrapbooks that will bring us that much closer to finding Dad. As Max said, keep following the signs.

"Amazing, right?" Christopher asks when I step back into the room. He's lounging on the bed, typing on his phone, with another beer in hand, dressed now in a tight Britney Spears T-shirt and frayed jean shorts.

"It was kind of spiritual," I say, drying off.

"Right? I *love* it here! Come on, let's go."

I throw on a white V-neck and slip into another pair of black skinny jeans. We're bouncing back down the stairs when a laugh echoes through the walls and wallops my heart.

"No way," I say.

"You gotta be kidding me," Christopher says.

"It can't be," I say.

But it is.

Max sits on the chaise lounge next to Aunt Luna, with a sparkling white Rose Tyler snuggled between them, talking as if they're long-lost girlfriends who've been reunited.

She looks up, lifts a sheepish grin. "My aunt wasn't home yet, so . . . surprise!"

"Awesome," I say, surprisingly happy.

"Great," Christopher says, surprisingly not.

19

Scrapbooks are talking time capsules.

"Ooh, okay, I'm not usually a dress-wearin' gal, but this one is a piece of divine," says Max.

"Because it's blue?" I ask.

Christopher grunts. He's been simmering on the end of the couch since we started flipping through the books, and I have no idea why. He's on his fourth beer now, so maybe that's it.

Max squishes between us. Her hair's turbaned up after her shower. Strands of blue peek through, falling over her shoulders.

"I mean, it's so hard to believe," she says.

"What is?"

"They had one day a year to dress freely like this." The page crinkles, and some of the tape's come unglued, so pictures slide down. "Halloween was one of the only nights they could legally be themselves. So sad."

"Yeah."

Max turns another page. Faded photos of men in suits with skinny ties next to men and women in wigs and crinoline dreams. White gloves. Caked-on makeup. Like they're going to prom, but way late in life. Smiling so huge it explodes through the film even after all this time.

"I wonder if they were really happy," she whispers, lifting one of the pictures. "Like, they're smiling, but were they happy?"

"Why do you say that?" I ask, leaning in. She smells like Aunt Luna's shadow, powdery and sweet, after hugging her for so long.

"I don't know. I guess I know a fake smile when I see one. It's easy to put one on for others, even when you're screaming inside. Just so they'll leave you alone. I've had practice."

"Me too," I say.

"They seem happy to me," Christopher says.

Max replaces the photo, tucking it under the cellophane. "Wouldn't you be if you finally got to put on the dress that's been taunting you in your closet for three hundred and sixty-four days?"

"How do you know they weren't happy the other days?" Christopher asks her. "They didn't know they could live any other way."

"You're right," she says. "They didn't. And that's the greatest tragedy of them all."

He glugs the rest of his beer. "Maybe it's better people don't know what they're missing."

"Hmm . . . not sure I agree with that," she says.

They stare at each other.

"Makes you wonder what they'll say about us in fifty years, doesn't it, heh-heh," I say.

"Yeah, it does, Fig," she says, turning the last page. "Nothing yet?"

"Nothing."

"Well, don't give up. That's what Rose Tyler says in 'The Parting of the Ways' episode, remember?"

"*Doctor Who* has the answers to all of life's questions," I say.

"It certainly does." She folds the book closed like a deflated accordion and bends over to pick up another one. There's a vibrant pink lotus tattoo in open bloom on the small of her back. I swear it pulsates, unfolding right before my eyes.

Christopher clears his throat. I look up. His eyes are wide staring back at me and his left eyebrow is lifted. I don't know what this means. "What?" I mime.

Max pulls up her striped pajama bottoms and sits back between us, beginning again.

This has been the recurring scene since we walked into the living room. Lenny found nine scrapbooks labeled 1966 (hundreds more are stacked in that tiny closet, dated other years) and we've been riffling through them like an archaeological dig, excavating people's lives through photographs and clippings, notes and doodles, dried-up corsages, locks of hair (someone even taped their beaded cross on a page, writing, *My Goddess now comes in the form of a Hippie Aunt*), and on and on. Next to each item: a time-stamped date and signature, and an inevitable note of gratitude like Aunt Luna really is a saint. And after sifting through six scrapbooks, I'm a convert.

Aunt Luna sat with us for the first one, recalling stories of some, not recalling stories of most, wiping a few tears, laughing. But it's after midnight now and she's long gone to bed, as have most of the hipster revelers. Although a few remain conversing around an outdoor firepit. And that one guy's still staring at a tree.

Then there's the question of Max, who is still just that: one big swirling blue question mark. We only know four more things about her after Christopher turned his interrogation lamp on her. He kept asking where she was from and what school she goes to— presumably having forgotten because he's had one too many beers— and she jokingly showed us her driver's license, which she always carries in her pocket.

Her name is Maximillian Whitaker. She turned eighteen on February 19. She's 5'4", 153 pounds. And she's a real-life LA Valley girl:

428 Chula Vista Way in Valley Glen, an address I implanted in my brain. (Thinking maybe we could hang out when we return? Perhaps a bit stalkery, but still.) That's all we know.

But now that we're between scrapbook number six and seven, the interrogation continues and I'm still not sure why:

> **Christopher:** What happened to your aunt again?
>
> **Max:** Dunno. She texted and said she wouldn't be back until tomorrow.
>
> **Christopher:** So she was going to let you roam the streets?
>
> **Max:** I think she forgot.
>
> **Christopher:** And what were you going to do if we weren't here?
>
> **Max:** Doesn't matter, because you are here.
>
> **Me:** She's staying, Christopher. Can we please move on?

Christopher grunts.

Max draws hearts on the dusty scrapbook cover with her finger. "I'll go text her again," she whispers. "Thanks for letting me stay the night." She walks into the kitchen.

I turn on him. "What's your problem?"

"There's something about her."

"What?"

"I don't know."

"Need something concrete here. And hurry, before she comes back."

We peer into the kitchen. Max paces, scratching her hair under the towel turban and typing on her phone. "You're too trusting of people, Fig. Always have been."

"What's wrong with that?" I mumble. "Besides, it was your idea to get in her Jeep. We don't have time for this, Christopher. We have to get through these scrapbooks."

He leans closer, his eyes boring into mine. "Why'd you tell her that stuff in the car?"

"What stuff?"

"About your dad. That you felt alone, even with me."

"I didn't know you were awake."

"Does that matter?"

"No, but I mean—"

"You've never told me that, Fig. I've known you two years now, and you've never mentioned anything about not belonging or—"

"I'm sure I've—"

"Nope. Not once. You tell her, a total stranger, but not me, your boyfriend of two freaking years. That's what I'm talking about. You've disappeared from our—"

"So have you!" I catch myself. "Look, I'm sorry. I didn't realize— This isn't the time to talk."

"It never is."

"Everything good?" Max asks, standing in the doorframe.

We sit back.

"Yeah," I say, turning to her, smiling. "Fine."

She squeezes between us. "Scrapbook number seven," she says, as Christopher stands. "I need another beer," he says. And he's gone.

"Did I do something?" she asks me.

"No." I look after him. "We're just . . . I don't know what we are right now. I'll go talk to him in a bit. Let's keep going. If you want to."

"Oh, I am loving this," she says.

"Me too," I say. We share a smile.

And we begin again.

Page after brittle page, a new person from another time sits with us. Talking to us. Laughing. Crying. Sharing intimate secrets or long-lost dreams, or warnings of street corners with undercover cops . . .

A cartography of souls.

Hours pass, it seems. Christopher's been hooting it up with the hipsters outside. My eyes feel heavy and dry. Pinned open like that *Clockwork Orange* movie but of my own free will. Because I'm determined to find something, anything. My cheek somehow finds its way to Max's shoulder. She doesn't fidget to brush it off, so I keep it there.

With each turn of a page, my heart stretches tautly. Because after all this time, we still haven't found—

"Wait. Go back," I say, lifting my head. My eyes zoom in and out like a camera lens: Pictures of a late-night diner. Patrons squished together in booths. Girls dressed to the nines, laughing. Boys in tight white tees and jeans, smoking. Waitresses in starched linens, scowling. And underneath them, a handwritten note on a business card, stamped with a steaming cup of coffee:

THE PLACE TO BE WHEN YOU WANT TO BE SEEN:
COMPTON'S CAFETERIA, 101 TAYLOR ST. (AT TURK)

Luna,
    Thank you for believing in me, for showing me the Path. I wish I could've said goodbye before you had to go. I won't let you down.
                Alex 7/17/66

"Oh my God," Max says, "that looks just like you, Fig."

"That's my dad."

Alex Griffin waves back at us, wearing a tight angora sweater, a bouffant blond wig, and thick eyeliner like Cleopatra, crowded together in a booth with the same group of friends, each trying to outdo the other by making funny faces at the camera.

My heart somersaults.

Another envelope's glued to the page next to the business card.

"Open it," she says, our heads touching.

I break the seal and carefully lift more folded spiral notebook pages.

Max's smile stretches across her face. "Well, I think we just found your next clue."

The words bleed through the paper. Max reads them aloud.

July 2, 1966

> *Been two months since I was last here at Compton's Cafeteria. Feels like two years. Had to come back for so many reasons. Mainly because it's the only place I feel safe. But Ezzy's not here.*
>
> *Rage simmers in my heart. Like the anger blazing through the country. Everyone screaming to be seen: Vietnam protesters; civil rights agitators; feminist demonstrators. A revolution of the soul pouring out onto the streets!*
>
> *But what about us? During the day we need to hide in the shadows. It's only safe to come out and play at night. And just barely. Ezzy tried to warn me. You can't go anywhere without getting caught.*
>
> *I feel stuck. Like so many of us, lost. I thought things would be different in San Francisco. Guess some things are. Not like back home. (Wherever home is anymore.) I also guess you take yourself with you no matter where you go. But I'm so fucking tired of running. We all are.*

I tried working real jobs. At Woolworth's. As a bookstore clerk. As a shoe salesman. Got found out each time. For being too effeminate in boys' clothes. Too masculine in girls'. Too everything I'm not supposed to be, even though I AM.

The first time, I maybe swiped a few lipsticks to give to the girls. Okay: guilty.

The second time, an angry hippie came in and called me a queer. Punched that patchouli-smelling good-for-nothing through a pile of books.

The third time, I got caught trying on a pair of heels.

Fired. Fired. Fired.

So I did my first trick last week. Had to make money somehow. Writing sure as hell isn't paying any bills. Not yet. And I'm not about to end up in one of those sidewalk tents. I walked around Union Square for a few hours, and next thing I know, some mustached man says:

"Got a light?"

"Yeah."

"Wanna light me?"

"Okay."

And he brushed up against me and I felt his basket push against my thighs and I nearly fainted right there on the spot. The caress of another man. The forbidden connection.

I made fifteen dollars. I would've done it for free to be touched like that. But here, love ain't free.

Next day, I tried it again. Because maybe this is what a junkie feels like. The rush.

That's when I got caught. Penal Code Commandment: 650.5: Thou shalt wear three articles of clothing that match

your biological sex. Thou shalt not "personify" someone.
Amen.

What they don't realize is you can't personify something
you actually are.

"Don't resist, just go limp." That's the rule for getting
arrested. Spent two days in jail. Two nights in the cell
with other queens and male hustlers—the "dangerous
deviants."

That's when I heard her name.

"What'd you say about Esmeralda?" I asked.

She looked at me—makeup smeared all over, hair cut
like some kindergartner chopped it up when Teacher wasn't
looking. I know the cops did that to her. I've heard stories.

"What's it to you?"

"She's a friend."

She flipped back over on the cot, pulling down her dress.

"She got beat," someone else said. Some white boy
hustler. "Pretty bad."

"By whom?"

"Who you think? The pigs."

"Is she okay?"

He disappears in the corner. And what he says fills me
with such fury and fear, such helplessness, I punch the concrete
wall until I break my knuckles and bleed through the bars.

My blood, the only part of me that's free.

That was five days ago. They sent me to the hospital.
I was bandaged. Psych-checked. Evaluated. I know all the
goddamned answers to all the goddamned questions to pass
their test. To stay hidden.

Keep quiet. Don't speak. And you'll be safe.

That's why I sit here. At Compton's Cafeteria. In the far back corner, behind the buffet that's piled high with steaming plates of fluorescent food. Lost in my spiral notebook, writing. To escape this mad, mad world.

And I look around to see the beautiful hair-fairies wearing crinoline dotted with daisies and gorgeous transcendent transsexuals smoking. Boy hustlers and butch dykes laughing.

Free. Together. One.

And I sip this coffee, and I feel it again.

Like the last time I was here.

That I found my family.

That I am home.

And I will fight for every single one of them for as long as I live.

20

Sleep was impossible last night. Although when I drifted off, I dreamt about Dad in prison, wearing eyeliner, finding a new voice, bleeding freedom. When a hustler showed me their mirror, it was actually me. And in the reflection, carved in the concrete prison walls, I saw the phrase that continues to haunt me: *If broken hearts are maps to the soul, why do I keep getting lost?* I startled awake, wondering where I was, who I was. Charting unfamiliar territories inside and out.

City lights gleamed through the om-symbol window. Max slept on the floor, with Rose Tyler snuggled into her. When Christopher stumbled in around four in the morning, he fell onto the bed fully clothed and immediately wrapped himself around me—he hasn't let go since.

I breathed, allowing more of Dad's being to sink into my own. Recognizing the fears and frustrations as mine, the unquenchable thirst for purpose. And for a soft moment, feeling the chasm in my broken heart begin to close.

I couldn't stop thinking about those scrapbooks: how difficult and dangerous it was to live then; how, as a queer person, you'd be thrown in prison if you sneezed; how hard it was to know the meaning of love.

One thing about Mom, she always encouraged me to *love whoever you want to love, freely*. Like she once did. (Growing up, she had a girlfriend for a few years; when that ended, she had a boyfriend for two more; when that relationship didn't last, she declared to the universe, *I can't hold on to love!* and that was that.)

But I know not everyone is as fortunate as me. Even now, so many people I know are still scared to come out. That's when I started thinking about Christopher. How he told me he felt imprisoned, drunken stupor or not. How maybe he's feeling as stuck as Dad.

So, as soon as the Sunday-morning light began filtering through the window, casting the stained-glass om symbol on the wooden floor (and after Max tiptoed downstairs for breakfast, with Rose Tyler gleefully trotting behind her), I nudged Christopher awake.

"Christopher?" I slip his arms off, sitting up.

He stirs and whispers back, "Love you, babes."

"Can we talk?"

"What time is it? Didn't I just fall asleep?" he mumbles.

"Seven sixteen. And sort of, yeah."

"Five more minutes?" He snuggles closer.

"Sorry. Can't." And I'm off. "I know you hate when I say sorry. But I am. I'm sorry about last night. About not letting you in. Not telling you everything about me—I don't know why I don't—" I watch the om symbol slowly travel across the floor. "And that's obviously something for me to look at, which, honestly, I've been doing since we went to bed—and, well, I came up with more than a dozen reasons. But also, you know how your mind can spin out of control at night, like how you can fall down a rabbit hole and suddenly you're wondering why people sneeze or something—well, the point is, I'm sorry." I massage his hair. "And I just want you to know you don't have to hide anything from me. Whatever you're feeling, I'm here for you, too. If you want." And then I add, "It's not because of you I feel alone. And I want you to know you're not alone either. Okay?"

He hasn't moved. "You hear me?" I ask.

He slowly raises his head, gazing up at me. "Thank you," he says softly. His cheek settles back on my chest, and we lie there, holding each other. I can tell by his breathing he hasn't fallen back asleep.

I guess, sometimes, silence says more than words ever could.

After the om symbol has landed on the opposite wall, I kiss the top of his head and wriggle out from under his arms. "Meet us downstairs in twenty?" I say.

He smiles, even though his eyes don't. "I hope we find your dad today."

"Me too."

Exactly twenty minutes later, I'm standing in the garden with Max and Aunt Luna. They're examining a wall of succulents, talking about the Fibonacci sequence in nature, something about sacred geometry connecting all forms of life (???)—turns out, Max's dad was a genius mathematician who taught at Caltech—when Christopher saunters outside, freshly showered and smelling as sweet as the garden.

"Morning," he says, his voice still gravelly. He's wearing the same clothes from last night, disheveled but awake. He wraps an arm around my shoulder. "You ready?"

"Good morning, darlin'," Aunt Luna says. "Sleep well?"

"Pretty good. You?"

"Oh, 'to sleep, perchance to dream,'" she says. "I was butterfly-stroking through the great blue sky, free as a bird. Coffee?" She looks like a tropical drink: Her neon muumuu billows in the breeze, her straw hat flaps like little wings.

"I'm good, thanks." He stretches, turns to Max. "Glad you're sticking around to join us."

"You kidding? I wouldn't miss this for the world," she says, beaming. Her blue hair comets down her shoulders, just as fiery, and she now wears a light purple long-sleeved shirt that keeps billowing from her chest.

She's been bubbling joy all morning, more excited than I am about our day's adventure. I'm glad I asked her to join us. The plan: Find Compton's Cafeteria and ask around for Dad. Admittedly not much of a plan, but it's all we've got and I'm not turning back now. I keep reminding myself to *follow the signs*, so we are.

"Well," I say, the word jittering out. "Guess we should go." I pick up Rose Tyler, who's been bouncing around the garden, playing tag with a grasshopper. "You be a good girl."

"We'll take care of her," Aunt Luna says. "Now, time to put on my Sunday finest and head off to church!"

"What church do you go to?" Christopher asks.

"Oh, darlin', you're in it. Just got to get my gardening gloves!" She hugs Rose Tyler to her chest. "I'm sure you'll find everything you're looking for out there." She starts to shuffle back inside, pausing briefly to whisper something to a dangling trumpet flower.

"I hope you're right," I say, opening the front gate.

"You're in San Francisco," she yells, waving us off. "You always find what you're looking for here. It's just never what you went out to seek."

And with that, we're off, to hike across town to the Tenderloin.

I sling my backpack over my shoulder, filled with Dad's letters and the framed photo and my lucky talismans and questions I hope to finally answer.

21

Max leads the way, twisting a foldout tourist map she'd bought at Walgreens, *Because it's way more fun than a silly old phone map,* she said. A point that Christopher refused to argue. We hike up a paved mountain to the Castro, which is apparently crossing the border into Gayland, USA. I have to pull Christopher along every few steps because (1) he's distracted by a shiny new sex toy, or the LEGALIZE GAY T-shirt in the window, or the boys standing on the corner in tiny red briefs—that's it, tiny red briefs—passing out postcards for an all-night orgy or something, and (2) the boys won't stop pulling at him, ogling his rippling muscles and God knows what else.

We grab a trolley car to take us across town, and Christopher sits with his head in his hands as Max stands in the aisle singing, *"Clang, clang, clang . . ."* People sneer or scroll through their phones, and I hear one person say, "She should win the award for origi-fuckin'-ality," and an old woman hands her a dollar because I think she thought Max was homeless. Or she just wanted to shut her up.

Thirty minutes later, we jump off.

"We're here," Max says, twirling around to face us. "Welcome to the Tenderloin!"

Uh . . .

In my dreams, smiling families walked the streets passing out baskets of fresh-baked goods. Children skipped alongside them holding dollies in their hands. Sidewalks glittered and the air smelled of hope. But unless you count the severed doll head I spotted in the alley that looks like it's been recently peed on and used for toilet paper, then no.

And in a flash, my heart begins to race. I can't catch my breath. Could be lack of sleep, or oxygen. Could be the overpowering smell of feces coming from the alley behind me. I'm not sure. A woman who has seemingly never bathed bumps into me. "Outta my way," she screams. She has two teeth.

"Sorry." I back up against a brick wall that's covered in graffiti and layers of peeling posters spiral down. Sounds muffle all around me. I can't even begin to glean one to bring me back. I'm wheezing. Or having a stroke. I grab my chest. I remember this feeling. After that day in kindergarten, my mom sent me to the clinic for a few weeks because I was having these attacks, like the earth was trying to swallow me.

"You okay?" Max asks. Her voice sounds cavernous.

Christopher holds my hand. "Fig? What's wrong?"

"Just need a minute." People scowl as they push past, their faces closing in on me, and all I want to do is crawl in that alley and hold on to that doll head, so I close my eyes and breathe. "I think I'm having . . . a panic attack."

"Oh, sweetie," I hear Max say, "I understand. It means you're getting closer to the truth. Keep breathing, you're going to be fine."

So I do.

A few minutes pass and I open my eyes. I blink a few times because it looks like Christopher's spinning through space. "Where's Max?"

"Asking for directions," he says. "What's wrong?"

"Overwhelmed, I guess. Because we're here. And maybe Dad is, too. Or probably not, I don't know. Maybe this is a bad idea. After all this time—I'm scared to meet—"

Max calls out, waving us forward. She's standing at the corner a block ahead.

Christopher clutches my shoulder, sweeps a few hairs behind my ear. "You want to chill for a bit? We don't have to—"

"No. I can't go back now."

Maybe Max is right, maybe we're close to the truth.

I keep breathing, shove my feelings aside. We weave through swarms of people and reach her just in time to hear her mutter, "Look for the patterns, look for the patterns." She paces, staring at the ground.

"Everything okay?" Christopher asks.

She says nothing, points behind her.

"What is it?" I ask.

We peek over her shoulder. Someone sits on a bike waiting at a stoplight. Another someone sits on a curb holding a cardboard sign. A woman screams at a postal box.

"What?" I say again.

Christopher grabs my hand and says, "We'll keep looking. I promise."

"What are you talking about?" I lean over, scanning for any new clue as to why they're looking at me like a three-legged dog, when—

Oh.

Oh no.

I see the street signs first: Turk and Taylor.

And my eyes jerk around searching for Compton's Cafeteria. Because I see now.

It's that boarded-up building that is no more.

22

The light changes.

I sprint across the street.

"Fig! Wait!" Christopher.

"Where are you going?" Max.

They run after me.

I try the doors. They're bolted shut and barely shake when I pull them. *No.* Each window is covered in a white laminate film from the inside, smothered in layers of dirt and dried soap on the outside. Like a cloudy crystal ball. Seeing nothing.

Except me.

Staring back at me.

I pound the window with my fist. "Shit!"

"BASTARD BITCH SLUT." The woman yelling at the postal box joins me.

I walk away.

What the hell did I expect? Dad, holding the door open for me, wondering what took me so long? A cafeteria brimming with all my answers?

My body is earthquaking, sinking. *I can't go back without knowing something,* I think. *I won't go back to that loneliness.* I steady myself against the window. Breathe.

"Babes? Don't worry. Sometimes plans don't always work like we want them to."

"He's right," Max says softly.

I want to punch them.

"Where are the letters?" Max asks Christopher.

"Fig, hand me your backpack," Christopher says. He wrestles the bag off my shoulders, starts digging through it to find the notebook pages—for what exactly, though, I don't know. My face presses against the glass, trying to see something, anything.

A guttural cry starts to flood through me. I pound the window again to stop it from gushing out. Max's reflection squeezes my shoulder, whispers, "*Never give up, never give in . . .* From the 'Day of the Doctor' episode . . ." She lifts her beautiful crescent-moon smile, flickering between happy and sad, sad and happy. I blink a few times, watching her. Like she's a flipbook. It's doing something to my brain. I close my eyes, reciting the mantra in my mind.

"Hey! Check this out," Christopher yells. He's crouched over a bronzed plaque embedded in the sidewalk. "This was the same year as your dad's letters."

Max pulls me away from the glass.

"What is it?" she asks, hiking up her jeans and bending down.

Christopher reads: "'Uptown Tenderloin Lost Landmarks: Compton's Cafeteria Riot 1966. One August evening in 1966, transgender women and gay men banded together to fight back against'"—he brushes some leaves away—"'oppression after a police officer harassed one of them at Gene Compton's Cafeteria. This confrontation was the first known full-scale riot for transgender and gay rights in U.S. history—'"

"Whoa," Max says. "I've never heard of this. Have you?"

"No," Christopher says. I squat down to join them. The gold letters on the marble plaque glisten in the sun.

"Maybe your dad was here for this, Fig," Christopher says. "That would be amazing."

"Maybe."

"Who's your dad?"

I think a raven just spoke. No. We look up to see a striking eight-foot-tall woman towering over us. Could be her heels, but—

"Alex something," Max says, standing. "What's your last name?" she asks me.

"Oh. Uh, Griffin."

It's hard to tell how old the woman is, in her seventies at least. Although the deep wrinkles on her face reveal someone who's lived several lifetimes, rather than several decades. "I don't know her. But I was there."

"Really?" Max says.

"Wow," Christopher says, brushing dirt off his knees. "That must've been scary."

"Well, coming out can be, can't it." She lifts a thousand smiles. "But you can't hide your whole life. The truth shall set you free," she exclaims to a passerby who shrugs her off. She's wearing a pleated, tawny-brown pantsuit that flares at her heels, blending into her skin like a silken glove. Her white blouse, tied in a bow around her neck, flutters in the wind. Her rose-tinted silver hair falls loosely on her shoulders.

If I squint my eyes, she looks like a wrinkled version of one of those scrapbook pictures, dusted in pink blush and radiance. "My dad used to come to Compton's," I somehow manage to say. A few aftershocks tremble within, but I'm determined to get answers. "What was it like?"

The woman clicks open her purse, flicks a cigarette into her mouth, and lights it. Puffs of smoke fly out with each word. "It was Oz, honey. The only place we ever felt safe."

"What happened that night?" Max asks.

"What didn't happen? All hell broke loose. It was the most unbelievable— You kids really wanna hear about this?" Her eyes sparkle, even through the tough veneer.

"Yeah, we really do," Max says. "Don't we?"

Christopher and I nod, as he intertwines his arm with mine, pulling me close to him.

The woman shakes her head and turns to the window, blowing smoke at her reflection. "Well, us trans girls were done, you know? Sick of being harassed, chased all over holy hell for doing nothing. For just putting on a goddamned dress." She fluffs her hair, running her fingers through the dyed straggles. Her ring gets caught. She tugs it free, along with a few strands, floating them to the sidewalk.

We stand behind her, gazing into the window, mesmerized. She continues. "It was hot as hell that night, I'll say that. Hard to keep your makeup from dripping all over; I'll never forget plastering myself in powder. Funny, the things you remember. I was so young."

As she talks, the cloudy film on the window parts and the cafeteria springs to life, bustling with laughter, Dad's letter materializing before our eyes. The cafeteria lights blaze on. Patrons fill the leather booths. Waitresses zip through the aisles. Forks clink on plates.

"I wore my finest wear, of course, this brilliant blue vision to die for. I'll never forget that dress. Thinking I looked like a morpho butterfly, all translucent and free." She laughs at herself. Digs through her purse. Pulls out a gold tube of lipstick. Turns it slowly to reveal the rubiest color I've ever seen and paints her lips. "We showed up like clockwork every single night, no matter what. To make sure we were all accounted for, you understand." She pauses, puckering her lips, lost in the memory. "And there were lots of cops there that night— you always knew they were cops because of their shoes—wing tips gave 'em away—but this one grabbed my girl's arm, 'bout to haul her to the hole, you know, because she wasn't wearing men's clothing like she was *supposed* to be." She drops the lipstick back in her purse, shaking her head. "But I don't know, I guess something snapped in her that night, because the next second, she tossed her hot coffee in his face, and you have never heard such a howl. The dam finally broke free.

"And I thought, *It's about goddamned time.* Something flew past my head. Nicked my ear. Glass shattered. And the screams, Lord, the screams. Like sister warriors calling out to each other, I don't know." She cackles, smoke twisting all around her. "And I just started throwing whatever the hell I could grab ahold of. Like they were grenades. All of us did. Glasses and saltshakers and forks and trays. Windows were smashed and people ran out. Someone set a newspaper stand on fire. The whole street erupted, honey. It was absolutely glorious."

She glances at our reflections in the window. "This kinda thing never happened before, you understand? We were so used to being kicked around, thrown in the clink, it never occurred to me we could fight back. Not like that—this was three years before those Stonewall girls—so we'd never known anything like it. But hell, if you don't fight for what you believe in, who will?"

She straightens herself. Life on the street buzzes back behind us. "After that, a lot changed for us girls. The community started coming together to help us. People started paying attention to our needs. Our lives were finally being looked at as human, not as some deviants of nature. It was the spark that ignited the movement as far as I can tell. We didn't know it at the time, of course. But we were tired of hiding . . . yup, best night of my goddamned life." She stops, gazing at Christopher. "Was it scary, you asked?"

Christopher looks up, his brow furrowed.

"Hell yes it was. But that fear was tiny compared to the freedom we all felt. Because we finally stood up for our truth."

The three of us hold each other, enthralled by this woman from another time.

"You really did make history," Max says.

"Oh, we were only doing what we had to do to survive."

Christopher whispers in my ear, "We should go, Fig."

"My dad got thrown in jail once," I blurt out. "We read a letter. You must've known who— There was someone who helped. Everyone knew her—damn, what's her name? Where's the letter?" Christopher hands it to me and I feverishly scan the pages looking for it.

The woman tosses her cigarette to the sidewalk, squishes it with her heel. "We all got thrown in at one point, honey. Sorry I can't help you. But thanks for listening to an old lady reminisce. No one ever looks at that plaque anymore . . . they walk right over it. And when I saw you there . . . Anyway, best of luck."

"Esmeralda!" I yell.

She stops, turns. "What'd you say?"

"Esmeralda Esperanza. That's the name I was trying to—"

She instantly crosses herself and pulls out a sapphire-beaded necklace from under her blouse, kissing it. "Mercy, haven't heard that name since— Your daddy knew Esmeralda?"

"Yeah."

"Well, that's just . . ." She studies us for a long time. Then she straightens her pantsuit, tucks her purse under her arm, and starts walking away. "Follow me."

We don't move.

"You don't think *that's* Esmeralda?" Max whispers, sounding giddy.

"No," I say. "Do you? That would be too weird. No."

"Well?" the woman yells. "You comin' or what? I have something for you." She tosses the words over her shoulder and vanishes around the corner.

Christopher twitches uncomfortably, looking after her.

Max's grin is revolutionary, taking over the city. "I think maybe we found our next clue."

23

We follow her a few blocks.

With each step, a cautious hope slowly returns. Christopher gets more jittery for some reason, although he won't tell me why. And Max is clearly in her element, adventuring into the unknown.

The woman stops in front of a brick building that looks like a converted hotel with a faded Coca-Cola logo painted on the side. She clicks a touch-tone keypad, and when the door buzzes open, she flies in. Max grabs it before it shuts.

We charge forward, climbing marble stairs. The clicks of stilettos and our rubber-sole squeaks are the only sounds in the building. The woman walks down the hallway, all of us heaving and panting, and stops at door 428.

"Well, ain't that something else!" Max whispers in my ear, dabbing her forehead.

"What?" I wheeze back.

"That's the same number as my house. Another sign, Fig!" She squeezes my shoulders.

"You sure about this?" Christopher says in my other ear, lifting his shirt to wipe sweat from his face.

"Not at all," I say.

The woman holds the door open for us as she kicks off her heels. They thwack against a skid-marked wall. "So much better," she says, bouncing up and down to rub her feet. She's suddenly inches shorter, same height as us.

"Why do you even wear those?" Max says, closing the door behind her. "I can only do comfortable."

"There's power in them things. One wrong move and that heel's going into your jugular. Tea?"

We're going to die.

Max laughs. "None for me." Christopher and I shake our heads.

The woman plugs in an electric hot plate by a sink in the corner, fills a small kettle.

Christopher whispers in my ear, "What are we doing here exactly?"

"She said she had something for us," I whisper back.

"Make yourselves at home," the woman says. "However much you can anyway. Now where the hell is it . . ." She riffles through cabinets, pushing aside boxes of cereal and such, searching.

Besides the small kitchen in the corner, there's an unmade sofa bed, a small desk by the window, a bathroom peeking through an open door. Otherwise, the apartment's filled with jagged stacks of books. Hundreds of them. Like we've stepped through a closet into a secret used bookstore.

"Who's this?" Max asks, pointing to a framed picture hanging on the wall by the front door. Two people, wildly smiling, ride a motorbike with their hands sailing in the air. One is clearly this woman, decades younger, with fire-engine hair blazing through the sky.

"Oh, that's me and my Freddie. Greatest man who ever lived. Died in the eighties, like all the other good ones. God rest their souls. Never found another love like him. Still, I don't give up hope." She slams a cabinet door and opens another.

"Me either," Max says, inching past me. "This is quite a collection. Have you read all these?" She grabs a book from a stack.

126

"Every single one," the woman says. "At least twice. People give us their old books at the library; I grab them. Don't care what they are."

"Oohh, you work at the library?" Max says.

"Mm-hmm. San Francisco Public."

"Always thought that'd be an awesome job."

"It is." She throws open a drape to let the sunlight stream in. Sort of. It reveals a barred-window view of another brick wall a few feet away. "Sorry about the mess, wasn't expecting company." She gathers newspapers off the sofa bed and dumps a mound of cigarette butts into the trash, still in search of whatever it is she wants to give us.

"You should see my room," Max says, flipping through the tattered pages. "Oh, Maya Angelou, how you weave my heart with your words— Fig. Christopher. Sit."

Christopher doesn't move when I try to pull him forward. *"I'm fine,"* he says, even though it's clear to me he's anything but.

I sit on the edge of the sofa bed, thigh-to-thigh with Max. "So, um . . . are you . . . Esmeralda?" I ask the woman.

"Oh no, sweetheart," she says, smiling. "Name's Gracie. Gracie Thompson at your service." She twirls her hand down in front of her, bowing. "No, Esmeralda left that shell of hers long ago, God rest her soul. But your daddy knew Ezzy, huh?"

"Oh . . . yeah."

I look around. A few bricks peek through layers of GAY LIBERATION and FLOWER POWER posters smothering the walls, along with an emporium of knickknacks and endless framed photos of "Gracie and Friends."

The kettle whistles. I jump. Gracie pours herself tea, lights a cigarette, and leans against the sink. "What'd I do with that thing?" she mumbles to herself.

Max stands. "You've certainly seen a lot," she says, perusing the wall of photos, her hands interlocked behind her. "It's like a wall of living dreams or something. Look at all you've done, what you've been a part of, all your friends, it's—"

"Hard work is what it is. Every second of it. Lonely even." She blows smoke out the window. "Shit. Those days of dreams are long gone. Forgotten. Thrown in the trash. Some days it feels like I still gotta hide in the shadows."

"But what you were a part of—" Max says, straightening a crooked picture on the wall. "You don't have to hide or be forgotten if you don't—"

"You ever think maybe I *want* to hide?" Gracie snaps. We whip around. "What do you think I did all that fighting for anyway? To fit in. To walk down the street one day and *be* forgotten. Hell, I'm still scared to loiter too long in the streets, afraid they'll arrest me because they think I'm a hooker. That's not paranoia. That's fact."

"I'm sorry," Max says. "I didn't mean—"

"I see how people look at me still. Staring at me when I walk by. I don't *pass* like some of them other girls, whatever the hell *that* means. But I'm so much more than just being a beautiful trans woman. Obviously. Finding clothes at thrift stores and making my own couture for starters—"

"You do have impeccable taste," I interrupt, without thinking.

"Well, you do, too, if you see it in me." She shakes her head, laughs. Then she clears her throat and stubs out her cigarette. "Sorry—I don't mean to rattle on. I'm not used to talking to people about this kinda stuff anymore. Talking to people about anything really." She studies her wall of memories, as if she's reliving them. "You're right, doesn't do any of us any good to hide. Only eats us alive inside." A tear suddenly crawls down her cheek. "It's sometimes hard for me to let go of that time in my life, I guess. That freedom I felt. Even if it was hell some days, I sure do miss it. The laughs, the innocence. All my friends who've left this world." She turns to us, streaks of mascara now streaming down her face. "But we have to let go eventually, don't we? Otherwise, we miss the whole point of living. Or why we fought in the first place."

We don't move, each of us similarly stunned.

She grabs a wadded-up paper napkin from the table and dabs her face. "Good Lord, look at me, going on and on about things gone by. Let me find this damn thing so I can get you kids on your way."

She pushes past me, shoving books and pictures and knickknacks aside, searching. "Maybe I knew your daddy, maybe I didn't. It was a crazy time, you know? But one thing I know for sure, if your daddy was friends with Ezzy, then she was one of us. And any friend of Ezzy is a friend of mine—where the hell is it?"

"Fig?" I turn to Christopher, who's still stuck at the front door. His eyebrows bunch together, like he's on the edge of rage or tears, I can't tell. "Can you come here for a sec?"

I sneak over as Max asks more questions, holding books and trinkets and picture frames that Gracie keeps piling in her arms.

"What's wrong?" I whisper to him.

"I don't feel— I have to go."

"What? Why?"

"I just— I have to get out of here, Fig." He peers over my shoulder. "I don't know, I'm feeling, like, claustrophobic or something. I'm sorry I can't help you."

"Okay. Wait downstairs and I'll be down as soon as she—"

"No. I need to be alone." He's so fidgety, he can't even meet my eyes. "This is all too much."

"What is?"

"I want to walk around the city. I'll text you later to meet up."

"You don't want me to come with—"

"I'll be fine." And before I can reply, he's opened the door and slipped out.

"Fig?" Max's voice startles me. I turn to see her sitting on the sofa, juggling a stack of books and memories, wide-eyed and bursting with glee. "Everything okay?"

"Yeah. He . . . needed some air."

"Where's that picture of your dad?" she asks. "Maybe that'll help jog Gracie's memory. Did you bring it with you?"

I rummage through my backpack. "Good idea."

"Ah, here we go!" Gracie yells, before walking back over to us.

I flash her the photo.

She gasps. "My . . . friends. Where on earth did you find this?" Another tear trickles from her eye.

"This is my dad."

"Where?" Gracie peers over Max's shoulder, following my pointing finger.

"Holding that broom and sign," I say. A sign that reads DRAG IT OUT INTO THE STREETS!

"Alex Stryker is your dad?"

I look up at her. "Alex *Stryker*?"

"That's her name, honey. My goodness. I see it now. Your eyes. Her chin . . . we used to call it her little butt chin." She laughs through a few more tears. "My Good God, I've never seen this picture. She was something else. Yes, ma'am, she fought as hard as the best of them."

"Was?" I ask. "As in . . . Alex is dead?"

"Oh, I don't know. Haven't seen her since that time. We all kinda went our separate ways, you know how it goes. Or maybe you don't yet, but you will."

"What else can you tell me about her?" I ask.

"Gosh, it's been so long . . ." she says, still lost in the photo. "One thing, she'd drown herself in patchouli. Used to say it was the nectar of the goddesses, whatever the hell that means. But you smelled that, you knew she was in the room somewhere. Oh! And she had a sweet tooth that would knock you silly. Just now remembered that. You always hid your slice of pie when she showed up." She giggles to herself, tracing the figures, her eyes distant and longing. "And that laugh of hers. I can hear it now, like there was no tomorrow."

I'm absorbed in her recollections, making Dad more of a tangible being and less of an abstract nebula in my mind. Or maybe it's the opposite. Maybe the more I learn, the more wonder is revealed.

"So many lost friends," Gracie says. "So many lost memories."

I don't realize a tear falls down my cheek until Max wipes it away.

"This is what I wanted to give you," Gracie says, plopping it in my hand.

"A sugar shaker?"

"You wanted a piece of history," she says. "This here's a real piece of history. One of the things that started it all that night. This thing? Hard as a rock. Could smash through a window, crack a skull open, knock someone out in the blink of an eye, you name it."

"Wow," Max says, standing. "This was used in the riot?"

"Mm-hmm." Gracie puts her hands over the shaker. "I wanted you to have it, since you all were so sweet to talk to me out there. I don't know . . . I walk by that spot every day of my life. Never a soul even paying attention to it. People stomp all over that plaque like it's nothing. Like they do to us still. What they don't realize is that we trans folks started it all—the riots, the marches, the movement—and we've always been stepped on." She stops herself, looks up at us. "Anyway, I saw you kids, and heard you talking about it, and then you said Ezzy's name, and it was like a flood of memories passed over me and, well, I gotta thank you for that. It's nice to remember. To be remembered. Hell, it might've been the one your daddy used for all we know."

"You think my dad was there that night?"

"Oh, Alex was there. She was always there."

"This is incredible," Max says, interlocking her arm with mine.

Gracie nods, wiping away some black mascara that drips from her eyes.

"Thank you," I say.

"Wish I could tell you more about her," she says, walking us toward the door. "But one thing I know for sure?" She grabs my arm. "A lot of us didn't survive that time. And who knows what the hell happened to some of them. But since you're standing right here in front of me, I know she did something pretty damn good for herself. At least maybe it's a small piece you can hold on to. You know?"

She smiles.

My lips quiver.

And that's the moment I realize why we met Gracie Thompson.

24

"Janis Joplin played on the corner right there."

"Uh-huh."

"And Timothy Leary and his Merry Prankster bus traveled these streets passing out LSD to all the hippie kids." Max rambles on like a ten-year-old tour guide. Aunt Luna packed us lunches, so Max is taking us to Golden Gate Park for a picnic pit stop.

"Cool," I say.

"And Ken Kesey wrote *One Flew Over the Cuckoo's Nest* there, and Jerry Garcia—oh my God, like the actual Jerry Freaking Garcia—started the Grateful Dead right over there."

"Ah."

"You aren't even listening to me."

"Yes I am. Haight-Ashbury Fun Factoids! Woo-hoo!"

"You are literally walking through a time warp right now. Like, you're probably walking through some hippie ghosts and you don't even care."

"Those are not hippie ghosts. They are clouds of marijuana smoke."

"Same diff."

Max is right. No doubt about it, time has stopped in this five-block radius. Somehow the old, stacked Victorians are still painted in vibrant rainbow swirls, and the smoke shops and record stores remain untouched. Like we smacked into a psychedelic scratch-and-sniff coloring book. I swear even the streets are spray-washed with Nag Champa.

"No word from Christopher yet?" Max asks.

"No. He said he'd text when he was ready to meet up. But . . . I don't know."

"Is it something I did? You can tell me."

"Definitely not. He's done this before when he needs time alone, takes off on his own. But it's never been in a strange city." And never like that. Something was off with him. Something happened in that apartment. "I hope he's okay."

"He's tough. With those muscles, the boys he runs into will take care of him." She laughs, but I don't. "Sorry, that was a crude joke, I didn't—"

"No, you're good," I say, waving it off. "I'm sure he's fine."

She pulls me forward. "Come on. We're almost there."

Twenty minutes later, we find an empty spot on a hill and start devouring chicken salad sandwiches and homemade brownies. Below us, an impromptu drum circle, complete with a special appearance by the Whirling Dervishes of Hippiesville, conjures a dust storm. I lay the framed photo of Dad on the ground in front of us. *Where are you, Alex Stryker? And why did you sign the love letter to Mom as Alex Griffin?*

"That picture's incredible," Max says. "They're all so fierce and happy. I wonder what it's from." She swallows another bite of brownie.

"I don't know. Some protest. I'll look it up. And my dad's name! I can't believe, after all this time, I—"

"Do you think your dad's trans?"

"Maybe?" I lift the photo, twisting the frame. The still image pulsates. Like I can hear them chanting in protest. "It's one possibility of so many. Charlie taught me never to assume anything about anyone until they tell you who they are." I prop the photo up against my bag so Dad's face winks back at us. "But even if so, it makes me feel that much closer to them."

"Really? Why?"

"Gender's always been a big whatever to me, you know? I'm not huge on labels, but I guess I'm pansexual. I just love to love."

"That's beautiful," she says.

I shrug. "But I don't know why Mom wouldn't tell me, why she hasn't told me anything about this. She's . . . *Mom*. She threw a cotillion ball for me when I came out to her. And then there's Charlie, who's like her favorite child."

"You have another sibling?"

"Technically no, but Mom treats Charlie like they're hers."

"Is Charlie trans?"

"Charlie's nonbinary, and they've known since we were little. We met at this clinic when we were six—our moms put us there because we were both depressed—me because of my nonexistent dad, and Charlie because, well, kids can be assholes to people who seem different—like adults, now that I think about it—but when we found each other, we glued ourselves together and have been basically inseparable ever since. Except they're leaving to go to college soon and—" I take a breath. "I feel like I'm talking a lot, am I?"

"Not at all," she says. "Your voice is soothing, actually."

"It is?"

She shields her eyes, grinning with a mouthful of food. "Can I just say these brownies are amazing?"

We giggle.

"You know what else is amazing?" I ask.

"What?"

"I was beginning to lose hope, you know, but I kept hearing you say, '*Never give up, never give in.*'" I swallow more brownie. "And so, when Gracie showed up, I just kinda let myself go, for the first time in a long time. Because I didn't know what else to do. Hoping she'd have something that could help us. And it turns out, she did!"

"That's the way it works, Fig. That's what my dad always taught me anyway." She makes her voice deep and gruff. "'Pay attention to the patterns, Maximillian. Follow the signs. You'll never be steered in the wrong direction.'" She settles into herself again, staring up at the sky. "Damn, I miss him . . . that voice."

Trees and colors vibrate around her.

"How'd he die?" I ask softly.

"Cancer."

She doesn't offer anything more, so I follow her gaze. The clouds whiz by, creating an infinite sea of shapes. It's dizzying. I peer down at the hippie twirlers, who are, in fact, spinning so fast they're floating. I feel funny. My hands tingle like they're made of firecrackers. And my heart's beating so fast I swear the drummers are pounding my chest instead. What's going on with me?

"Fig?"

"Yeah?"

"These brownies?"

"Uh-huh?"

"I think they're made with hash."

I whip around. "Really?"

She snickers. "Uh-huh."

"Oh, okay. Are we going to die?"

"What? No. Well, eventually. But not right now."

"I've never had hash brownies. I've smoked weed a few times, but I didn't like it. I got in my head too much, which, trust me, is not something I need more of—and, um, I don't—my heart feels really—oh God. I had, like, twenty of them, I think? So, yeah, should we—"

"Hey. You're okay." She spins me toward her. "You only had three. But . . . it's a longer high, so we have two choices here: We can fight it or settle into it."

"Like life," I say, holding my chest.

"Huh?"

"Like life. You can fight it or settle into it."

"Oh. Well, exactly like that. What do you want to do?"

"I don't really see a choice here, do you?"

"None at all. So, just breathe with me. We're fine. Everything's fine."

We sit cross-legged, facing each other. I watch her breathe. It's supernatural. Each time she inhales, her face glitters a little brighter. Like she is the Andromeda. Look at her. Just a big, beautiful galaxy full of shining stars. Who is she?

"Fig?"

"Huh?"

"You're not breathing."

"Oh."

She smiles. It's the most glorious smile I've ever seen. "So. You're right here, okay? With me. Sitting on the hill. Just the two of us."

"Okay."

"Breathe with me."

I do.

I've never held someone's eyes, matching them breath for breath, but: *Whoa.* We are lost in each other's eyes. Lost in each other's other. Like we're creating a new dimension of Time.

"Wow," I somehow conjure out of my mouth because words seem stupid now.

"I know," she says.

"I feel so, I don't know, quiet inside."

"I do too."

"Haven't felt this way in so long."

"Yeah, me neither, come to think of it." And she leans in, kisses my cheek. "That was weird. Sorry. It just happened. So sorry."

"That's okay. Your lips are soft. Do it again." I close my eyes.

She pecks the other cheek.

Then, slowly, I feel her lips cushion mine.

I open my eyes. Hers are closed. She really is like another galaxy, her own space-time.

Then, she opens hers.

And we kiss.

Huh.

"That was . . ." I say. "Besides Christopher's, I haven't felt someone else's lips on mine in so long."

"How did it feel?"

"Like we've done it before."

She lies on the grass, picks little white daisies, and starts twisting them together. Humming a sweet something. I don't move. Lost in thought, lost in everything.

"What's wrong?" Max asks, swathed now in a few daisy bracelets.

"Nothing, why?"

"You're crying."

"I am?" I feel a tear trickling. "Oh, I didn't realize." I swipe it away, still looking at her, and I don't know why, but I instantly want to share everything I feel. My heart's twirling, like it wants to be set free. "Can I tell you something?"

"Anything." She lifts my arm, wraps a daisy bracelet around my wrist.

"And I don't want sympathy or—"

"I get it. Believe me."

"Well." I twiddle the bracelet. "Remember in the car I told you why I was looking for my dad?"

"Because you didn't feel like you belonged."

"There's something more. Something I didn't tell you, or that I've ever told anyone, and, well . . . I'm not sure—"

"You can trust me," she says, the kindness on her face washing over me.

And I do.

My voice trembles, matching the tremors in my heart. "Well, see, there's a part of me that's never felt whole, like I'm a half-person, without knowing who my dad was. And when I was little and first found out I was missing a dad, I felt this shame grow inside me, like I was embarrassed of . . . being me. That I wasn't a good enough person to have a dad." I look up, feeling the sun splash against my face. "And that feeling? It's made me so lost in my life, like I can't grab hold of who I am until I find out who Dad was. And I can't let that go no matter how hard I try. And I want to, so, so bad." Tears choke my words. I feel them streaming freely down my cheeks now, but this time, I don't shove them away.

She leans in, squeezing my knee. "I understand, Fig."

"Never told a soul that."

"Not even Charlie? Christopher?"

"No." I dry my face with my T-shirt. "I was thinking about that last night, why I don't tell him stuff. And I think . . . it's because he's never lost someone, you know? He has two parents who adore him. And as much as he'd like to understand, he never could. Maybe there's a part of me that resents him for that." I never thought of it like that before now. But it's true.

The words hang in the air like a thick fog; I wonder if it will ever clear.

"Some things you just can't explain, Fig." She lies down on her stomach, her feet weaving through the air. "My dad always used to say that when it's time for a person to go—" She puts on his voice again. "'Ain't nothing in the universe going to stop it from happening, Maximillian.'"

"Do you believe that?" I ask.

"I want to."

I watch her fingers caress a daisy's white petals.

"I wish I knew you when we were little," she says eventually.

"Me too," I say.

She twists more flowers together.

I close my eyes, letting the sun swim through me.

We sit like this for a while, lost in our own little worlds.

"My dad died of pancreatic cancer," she says. I look down to see she's now lying on her back with her hands twined behind her head. Her purple shirt has come unbuttoned at her wrists and ruffles up, re- vealing a part of that twisted tattoo on her forearm. "I took care of him best I could. Wiped up his sick, took him to the bathroom, that kind of thing. My stepmom wasn't much help, and—" Her voice is taut, strained. "It was hard. But I stuck to it. Every day after school, I'd visit him in the hospital, stay with him all night until he fell asleep. But one day, I just couldn't do it. I snuck out with a friend and got stoned until I passed out. I wanted to forget for one day, you know?" Tears flood her eyes. "That's when I got the text from my stepmom. *Your dad's dead,* it said. That's it. The one day I didn't show up is the day he left. I never even got to say goodbye. Guess we all have a some shame inside us," she murmurs. "Like Gracie said, it's hard to let go of it."

"It really is," I say. I want to wipe her tears away like she did mine in Gracie's apartment, but I don't move. Instead, I ask, "Do you have a picture of him?"

"I do." She unsnaps her wallet, pulls it out. And there's younger Max with braces, shorter hair, without the blue braids, wrapped in her dad's arms. He beams just as bright, with a movie-star tan and eyes the color of a crystal sea. Their joy is transcendental, hugged together like he never wanted to let her go.

"You have the same smile," I say.

"People always said that."

The picture's folded over on the right side, creased so hard it's barely hanging on. I undo it to see a white woman standing beside them. Separated, but gripping her dad's shoulders, wearing too much makeup and a forced smile. "Who's that?"

"My stepmom. She never liked me that much."

"That can't be true."

"It is."

I pass the photo back to her. She folds it over again so only Max and Dad gleam through.

We nestle in the grass, our breaths sinking into the earth.

I hold her hand. "Your fingers," I say. "They feel like dandelion seeds. Like I could blow on you and make a wish."

She doesn't say anything, clasps our hands tighter.

"It's weird, isn't it?" I say.

"What?"

"I barely know you, but it feels like I've known you forever."

"Maybe you have, Fig."

"Yeah, maybe we have."

We look up, lost in the clouds.

25

Later, the sun's setting, casting a pink phosphorescent glow over the city. Max and I walk down Castro Street back to Aunt Luna's house, still holding hands. Hers is supremely soft, like she tried every lotion in Sephora. Christopher's are more calloused, from lifting. I love tracing the rough lines in his palms. We only ever hold hands in private. Holding Max's hand is different. Safer. No one stares. I wonder if she knows the significance of hand-holding.

Still no word from Christopher. The worry building up inside me is suffocating. I've texted a thousand times, called a thousand more, but it goes straight to voice mail, like he's purposely turned his phone off. Max has convinced me not to call the police to file a missing person report, reminding me it's only been a matter of hours, that I told her he's done this before. Which is true. But it feels like it's been a few days.

I think we're still high.

We walk through the gates of 1967.

Rose Tyler leaps into my arms, her tongue gobbling my face. "Hi, my sweet girl. Did you have the best day ever? You're smiling. Look at you smiling. Oh, you are the cutest."

Max furrows her brow as she looks at her phone.

"Max?"

"Huh?"

"You okay?"

"Yeah." She shoves her phone in her back pocket and walks up the stairs. "I'm gonna shower. I feel disgusting." And she's gone.

I turn to Rose Tyler, who's still lapping my cheeks. "Settle down, girl. I know. I missed you, too." I kiss the top of her head.

We sit on the couch. Alone.

I check my phone. No news.

A new pile of opened scrapbooks sits on the coffee table. I flip through one dated 1983. Some Polaroid pictures of a twenty-seventh birthday party, but no one's smiling. Except Aunt Luna, of course.

I check my phone again. Nothing.

I pace the living room. Read book spines. Smell unlit candles. Dangle my fingers through twinkle lights. I'm fidgety and twitchy and headachey, and for future reference: After a thorough scientific and mathematical examination of every statistical probability, I have come to a direct and absolute conclusion that getting high is akin to a thirteen-year-old boy getting circumcised. It should never happen ever.

That said, no thought, no feeling, nothing can distract me from the fact that I still haven't heard from Christopher.

I sit back down on the couch. *Let's do something constructive,* I think. I search "Alex Stryker Queer History San Francisco" on my phone to try to unearth more answers about Dad. Okay, this might be too much for my brain to handle at the moment.

But this link looks promising. It reads: *Want to know where you came from? Make an appointment to visit the GLBT Historical Society Archives in San Francisco.* I click it, and within minutes I see they're open Mondays. Excellent. I schedule a time for bright and early tomorrow morning.

That done, I check my phone. *Again.* It's only been sixteen minutes since the last time I looked at my messages. Being high is stupid and sucks. Does time move this slow in real life and I'm just now noticing it? I see the eleven texts I've already sent him, and start to write another one, but stop. No. He's fine. He does this. But I can't shake the feeling something is different this time.

I walk into our room and find Max with her hair rolled up in a towel, back in her striped pajama bottoms and another long-sleeved plaid shirt. She looks in the mirror and rubs lotion on her face, fragrancing the room like a rose garden.

"Hey," she says, with her galactic smile. "Any word?"

Rose Tyler bounces out of my arms and into hers. "Nothing," I say.

"He'll turn up. I promise. Take a shower. It'll help."

"Yeah."

Max grabs my hand as I walk past. "Thanks, Fig. For all of this. Today was everything."

"It really was," I say. "Oh, and I made us an appointment to go to these historical archives tomorrow. Following the signs and all that. If you want to come with me, I mean."

"Are you *kidding*?" she squees. "I so want to be there the moment you find your dad."

"If we ever do."

"Oh, you will. Go take your shower."

Three months later, I finish. I swear I teleported to an Amazonian rain forest in there. Anyway, I forgot my pajamas, and those rancid safari–through–San Francisco clothes are not touching my skin again, so I wrap a towel around my waist and step back out to—

"WOOO-HOOOOO!"

"Very funny," I say. "Just need to get my pajamas."

"Why bother, Fig? It's just skin."

"Says the girl who's always dressed like we're in Siberia." I rummage through my bag.

"Touché." She lies in bed, leaning against the headboard. Rose Tyler snuggles in her lap. "Anyway, it's different for me. I'm a girl."

"And I'm a boy. What's your point?" I shimmy into my boxers under my towel, throw it to the floor.

"WOO-HOOOOO!"

"Stop it."

"This has been my ploy all along," she says.

"What?"

"To get you alone in your boxers, of course."

"Funny." I smell each shirt in my bag, and I don't know if it's because I'm forever high and my senses are now super-maniacal, but nothing smells fresh. Noted: doing laundry as soon as I get home.

Home.

That feels so far away, so long ago. But was it only yesterday we were stuck on the side of the freeway meeting Max for the first time? How is that possible? Seriously, *what is time*?

Max props an arm under her head to face me. Her hair drapes down her shoulders. Her breasts bounce freely underneath her shirt, which I try not to notice.

I lie on the bed next to her. Her face is a blank canvas, open, ready. She has a few barely visible freckles dotting her face, which I never saw before. She giggles.

"What?" I ask.

"Your hair looks like a blond fro without anything in it." She pats the top of it.

"I hate it. I always wanted straight hair growing up." Rose Tyler nestles into her, snuggling up her sleeve. "She likes you. That's her saying, *I trust you so much, human blanket*."

"She's amazing. Wish I had a pup back home. It would definitely help with my life."

"Tell me about home," I say. "Your life, I mean."

"Not much to tell," she says, ruffling her fingers through Rose Tyler's fur.

"Come on," I say. "We just spent almost the entire day talking about me, now it's your turn."

She smiles, still looking at RT. "Fine. In a nutshell, my real mom didn't want me, so my dad raised me alone. He met the stepmom several years later. I'm pretty sure Stephen King based Carrie's mom on her, the end."

"Oh."

"Uh-huh." She shifts on the bed. Strange to see her uncomfortable. Vulnerable even. Unguarded. Rose Tyler wriggles out from under her sleeve.

And that's when I see it: her fully exposed arm. It's not tattooed; it's scarred. Streaked in a million cuts. Some are letters, I think; words maybe, but I can't read them. They're more like thorny vines strangling her body.

I sit up. "What is that?"

"What?" She realizes what I see and rolls down her sleeve. "You shouldn't have seen that. I can explain."

"Are you a cutter?"

"Please don't look at me like—"

"Let me see." I try grabbing her arm but she flings it back.

"Don't! I'm not— Don't look at me like that, Fig. I hate it."

"Like what?"

"Like every other person does. Like I'm a freak."

"I'm not. I just want to—"

"Drop it. Please." She clutches my hands. "Let's talk about your dad and—"

"I don't want to—"

"Fine. I'll tell you whatever else you want to know. My fake mom's a religious wingnut who hates me and thinks I'm a—"

"I don't care about her. Are you okay?"

"No," she says, throwing my hands down. "No. I'm not okay. Is that what you want to hear? *She's a crazy cutter!* That's what they say." She jumps off the bed, starts throwing her clothes and makeup in her bag.

"What are you doing?"

"Leaving. I shouldn't have— I don't like people to know. I don't want to—"

"Stop." I grip her arms, turning her to me. "Max, stop. You're not going anywhere." She looks up. Her heart cartwheels through her wrists. "I don't care what anyone else says, I just care about you," I say, which surprises us both. "Show me."

I slowly inch her sleeve up. She shudders as I lift her arm.

A maze of cuts slash through each other like an intricate spider-web. They're scabbed over but still swollen. Bruised. I slowly trace them, barely touching her skin. I see words. Patterns carved into her arms.

Love. Joy. Peace. Kindness.

"What is this?" I ask, just above a breath.

She lifts her other arm, wipes her face with her sleeve. "It's nothing. It's—"

"What?"

She inhales deeply, staring at her forearms. "You ever hear of the water experiment?"

I watch her face, her eyes quicksanding with sadness. Like I'm looking in a mirror.

She continues. "It's from this Dr. Emoto, and he did all these different tests on water. He saw that water molecules respond to vibrations, right?

"Well, when water was labeled with negative words for long periods of time, they'd look at the molecules under the microscope and see they were all gnarled and fungusy-looking, like an infected cancer or something." She breathes heavily. Her arms tremor in my hands. I hold them tighter so she knows I won't let go.

"And then they labeled other waters with positive thoughts and said all these nice things to them—mantras, you know, sang lullabies, that kinda thing. And when they looked at *those* under a microscope, they were like perfect crystallized snowflakes. Perfection in the stillness, they called it. And the point is this—" She looks back down, her tears falling over my hands. "Our bodies are made of like sixty percent water molecules, right? And I thought, why not do this to my body? To help fix me. I mean, if I keep writing all these positive thoughts, and keep thinking that way, feeling those words seep into my blood, maybe, I don't know, maybe I can finally find my own perfection in the stillness."

"Oh."

"Crazy, right?" she says, with a little laugh. "No one knows. No one's cared."

"I do."

"I started it when my dad got sick. I don't really have anyone else to—" Our eyes meet again. This time, they're filled with a desperation, a longing to understand who she really is. I know that feeling. "I was so scared, Fig. Didn't really think I had anyone left. Some days I can barely get out of bed to— I didn't want to get into all this. I don't want to make this about me—"

"But it must hurt. Couldn't you maybe use a Sharpie or something?" Which feels like such a birdbrained thing to say, but it's all I can think of right now.

"Half the point is the feeling," she says, looking down, as I caress her palms. "To feel something again. Anything. I don't know, I was numb for so long. The first time was an accident, but then—" She glances up. "It doesn't hurt. Not really. Just scratches the surface mostly. I mean, a couple times I maybe cut a little too deep, but nothing serious. I quit doing it months ago."

"You're okay?"

She shrugs.

I lift her arms. Gently rub my hands over the words. Like I want to erase them, take the pain away. But I know that's not how it works; I know pain doesn't erase like that. I know because of my own.

"You're beautiful," I say, kissing her wrists without thinking.

"Fig."

"You are."

"I'm not."

We close our eyes. I inch closer. Until our hearts touch.

"Perfect," I say.

26

I lead Max to the bed and let her cry on my chest until she falls asleep.

I trace the etched words on her arms, whisper the affirmations in her ear.

Maybe she'll hear them in her dreams.

27

An hour later, Christopher fumbles in.

"I knew it!" he yells, tripping over a bag.

"Oh God." Max pushes off the bed.

"Knew what? Where were you?" I ask, jumping up, trying to grab hold of him as he flails around the room.

"Get off!" He shoves me; I stumble back onto the bed.

"Max, close the door," I say. She does, her eyes glued to Christopher.

"Pretty clever, you two. For a second you had me thinking *I* was the crazy one."

"What are you talking about? Why are you so drunk right now? What happened?" I try holding him again. He swats at the air.

"I've seen the way you look at her."

"Christopher. Stop it. Now."

He flounders toward me, wobbles inches in front of my face. "Well, I went to some gay bars and kissed a boy tonight. How's that?"

"Okay . . . why?"

"For one, you said you always feel like you're alone when you're with me."

"That's not what I—"

"And three, her tit-tay was in your hand. What am I missin' here?"

"It wasn't. You're drunk."

He turns to her. "Well, that's what it looked like," he sneers.

I glance over to Max. She's shaking, her face buried in her hands. She slides down the wall. I turn back to Christopher, who leans to one side, then jerks back upright. I grab his shoulders to steady him. "Am I still high? What is happening right now?"

"You're *high*?" he asks. "Since when do you get high? Who even are you, Fig? You keep talking about your dad this and poor me that. Meanwhile, you're missing out on our"—he waves his hands around me—"life."

"Why are you acting like this?"

He rubs his face, hard, like he's trying to peel off his skin, and says, "My head . . . I think I drank too much."

"I know. Why?"

"To forget."

"Forget what? I tried calling you. A lot," I say. "I thought you wanted to be alone. I've been worried about where you were and—"

"That's the million-dollar question, ain't it." He whips his arms up, pushing me away. "And where were *you*, mister?" He whistles and lands a finger somewhere on my forehead, burrowing his nail in. "We left each other long ago, didn't we?"

"Let's get you in the shower."

"I didn't mean for it to happen, Fig." Still burrowing. So hard, it stings.

"It's okay. Let me help you."

"You can't help me! Don't you get it?" He staggers back, catches himself against the wall. "You can't help—" And like that, he bursts into tears. A volcano of sobs. Like the sadness and anger have been dormant for years. "Shit."

"Christopher—"

"No, you can't." He crouches, his head buried in his hands.

I bend down. "Tell me what's going on. Where's this coming from?"

He bangs his head against the wall, staring up at the ceiling. His breathing heavy and thick. "Gracie . . . everything she said . . . about hiding and facing fears and how it eats you alive. She's right. I couldn't . . . I can't . . . I'm so fucking tired of hiding this from you and everyone," he says to me or himself, or no one—I can't tell. "Of letting him win, letting him make me believe I'm nothing."

"Who?"

Then, gently, he says, "I want to fight like her, Fig. But I don't know how."

"I told you, you're not alone."

He wipes his face, his eyes lost and far away. "He did something that . . . I'm so embarrassed, I don't . . ." He looks at me. "I'm sorry, Fig. I didn't mean it."

"Who are you talking about? What happened?"

He holds his hand to my cheek. Shudders a breath. Inhales to say something but scrunches his face instead. "I have to get out of here."

He jumps up and reaches for the door handle, but he keeps missing it.

"I'm not letting you leave again," I say. "Not like this."

"You can't stop me. And don't follow me."

He flings the door open and just as quickly slams it shut.

28

I snap up, bleary-eyed and confused. It's the next morning. And no, none of it was a nightmare. What the hell just happened?

Violet sunbeams filter through the stained-glass window. Max looks up from the bathroom sink, eyes swollen, hair tangled. She's brushing her teeth.

My phone rings. Charlie's face laughs back at me on the screen.

"Charlie."

"Fig!"

"I—"

"One. Are you safe?"

"I'm fine."

"Two. Christopher called me."

"He did? Where is he? Is he okay?"

"He's on a bus back home. What happened?"

"I don't know. He was wasted and saying all these things. I ran after him, but he was gone before I could catch up and he won't answer my calls. He's on a bus back to LA?"

"He is. Pretty hungover. Said he doesn't remember much of last night."

"Did he say anything else? Why didn't he come back here?"

"He's embarrassed, I guess. And sorry. Couldn't face you. He wanted to get home. He asked me to call you."

"I'm glad he's safe."

"You sure you are?" they ask.

"Yeah."

"He said you met a friend?"

"Yeah."

"Okay . . . Fig?"

"Mm-hmm?"

"You find what you were looking for?"

"I don't know, Charlie."

"Call me when you're home. Okay? We'll figure all this out. I love you."

"Love you, too."

I close my eyes. My head throbs. I call Christopher. Straight to voice mail. "Hi, it's me," I say, my voice strained. "Charlie called. I'm glad you're safe. On a bus and— I'm sorry. I know you hate when I say that, but if something happened to you, I don't know what I'd— Look, I love you. And if you don't want to talk to me, I hope you talk to someone. Don't hold that shit in, whatever it is. And I'm saying all this to a voice mail, great. Just— I don't know. I don't know." I hang up.

"He's gone?" Max asks.

I nod.

"Need a ride?"

I look up.

"It's the least I can do," she says.

"You're headed back?"

"Yeah. Don't know what I was thinking, really." She starts repacking her bag, folding jeans. Then a shirt. She stops. Staring. Lost. "Don't know why I thought I could run away. Don't know why I lied to you either. I don't have an aunt here. I had nowhere else to go, and when we met I—" She throws her shirt in. "I'm going back home if you want a ride."

"Thanks. Don't know where my car is. Christopher—"

"Right. That's right." She zips up her bag. "I can call some tow companies around here to see where it's at if you want to shower."

We look at each other. Like looking at the aftermath of a disaster.

My phone buzzes in my hand. Mom. No. I click it off. "Max, I—"

"Go shower. I'll make some calls."

"Thanks."

After a quick rinse, I streak the mirror free of steam. I close my eyes, shake my head, then look again. I don't recognize me. My skin's ashy and pale. Dark circles shadow my eyes. Sunken cheeks. If I saw myself on the street, I'd run in the other direction. Maybe I have been. Maybe I've been running from myself this whole time.

Meanwhile, my phone won't stop ringing in the other room, an incessant buzz. I step out. Max stands, staring out the stained-glass window, hands in her pockets.

"Didn't want to answer it," she says. "Probably your mom. She's been calling since you got in the shower."

Great. I pick up my phone. She's left thirteen messages. It instantly buzzes again.

"Hello?" I say, trying to muster a smile.

"JESUS CHRIST, ISAAC."

"Mom?"

"WHERE ARE YOU? ARE YOU DEAD?"

"No. I—"

"Of course you're not dead, you wouldn't be— Where the hell are you?"

"What? I'm at Charlie's."

"GODDAMN IT, ISAAC ALEX GRIFFIN!" She stops. Breathes. I hear someone on the other end of the line calming her. A voice I don't recognize. "Don't you lie to me. Where are you?"

"I'm— Did Christopher call you?"

"What? No. Where is *he*? Never mind. Answer my goddamned question."

"Mom, calm down."

"Answer me!"

"I'm in San Francisco!"

"What the hell are you—how are you—who are you— I don't even know where to begin." Her voice muffles. "He's fine, I guess. Sorry!" She yells back in the phone, "Are you okay?"

"Who are you with?"

"The goddamned police, that's who."

"What?! Jesus, Mom."

"Don't you Jesus me—how dare you—how—" She stops again. More deep breaths. Someone, a man, a *police officer* I guess, reassures her, tells her to relax. "They found your car, Isaac."

Oh.

"They found it abandoned on the freeway. I thought you'd been kidnapped. Or were—" She stops herself again. This time, she's crying. Hard.

I sit on the edge of the bed. Rose Tyler snuggles in my lap. "I'm sorry."

"How are you getting home?" she asks, clearing her throat. "Because you're coming home right now."

"Max is taking me."

"Who the hell is Max?"

"She's no one," I say, without thinking. I look up. She hasn't moved, except she's looking at her shoes now. "A friend, I mean. She's a friend. We're leaving soon."

"And you trust this strange friend I've never heard of before?"

"I do," I say, looking at Max. "Very much."

"Fine. Be safe. Text me every hour until you're outside this door. I'm not kidding even one bit here, you hear me?"

"Yeah."

"And, Isaac?"

"Yeah?"

"I love you." She's crying again.

"Love you, too."

We hang up.

"Change of plans?" Max says, after a long while, now looking out the window.

"I guess."

"I'll take Rose Tyler out and meet you downstairs." She throws her bag over her shoulder and walks out the door. Without looking at me once.

◆

Several minutes later, I'm in the garden.

Max stops talking when I step outside. Luna whips around, wrapping me in her silky pink muumuu, smelling like sunshine. She doesn't let go until I hug her back.

"My darlin'," she says, pulling away. "I'm sorry to see you leave so soon." She looks at me—scratch that, through me. "Oh, honey, don't you worry your pretty little head. This is the beginning you've been waiting for." She claps her hands. "Before you go, you must sign my scrapbook!"

"We really have to—"

"Oh no. That's the fourth rule of the house. I let you stay; you sign my book. Let me hold a little piece of your soul to keep it safe, remember?" She winks, pats my cheeks, and pulls me inside, where an open book sits on the coffee table. "I've been going through these things again. It's so nice, comforting. Gotta thank you for that. Have at it, honey. I'll see you out there in the great big beautiful wild one day, yeah?" She hums and floats away.

I look at the scrapbook. Max signed the previous page: *Thank you for showing me the truest meaning of love.* And she drew a rain cloud with positive water words dripping down on a scribbled version of her.

I stare at the empty page next to hers.

Thank you for your kindness, I write. *Thank you for helping me find a piece of my dad's story.* I sign it with my address and phone number, inviting her to stay with us, in case she ever visits Los Angeles.

Then I reach into my backpack and pull out one of my lucky talismans: the deflated yellow balloon from Griffith Park, from my coming-out party. A day consumed with joy and innocence, laughter that blurs the darkness. I tape it in the book, to always keep that part of me safe.

29

We are silent for six hours.

No jazz. No conversation. No crunching food wrappers.

Out the window, I watch the world flash forward. Wishing it would rewind so I can start all over again.

Or just stop.

When we start our ascent up Beachwood Canyon, just minutes from home, I say, "Pull over here." We're several houses down the street from mine, but I won't be able to say goodbye with Mom waiting at the door. "So, look, Max, I hope we—"

"I'm gonna stop you right there, Fig." She puts her Jeep in park, turns off the ignition, and faces me for the first time today. "You don't need to say anything. In fact, I really don't want you to. I just want you to listen, okay?" I nod. "So, here's the deal: I don't understand it, but it's like I somehow, someway, destroy everything and everyone good that crosses my path."

"What? You didn't—"

"Don't. Don't make excuses. I didn't mean to cause any trouble between you guys. It was so nice to see two people who actually care about each other. At least, that's what I saw when you were with each other."

"Max, you didn't—"

"And, God, you're awesome, Fig. Like more than awesome, really—and yesterday . . . well, honestly, for the first time in my life I forgot about me. I was someone else, someone I've been wanting to be, and . . ." She pulls her shirt down below her wrist, wipes her eyes. "Fuck, I'm sick of crying. *Arrgghhh.* Anyway. It's all to say thank you and I'm sorry. I really am. I had an amazing time and I really hope you can salvage what's left between you guys. Because you deserve all the happiness in the galaxy, Fig. You really do. And I hope you find your dad."

She turns and flips on the ignition.

"Can I say something now?" I ask.

"No."

"No?"

"No. I need you to get out of my car."

"But I wanted to—"

"Now. Fig. Out."

"But—"

"GO!"

"Fine." I grab my bag, tucking Rose Tyler under my arm. The second I close the door, she speeds down the hill. I don't move until I see the blue speck disappear into a sea of traffic. Gone. Like she was never here.

I dry my cheeks and walk the rest of the way home.

Oscar slouches in the driveway humiliated, plastered with an orange-neon TOW AWAY sticker on the rear window.

The front door flies open the minute Mom sees me stepping up the path. She's wrapped in a white, fuzzy bathrobe she stole from some spa, hands on her hips. Her face is swollen, splotched red. Her body, windblown. Like she's been ripped and tattered and tried to piece herself back together again, too.

I did this to her, I think.

When I reach the top step, she pulls me into her and kisses the top of my head over and over and over. "I love you, goddamn it."

"I love you, too, Mom."

She doesn't move, her eyes a swirl of red tributaries. "I swear to Christ, if I was a different kind of mother, I'd slap you so hard right now you'd wish you'd stayed in San Francisco. Get up to your room. You're grounded. Obviously. No. You're more than grounded, whatever the hell that is. Just go. Now that I see you, I don't want to look at you, understand?"

I nod.

"Get up there."

As I walk up the stairs, I hear her exhale a release so deep it's like she's been holding her breath for years. Just like me.

part three

THE FIRST
TOMORROW

30

I am alone. Again.

Home, but homesick. Like I don't belong here, or anywhere for that matter.

It's been a week since Oscar gave up on life on the side of the freeway. Like me. I've spent the past five days in hiding, barely moving from this spot. Not even to shower. It smells like a boys' locker room in here. Rose Tyler buries herself under the covers from the stench.

I called in sick to work and turned off my phone. I've hardly eaten.

Mom brought me matzo ball soup from Canter's one day. And chicken noodle from this place at the farmers market on another. Both of which I declined. Wrong move. Had to practically beg her not to take me to see Dr. Andrew and the "people she knows at Cedars." So the next time she brought me soup, I slurped it all down to appease her.

Other than that, we haven't talked or seen each other. (Although she slipped a note under my door this morning that said, *Meet me downstairs at 5:00 p.m. sharp!!* Since then, the house has been smothered in burning herbs. She's doing so many spells and incantations, she's either trying to find some clarity or summoning a demon to take me away.)

In short, spring break was a total bust.

I have a thousand more questions than answers about Alex Stryker since my return. Who else was Dad with in that picture?

What happened that day? And every day in between before meeting Mom? And then what? Alex vanishes into thin air? Or dies? What about me? How'd I get here?

But now, I don't have the energy to find out.

All I've been able to do is glare at the phony stars painted on my stupid, ugly ceiling. I can't name them to bring me back. And bring me back to what? My inescapable loneliness? Instead, the darkness between them has consumed me, filled me with this black hole of emptiness again. Even my dreams are vacant.

Maybe I'm meant to be a half-human forever, dangling through space, never feeling whole. Maybe I'm always going to have this hollow void inside me. Maybe that's who I have to finally accept I am.

Or maybe I've been missing the point all along. Maybe instead of finding the answer, I'm supposed to live in this insoluble question. Maybe I'm never meant to know the truth.

Or maybe the truth is—

I am alone.

Even Christopher's gone. I heard from him the night I returned: *I'm so sorry,* I texted. *I'm sorry too,* he replied. *But I need some space. I think you do too.* When I called, he didn't pick up, and we haven't spoken since. I ache for him, a kind of longing I've never felt before. But I can't decide if it's real; my feelings are all blurred together these days. I close my eyes and he's in my room again, snuggling next to me on my bed. I feel his heartbeat against mine, sink into his lips one more time, wipe his tears away, and tell him everything's going to be okay. But when I open my eyes again, he's not here.

I guess he's lost in the darkness, too.

Charlie tried calling a few times, but I can't be pep-talked into joy anymore. One day they texted *You need to tell your mom the truth about why you left,* but I deleted it.

And Max. She drove off without knowing the full story, that anything between Christopher and me had nothing to do with her. Just disappeared down the hill and out of my life forever. Seems to be a recurring pattern here. I suppose I could show up at her doorstep. (I time-stamped her address in my brain that day at Gracie's: 428 Chula Vista Way.) I could knock on her door, bring her a Happy Meal, and act like everything's fine. I'm good at that. Maybe she'd lift that perfect smile of hers and say, "This feels right." Maybe she misses me as much as I miss her.

But no.

Instead, we're left alone with our made-up truths about other people's lives and who we are.

Maybe that's it, though.

Maybe we only see what we want to see.

Maybe that's how we keep ourselves safe, protected, stuck.

Maybe, maybe, maybe.

31

It's 4:57 on Saturday evening. Three minutes until The Talk with Mom.

When I stagger out of my room, I notice two things: (1) The herbal smoke is overpowering. I have to swat through the haze to see my way down the stairs. (2) I hear a voice other than Mom's. Is this a trap? Has she called her friend Dr. Andrew to cart me off to the clinic again?

No, it's Charlie. Great. What is this, an intervention? I stop at the bottom of the stairs to listen.

Mom: "So, you know nothing? Why he ran away like that? Why the hell he took off to San Francisco of all places and lied to me?"

I strain to hear. Charlie knows better than to say anything. I'll be cataclysmically pissed if they do.

Charlie: "Well, it's—"

"Because I knew you wouldn't let me go," I say, interrupting them and stepping into the kitchen. That's the first I've heard my voice all week. It feels bruised. I clear my throat.

Haven't really seen Mom since Monday when I walked up the path. It's clear now what I've done to her. If the skeletal holes under her eyes don't give it away, the extra wrinkles surely do. But let's be real here. Maybe the fact that she's hiding secrets from me about Dad is causing her own inner turmoil.

Also, there's a forest fire on the kitchen table. No, it's Mom's huge bundle of herbs, smoldering. "Can you put that out? I can hardly breathe." These are the only words I shall speak.

Charlie sits next to her, hands folded on the table, now wearing a buzz cut (this is new) and a look of concern on their face that hurts my heart. They're paler than usual, too. I can't look at them, so I turn away.

"So that's it?" Mom says, after finally extinguishing the smoke. She takes another swig of wine. "You said you were with Charlie, and I believed you." She whips a tissue out of her stolen spa robe's pocket, blows her nose. "And, Charlie, I don't know why you lied to me, too, but—"

"I'm sorry, Ms. Griffin," they say. "It's . . . complicated."

"I don't know what's so complicated about telling the truth," Mom says, throwing her hands in the air. She stands, jostling her glass of wine and pacing the kitchen. I keep my attention focused on the floor, even though I'm seething inside. All this talk about telling the truth!

"Isaac, honey, I've been trying to give you space, your own time to figure out what you want to do. I'm going to straight-up ask: Are you on drugs?"

"What? No! God!" Crap. Wasn't meant to talk, but that came blazing out.

"Tell me the truth. I can help you. Dr. Andrew is a good guy, a friend, you know that." Oh, here we go. "He's at a really good hospital. I promise you won't be in trouble."

"I'm not, Mom."

"Then what? What is all this? Why would you disappear like that and lie to me? For the life of me, I can't figure it out. Why'd you go to San Francisco of all places?"

I don't move.

I look behind her to see Charlie widen their eyes and mouth, "Tell her."

"I feel like I don't even know you anymore," Mom says, after blowing her nose again.

"I don't know you, either," I say. And in that moment, a few memories flash through my mind. When we'd practice full moon meditations on the secret hill together, sharing each other's smile. When she gave me an extra candle on my birthday and told me I was too magical not to make another wish. When she held me in her arms and sang me to sleep, stroking my hair: *I hear the cottonwoods, whispering above* . . . Just Mom and me.

I study the cabinets as she once did, to avoid her eyes.

"I can't help you if you won't talk to me, Isaac," she says, her voice breaking. "We used to share everything. We were best buds, remember? I'm here for you if you'll just—"

"Where's Dad?" I barely hear myself ask it.

I look up. Her brow is furrowed. "What?"

"I want to know where Dad is," I say, my voice trembling.

She shakes her head. "What are you—why are you changing the subject?"

"I'm not."

No one moves.

Her phone buzzes on the table, startling everyone. She looks at the screen. "My agent. This goddamned deadline." Then, turning to me, she says, "We're not through here. You understand me?"

She picks up the phone. "Hi, Fern. I know, I'm working on—" She wipes her eyes with her tissue, starts tramping down the hall toward her office, glass of wine in hand. "Well, what sort of plot seems real to you? Mine sure as hell doesn't." And she's gone.

I'm left standing alone with Charlie, still unable to meet their gaze. I notice the stack of college brochures scattered on the table. ArtCenter College of Design in Pasadena. Otis College of Art and Design. San Francisco Art Institute. Among others.

We don't speak, but I know they're waiting for me to say the first words.

"You got a haircut," I say.

"Fig." I still can't look at them. It's impossible to hide anything from Charlie. So instead, I focus on the silver feather earring dangling from their ear. "Where have you been?" they ask.

"Upstairs."

"You know what I mean. Don't shut me out."

"I'm not. I needed to be alone." I pause. "Have you talked to Christopher?" When I finally look at them, their eyes are filled with such worry it makes me feel sick.

"A few times."

"Does he miss me? Is he okay?"

"Yes, he does. And he will be . . . will you? What's going on here?"

I crack my knuckles, shifting uncomfortably in place. "It's hard to explain."

"Try."

My blood simmers, but I'm on the verge of exploding into tears. I don't even know what to feel anymore. So that's exactly what I say.

"And?" Charlie still stares, their arms folded over their chest.

"And . . ." I look out the kitchen window. Palm fronds clap the sky in the blowing wind. "I don't know, Charlie. I feel so . . . confused. I wish I never left. I miss Christopher. I miss life as it was before—"

"Do you really?"

I think about Max gleaming on the hillside. I think about Gracie's tears falling on my hands. I think about Dad fighting for love, determined, like me, never to give up on the quest. And I wouldn't give those feelings back for anything.

"You said you found something in San Francisco," Charlie says. "What was it?"

"Alex Stryker," I say softly, still staring out the window. "That's Dad's real name. I meant to tell you."

"That's good news."

"And they might be trans, but I don't know for sure."

"I wondered from those pages. What else?"

I shake my head, start to walk away. "I don't really feel like— You should go, Charlie. I won't be able to take you to school next week, obviously. Oscar's dead."

"Fig." Their chair scoots out. I turn around to face them. Without makeup on, their jade eyes are more muted than usual. "How long have we known each other?"

"Almost eleven years."

"And how many times have I lied to you?"

"You'd have to tell me."

"Never. Not once. And what I'm about to tell you? It may hurt. But I'm telling you because I love you. Okay?"

"Okay . . ."

They lift my hands in theirs, rubbing their thumbs over my palms, our eyes locked. "I know we always said we were missing something from our lives."

"Yeah, and you found yours, Charlie. I didn't. You have two parents who love you for who you are." It comes out plainly, without a hint of resentment.

"But that's my point, Fig. It wasn't what I thought I was looking for."

"Easy for you to say."

"Hey, I know I'm lucky. I know some trans kids don't have what I have. But my folks only lit that spark within me. I'm the one who had to keep the flame going."

"What does that even mean?"

"It means it's up to me. Not anyone or anything else. You have to stop making this search for your dad the excuse for not living your life."

I drop their hands. I want to scream and throw the kitchen chair through the window and burn the house down with Mom's herb bundle and laugh in their face until I turn blue.

But I don't move.

"Because the real question," they ask, "is who are you if you stop searching?"

I open my mouth to say something, but no words come out.

"I know it's not easy to hear, Fig. But trust me, okay? Find whatever it is you need to find, and do it now, so you can move on."

"I don't know how," I say.

"Start with what you know, and take it step-by-step from there."

"Follow the signs," I whisper to myself.

"Hmm?" Charlie says. I shake my head. "And you know I'm here for you," they continue. "Whenever, wherever, however. You're not alone. Got it?" I nod. "I wish you could see your own light, Fig. It's so bright it's—" I feel a few tears falling. They wipe my cheeks, smiling. "You're going to be okay, I promise."

There's a part of me that knows they're right. But I'm afraid. Afraid to follow the signs to find the answers. Afraid to let it all go and see

175

what's left behind. Afraid that, either way, I'm not going to like what I see.

But I know I can't go back to the way things were before.

I picture Max and her riotous grin, standing on the sidewalk, saying, *I think maybe we found our next clue!* Feeling the hope and joy rise within me as we followed Gracie, knowing I had to keep going, that I could never return without finding the truth.

And I realize now I still need to.

We stand together—Charlie, drying my tears, twinkling a grin; me, feeling everything and nothing all at once—hugging each other tight.

32

I run upstairs feeling somewhat lighter. Like I have a mission again, a new sense of purpose. Charlie's right, I need to find the answers now. Decipher the clues to solve the eternal mystery of Dad. This is my chance to find out who I am. To quit rambling along my broken-heart map. When I do, I can finally finish this never-ending chapter in my life and start writing a new story. It's up to me to change it.

Maybe this is what Gracie meant: You have to fight for what you believe in, because no one else will do it for you.

So that's exactly what I do. Step-by-step, I follow the signs.

I start with the picture I found in the attic and dive headfirst down a rabbit hole of queer history. Unraveling a past I've never even considered before.

Turns out, that photo was taken during the Street Sweep protest in July 1966. Just one month prior to the Compton's Cafeteria riot that Gracie spoke about. Those people carrying brooms and signs were part of a group called Vanguard, the first gay youth and transgender organization in US history. Their mission? Street power. To help street kids and to promote a sense of self-worth. To fight. And this protest was organized to literally clean the streets. From what I can tell, the Tenderloin hasn't cleaned itself up over the years. But for those trans and queer youth who were thrown out with the trash, it was their home. And that was the ultimate point: ALL TRASH BEFORE THE BROOMS, one sign read. Police saw them as just another piece of garbage to be swept away, so they took to the streets to protest and prove them wrong.

And that was just the beginning.

The best part? Alex Stryker, my dad, was in the middle of it all.

I lock myself in my room for the rest of the weekend and keep digging. I've suddenly become a boy obsessed. Possessed, even. By the Ghost of Queer Past. Although names were mostly withheld from history, for fear of being caught and persecuted, I follow the Google breadcrumbs that lead from one story to the next, convinced this is the path to finally uncovering our truth.

And from what I've found so far, my dad was pretty badass and someone I *have* to meet one day. I only hope they're still alive.

Either way, one thing is clear: Alex Stryker was a part of history in the making. Knowing they were a rabble-rousing revolutionary, knowing that's who I come from, means that fighting spirit lives in me.

And that's something I can hold on to.

33

Monday morning, my radio alarm blares Prince's "Purple Rain." Good song. I switch it off after watching the numbers click over a few times.

No wake-up call. No motivational quote. No Christopher.

Rose Tyler licks my ears.

I stack the papers I printed out over the weekend, a trail of historical tidbits I'd found connected to Dad, stash them in my desk drawer to hide from Mom.

And at long last, I shower.

Downstairs, Mom's dressed in velvet yoga pants and a tight spaghetti-strap shirt. She's wearing her thick Ray-Bans, studying a crossword, hair twigged out on her head like a scavenged bird's nest.

We don't talk.

I drink orange juice.

I eat a bagel.

We say four words. Her: *You ready?* Me: *I am.*

We slide into her Prius and sit in traffic.

I hate riding in her car. It smells like a used litter box. I roll down the window some.

Mom listens to *NPR: Morning Edition* until we pull into the school lot. We say six more words. Her: *I'll pick you up after?* Me: *Fine.*

I navigate the hallway.

I don't see Charlie.

At my locker, I fixate on my textbooks for too long. Then the mirror for even longer. I'm hoping to see Christopher walk by.

But he never shows.

Until.

At the end of the day, I see him sitting on the steps outside of school, scrolling through his phone. There's no choice but to walk past because Mom's waiting in her litter box.

I tap his shoulder.

He looks up.

I smile.

He doesn't.

I clear my throat. "Can we talk?"

He doesn't move, just keeps staring at me, so I take that as a yes.

"Look," I say. "What happened in—"

"Fig . . . don't."

"Don't?"

He stands. He's wearing his favorite Bob Marley tank top, and I want to throw myself into his arms, smell his mint aftershave and favorite cucumber-scented soap, hear him whisper sweet nothings in my ear. Instead, he says, "Isaac, I miss you. A lot. But let's not right now, okay? I'm sorry about that night in San Francisco. I really am. But I'm not ready to talk about it. I need a break from us. Some time alone. Let's give that to each other."

I swallow.

"I'm sorry, I gotta go," he says. "Take care. Okay?"

Take care? It's worse than I thought. No, it just got worse. I watch him jump into Jadyn Brooks's car—the white kid who played his love interest in *Rent*. He turns away from me and they fly off into the sunset, in Jadyn's vintage green Bronco no less.

I slide into Mom's car, covering my face as much as I can. (1) Because of the god-awful smell and (2) to hide the tears that are sure to burst through at any second. Not because we're officially broken up now, I guess. But because I realize I was holding on to something between us that's been missing for a while. And it's time to let that go.

Maybe that's a good thing.

Mom and I say six more words. Her: *When do you work again?* Me: *Saturday.*

It's clear Christopher has moved on, and I need to do the same. I need to figure out what's next for me, what I'm going to do with *my* life. So as soon as we're home, I run upstairs and shove all my feelings down a Google rabbit hole.

I spend the rest of the day diving deeper into research, determined to find more answers, emerging only once for dinner. Tonight, it's kung pao chicken from P.F. Chang's. (Mom says I have to eat with her from now on, even though the only conversation we make is clinking silverware on dishes.)

She disappears into her office, doing rewrites on a script.

I disappear into my room, lost in a maze of history.

The end.

But then: A text appears on my phone.

Isaac Hayes, it says.

Who is this? I write.

You said all Isaacs were born cursed. Isaac Hayes. Prove me wrong.

A smile crests my cheeks.

I can think of a few reasons, I write.

Hiya, Fig.

Hello, Max.

34

Turns out, at some point during our trip, Max used my phone to call hers so she'd have my number. *Just in case we ever got separated,* she said. I'm glad she did.

We've been texting every night since. It started out simple. (We both avoided talking about anything that happened when we were last together.) (But to be honest, I was too ecstatic to hear from her to even care.)

TUESDAY

Max: How r u? How was ur day?

Me: Loaded question. How was urs?

Max: Same. Maybe we start off easier.

Me: Good idea.

Max: I've been DYING to know more about that picture of your dad.

Me: Where to begin?

Max: Tell me EVERYTHING.

So I catch her up.

Me: And as it turns out, Vanguard was meeting at Compton's.

They were sick of the way the managers treated

trans folks, so they picketed.

And get this.

Soon after that Compton's uprising,

the same managers tried to ban trans customers,

but Vanguard rioted and broke all their new windows.

AGAIN.

Max: Ducking awesome.

Me: Ha. Right?

Max: Hate autocorrect.

Me: And they started a more militant movement

after that.

Got money to help trans poverty.

Even started the first trans support group in US.

Max: The definition of street power. ✊🏿

Amazing ur dad was part of that.

Me: I know. Damn, my thumbs hurt from typing so fast.

So excited to share it w someone.

Max: Know where ur dad might be?

Me: Not yet. But I'm not giving up.

Max: And never giving in.

Me: Following the signs like ur dad said.

Max: He'd be so happy you are.

WEDNESDAY

Max: I've been wondering.

(I did not get this until three hours after she'd sent it.)

183

Me: Sorry. Been listening to an album. Didn't hear phone.

What have you been wondering?

Max: What album?

Me: Kind of Blue

Max: Wait. What?! By Miles Ducking Davis? No way.

Me: Yes way. I downloaded it the other day.

Max: what do u think?

Me: Amazing. So raw. Soothing even.

I feel like I'm floating in trumpet clouds when I listen to it.

Max: Right? It calms me too.

Me: Thanks for inspiring me. 😄

Max: I'm glad I could. 😄

I was wondering about ur mom.

Me: What about her?

Max: How did it go when you got back?

Me: Oh. We're not talking. She grounded me from life, so.

Max: Ah. Got it. Same.

Me: What happened when u got home?

Max: Armageddon.

A screaming match that obliterated civilization.

Fake Mom took my car away.

Basically locked me in my room.

The end.

Me: Shit.

Max: Yeah. But whatever, only four more months till I'm free.

Me: What happens in four months?

Max: Going to Caltech.

The proverbial daughter follows in her dad's shadow, haha.

Me: What? This is amazing! Studying what?

Max: Astronomy. Great excuse to live every day
in the stars.

Me: So cool!

Max: Yeah, only really saw the stars when Dad took me
to the desert once.
They're impossible to see here.

Me: Worst part about living in LA = why I work at
the Observatory I guess, haha.

Max: Oooo, what a cool job!
HBU? Where you headed in the fall?

Me: Nowhere.

Max: Nowhere?

Me: Don't know what I want to do with my life yet.

Max: U got nothing but time.

Me: Can you tell my mom that?
Or the whole world for that matter?

THURSDAY

Me: Hello you.

Max: Hey.

Me: What's up?

Max: Hard day. Weird day. U?

Me: Same. Always. U ok?

Max: Can I call you?

Oh.

I contemplate the text. For too long. *It's stupid,* I think. *When did talking on the phone become such a thing? This is all people ever did.* But now, I don't know, the intimacy level just rose, and I think I'm having a hot flash.

> **Max:** Or not. It's cool.
>
> There's just something I wanted to talk about.
>
> Easier than texts.
>
> **Me:** Sorry. Sorry. *slaps head* Of course. Yeah. Call me.

So, two seconds later, she does.

"HEY," she screams before I can even say anything. Then she does the laugh: her laugh that makes rain burst from clouds. It's transcendent. "Little quick on the draw there, I guess."

"Ha. Yeah. Hello. Officially . . . I missed that laugh."

"You did?"

"Yeah."

"No one's ever said that to me before."

"Oh . . . well."

We're silent. It's strange, I guess, to be speechless on a phone with someone. But it's oddly comforting, too. Hearing her breathing in my ear. That's probably weird to say, so I don't.

"It is funny," she says finally.

"What is?"

"Why is it so hard to talk on the phone? And I'm the one who wanted to."

"*Right?!* Sorry. I mean, I was just—"

"Maybe we should imagine an old rotary thing or when you screamed into those horn-shaped tube things."

"Or two cans and a string."

"Ha."

"But it's nice," I say.

"Yeah. It is," she says.

I lean back on my bed. "Your voice sounds different than I remember."

"Really?"

"Yeah. A little deeper. Like Isaac Hayes." There's that laugh again. A bass drum in my ear that strikes my heart. She sniffles. "You okay?"

"Yeah, why?"

"You sound like you're crying." *Are you cutting again?* I want to scream. But I don't.

"Just tired, I guess." She sniffles again. "And Fake Mom's in the other room on her third gin and tonic, so yeah."

"Ah. You sure you're okay?"

"Helicopter much? I'm fine, Fig. Sheesh."

"Sorry. What'd you want to talk about?"

"So, okay." She clears her throat. "Damn, I thought this would be easier, but clearly that ain't the case."

"What?"

"It, Fig. The big *it*."

"Huh?"

"About what happened the last night we were together."

"Oh." I sit up in bed. Rose Tyler wiggles off my lap, snuggles herself under the covers. "I'm glad you brought that up, because—"

"So, listen." She takes a deep breath. "Like I said, I'm really sorry if I messed up anything between you and—"

"Max, if you'll just let me—"

"And I'm *really* sorry if I messed up a friendship here. Because honestly—it's weird, I know—and probably totally selfish of me—and probably totally stalker of me because we barely even know each other, at least in this lifetime. But being with you is just, I don't know, fun. It's easy. And, God. I loved joining you on your adventure and watching you get excited about new discoveries about your dad, and honestly, I haven't stopped thinking about you since I drove off. That's weird, right?"

"Oh, well, no."

"And right now . . . I've felt such chaos in my life since my dad died, like I'm constantly spinning in circles, trapped in some vortex. I really need easy in my life, Fig, and you helped me find a way through, and I'm hoping we can at least salvage that. Our friendship. Together, I mean. There. Now you." She's panting.

"Wow."

"I know."

"I can talk now?"

"Yes, you can."

"Good." I take a breath, trying to absorb what she just said. "Because I feel the same."

"You do?"

"Yeah." And then I quite literally tell her everything. From navigating a broken-heart map to how Christopher and I met to where we're at right now and all the stops along the way that brought me here. "And I miss Christopher like hell, Max. I really do. And I worry about him. But he asked for space, and I have to respect that. Charlie says he's doing okay, better than before actually, so . . . I guess I get it now. We needed to go away so we could see ourselves more clearly. Like, we were both so lost in our own stuff, we couldn't even see each other anymore."

"I get that," she says softly.

"So, yeah. What you just said? About how strange it is we've only met and it's like we've known each other all this time? You took the words right out of my mouth."

"Really?"

"Yeah." RT peeks her head out from under the sheets. I scratch her ears as she licks my hand. "Knowing you're there helps me know I'm not alone," I say. "And it's been so long, I almost forgot what that feels like."

"Wow." Max sniffles. My heart beats in time to her breath.

"That's why I love going on adventures," she says. "I don't want to miss seeing people's joy. I don't want to miss out on mine." She blows her nose. "So, good, okay. Now what?"

"We talk, I guess."

So we do. About dreams we want to create. And the dreams that haunt our sleep. About how pain never goes away. How joy can be found in the strangest places. About feeling lost in a world where everyone else around you has been found. About my favorite memories from childhood (when Mom took me to Griffith Observatory for the first time) and her favorite memories with her dad (Joshua Tree, wrapped in his arms under a blanket, with shooting stars blazing across the sky—that's when she decided to become an astronomer, so she could always feel that tingly giddiness inside her). We talk about God and whether one exists, death and the life we try to live in between. And on and on and on until 2:37 a.m. At least that's the last time I checked my clock before drifting off to sleep.

I wake to the sun winking through the blinds with the phone lying next to my pillow, still on. She's asleep. So I flip over, staring at the stars above my head, listening to her breaths.

35

I had that dream again last night.

The one where I'm driving along the edge of a cliff, the waves crashing against the rocks below me, trying to find my way back home.

A hitchhiker holds a cardboard sign this time. *If broken hearts are maps to the soul, why do I keep getting lost?* He lifts a thumb, then flips me the finger when I drive by.

I stick my head out the window with Rose Tyler, feeling the wind rush through me.

"Time is a sickness," I hear. But when I sit back inside the car, no one's there.

The voice was my own.

The winding road suddenly veers.

I lose control of the car.

We fly off the edge of the cliff and sail through the air.

"This is the way it ends," I scream.

I open my eyes. Sweat pours. Heart pounds. Breath stops. Rose Tyler licks.

I sit up, clench the pillow to my chest, wondering where I am.

Who I am.

Even with the answers I've found, I still don't know.

I'm so sick of being lost.

36

On Friday, I see Charlie in the halls, but for some reason, I try to avoid them.

Until I can't.

They grab my arm from behind, startling me. Their eyes glitter silver like little comets.

"What have you found out, Fig?" they ask.

"Oh, this and that," I say, forcing a smile. I wonder if they can tell. "I'm so close I can feel it." It's the first time I've lied to them, and I don't know why.

"I miss our car rides. I miss our talks. I feel like I'm being grounded with you."

I nod, still smiling.

"So, listen, I'm off to New York this weekend for some early orientation thing, but I'm a phone call away if you need anything."

"Sweet. Have fun," I say. "And I will, for sure." Smiling hurts.

They look at me one last time. "You sure you're good?"

"Mm-hmm." I know they want to say more. But they don't. They kiss me on the cheek when the bell rings.

At lunch, I see Christopher laughing with Jadyn but sneak out before he notices.

I sit on the steps outside, alone. Rubbing my chest, feeling the world cave in on me again. I text Mom I'm not feeling well, and she writes back saying she'll pick me up in twenty.

I know now why I lied to Charlie, why I'm hiding from Christopher. They're both filled with new adventures and I don't want to take away their joy. Because even though Alex Stryker is less of an enigma, I still don't feel the connection to *me* I've been longing to find. What I really wanted to tell Charlie was that I spent all night trying to uncover more answers, and found nothing. That I'm tired of finding nothing. That I don't even know what I'm looking for anymore.

That, unlike them, I think I'll be lost forever.

37

I feel like I'm drowning.

This is what I write to Max the moment I jump in Mom's car.

Seconds later she replies: *Can I call u?*

20 min. I'll be home.

And exactly twenty minutes later, she does.

"Are you suicidal?" she asks immediately upon me answering.

"No."

"Are there prescription drugs or drugs of any kind nearby?"

"No."

"Have you been drinking?"

"No."

"Are you hyperventilating?"

"Yes." I'm pacing my room, sucking up what little oxygen seems to be available. My head throbs. My heart: reported missing. It burst from its cage long ago, running wild. Still trying to find it. "Help."

"Okay, I got you," she says. "I'm a solid A when it comes to freak-outs. Is there a window nearby?"

"I'm not jumping."

"No, no—I mean, good, that's good—but open it. Give yourself some extra air."

"Right." I fling the window open. The breeze is slow and thick today, layered in smog, but it's something.

"Breathe," she says. "Like in the park. Remember?"

I do.

"Good. Just like that. So, here's the thing, Fig," she says softly, still breathing with me. "Sometimes we need to drown. Otherwise, how could you ever really know the difference? How could we know how good it feels on the days we might be floating and not drowning, right?"

"Uh-huh." Her voice sails through me.

"Today, I happen to be floating. Some days I'm not. Like yesterday was a really hard day for me and—"

"I didn't realize that's what you meant. You should've said something. I would've totally—"

"I don't like to ask for help, Fig. It's a thing with me."

"Oh."

"But I love to help. And I'm your life preserver right now. Like in *Titanic*: I'm Rose and you're Jack right now, and—"

"Bad analogy. He dies."

"Excellent point. Forget that. I'm just a big ole blown-up rubber duckie floating in your pool. Grab me. I got you."

I laugh. "You're ridiculous, but thank you." I sit on the windowsill, my breath at last back in my chest where it belongs. In the distance, the ocean's horizon glitters through the smog.

"Good to hear your laugh," she says. "So, we got that clear, then?"

"Yeah. Are you at school?"

"No. Didn't go today. What's going on?"

"Everything. Nothing. I don't know. It's like ever since I left and came back, I've been a carbon-copy version of myself. Like everything's the same but totally different."

"I get that."

"You do?"

"Oh yeah."

"And every time I feel like I'm getting close to figuring it all out, or whatever, I smack into this brick wall."

"What's your brick wall today, Fig?"

"I don't know. I guess . . . Everyone's moving on without me. Charlie's leaving. Christopher's laughing again. And here I am, still stuck in the same fucking spot. I thought by finding Dad, or anything at all about them, I'd finally know *me*. I'd finally feel like I belong in this fucking world. But I was wrong. I still don't." Rose Tyler leaps up, snuggling in my lap. "And I know Charlie means well, but—they say I need to let all of this go, to talk to my mom, but I can't."

"Let all of what go? Talk to your mom about what?"

"My dad."

"She doesn't know?"

"It's a long story. The point is, how can I just let this go, Max? After all this time of searching?"

She's quiet. For some time.

I pull the phone away to make sure the call didn't end. She's still there.

"I'm going to go out on a limb here," Max says.

"What?"

"Can we FaceTime?"

"Oh."

"I know it's weird. It's like sexting or something. But if we already know that isn't part of the equation from the get-go, then why not?"

"I mean—"

"Honestly, Fig, I just want to see you right now. If I were there, I'd hug you, but I'm not, so this is the next best thing—I guess—or we don't have to."

"No, I want to see you, too."

"Okay."

She immediately hangs up, and seconds later her name appears. I click Accept.

"This is—" I start.

"Totally strange to see you on my phone," she says. "In my bedroom, no less. Anyway. Hi."

"Hi, you."

She's propped up against a wall. A painting of some sort hangs above her head, but it's too dark in her room to see what it is. Her hair's faded: Powder-blue tips cling to her cheeks. She's still wearing a long-sleeved shirt. And she's makeup free. Softer. Unfiltered.

"You look different than I remember," she says. "Even though it's only been a couple weeks."

Right, she can see me, too: blubbery, wild, and woolly me. I pat my hair down, wipe my face. "How so?"

"I don't know. More open or something."

"Huh."

"See? You're okay. You're even smiling right now."

"I am?" Oh, I am.

"Is there a ghost behind you?"

"What?!" I flip around. Rose Tyler leaps out of my lap. Nothing's there. "I don't—"

"That white shirt hanging over your head. It looks like a ghost."

"Oh. Right. That's my work shirt. Have to work tomorrow."

"I haven't been to the Observatory in forever. I went on a field trip when I was little. Barely remember it."

"You haven't been there since you were little? And you want to be an astronomer?"

"Life flew by, Fig. Then Dad got too sick to take me back."

"Ah . . . Well, I can get you in, kid. I got connections."

"Oh, cool!"

"Yeah, it's free actually, so . . ."

"Right."

"But I've been thinking about it a lot this week. And I have a surprise for you. If you want to meet me there sometime. Maybe even tomorrow."

"A surprise?" she asks, shifting up some. "Tomorrow? Let me check my sched— I'm free!"

"Good!"

She laughs. That laugh. I need to invent a new word for her laugh.

"Show me your room," she says.

"Oh. Uh. Well—"

"Is it a mess?"

"Well, no, it's never a mess. It's—"

"Then show me."

"I mean . . ." I turn the phone away.

"Aww, there's Rose Tyler," she says. "Let me say hi to her."

Rose Tyler's curled up on my pillow. Her ears snap up. Max *coochie-coos* and *wubba-wubbas*.

"Anyway, what else . . ." I turn the phone back around.

"Wait. Stop."

"What?"

"What's that wooden box on your nightstand? It looks like an ancient treasure chest."

I show her.

"Is that a quote from *Doctor Who* etched on there?" she asks.

"Indeed it is."

"I knew we were long-lost soul mates. What's in it?"

"Things I want to keep forever safe. My lucky talismans, a bunch of letters to my dad, stuff like that."

"Hmm. Show me more."

"Nope. Your turn. I want to see what the Magnificent Max's den looks like."

"You're cute. And no, you don't. My room's been classified a disaster area."

"Well, show me something. It's only fair."

"Fine." She shuffles out of bed and lifts her phone. On her nightstand, next to a few empty pudding cups, is a framed photo of her, standing outdoors against a backdrop of stars, arms outstretched like she's holding them in her palms. Or generating them. And because of the way the light hits the camera, beams shoot from her hands, an explosion of ecstasy. Like she's a supernova.

"Whoa. That picture of you," I say.

"I know. Dad took that of me when we were in Joshua Tree. Pretty spectacular, right?"

"It's beautiful."

"I was going to show you my painting. Please ignore the trash. Butterscotch pudding and I are having a strange love affair these days."

I laugh. "Duly noted."

She turns her camera to show me the picture above her on the wall. "Don't know if you can see this," she says.

"I can. It's cool." It looks like a cross between Van Gogh's *Starry Night* and *Sunflowers*. On it, she's written her dad's familiar phrases: *"Pay attention to the patterns. Follow the signs."* And added some I can tell she's maybe made up herself: *"Hate is for fools; love is wise." "We're all stories in the end." "The world is an infinitely better place because you're in it."*

"Just little reminders to myself," she mumbles. "I painted this."

"You did? Wow. Do your talents know no end?"

She nestles back on her bed, clutching a pillow close to her chest. "It's nothing. So, that's all you get. Show me more of yours."

"Uh, well, here are my walls. Not really much on them."

"Wait. What's happening on your ceiling there?"

"Oh." I lift the phone to show her. "My favorite constellations. I've been working on Cepheus forever. Haven't been inspired to finish it."

"Holy craptastic, Fig. That is A. May. Zing. You did that?"

"With my mom."

"It's sublime," she says softly. "Hey, turn the phone back around so I can see you." I do. She's smiling so big it makes the screen grow brighter. "Feel better?"

"I do, actually, yeah."

"Good. That was the point." She's turned her lamp off. It's completely dark in her room, even though the sun's still out. Only the pale-blue glow of her screen illuminates her face, and nothing else. "I wanted to ask you something, then."

"What?"

"Remember when we were with Gracie?"

"Of course."

"And what she said. About how when we face our fears, we finally feel free."

"Forgot she said that."

"Why don't you talk to your mom, Fig? What are you scared of?"

"Oh." Didn't expect that.

"I don't mean to pry. I only wanted—"

"No. It's fine. It's—"

Someone shrieks behind her. I jump. Max whips her head around. It's muffled, so I can't decipher words, but it sounds like someone's being exorcised.

"Shit," Max says, turning back to me.

"What was that?"

"I have to go," she says. "Bible study with Fake Mom."

"On a Friday? I didn't even think you liked—"

"I don't. But trust me, I'm much better off doing it than not." More muffled exorcisms. "You're okay, right?"

"Yeah. You sure you are?"

"I'll be fine. Bye, Fig."

She hangs up before I can say goodbye.

I nuzzle next to Rose Tyler, looking out the open window. A breeze wafts through, carrying with it the faint scent of fresh jasmine. The sun hits the clouds, swirling amethyst through the sky.

What *am* I really scared of?

Maybe it's not that I'm scared of hearing Mom tell more lies. Maybe I'm scared of her telling me the truth. That Dad wanted nothing to do with me after all. That Dad chose a different family to love and left me in the cold. That the legend of Alex Stryker is just that: a fairy tale without a happy ending.

There's only one way to find out, I guess.

Tomorrow, I talk to Mom.

38

The next morning, it's Saturday and Mom's still in permanent hunched-over-crossword-puzzle pose. Smoking again. Not sure she's moved from that spot for a few days. She smiles when she sees me. First one in a long time. Her face looks like her revisions: marked in red, every line crossed over. I try not to think about being the cause of that. Still.

"Morning, honey," she says.

"Hi, Mom."

"Want to do this crossword with me? For old times' sake?" Her voice crackles. Sounds like she's been screaming at her computer again all night.

"Uh . . . I . . . uh . . ." I also had another sleepless night, but this time I feel like I somehow ate seven hundred Aunt Luna brownies without realizing it: I'm twitchy, and my heart's currently in a high-speed chase with my brain. I've been rehearsing this godforsaken speech over and over again all night. About how I don't want any more secrets between us. About how she needs to start telling me the truth, because I know she hasn't been.

But nothing comes out.

So I walk to the window, shoving my hands in my pockets.

"You okay?" she asks.

Morning dew glistens in the trees. Orange blossoms flurry through the sky.

And the combination of the two takes me to another yesterday . . .

✦

We spent our Saturday mornings lounging under the canopy of orange trees. Some flowers would fall and tickle our cheeks.

"Oooh," Mom said, "an angel kissed you and got their wings."

"Huh?" I asked.

"You know, in *It's a Wonderful Life*, Clarence says angels get their wings when bells ring? Well, that's in Bedford Falls. Here in Los Angeles, an angel gets their wings when an orange blossom falls and touches your skin."

"Really?"

"Of course. How else could anything smell so sweet?"

"It's just a movie, Mom."

"What makes you think this isn't?" Then she grabbed my hand, squeezing it. When she lifted hers away, a bunch of blossoms landed in my palm. "Oh. Wow. You really must be something magical."

"Yeah," I said. "I am."

✦

"Isaac? You hear me?" Mom's voice snaps me back.

"Huh?" I turn.

She peers over her glasses at me.

"Sorry," I say. "Distracted today." I pull a chair out and sit down. This startles her.

She leans back. "So you are going to sit with me this morning?"

I shrug, start flipping through the college brochures on the table. Why can't I just ask her? This is harder than I thought. It's one thing when you have an imaginary mom in your head all night. It's another thing entirely when she's sitting right in front of you.

She riffles through a pamphlet. "You always loved the ArtCenter in Pasadena. The campus is gorgeous. Especially in the fall. All those leaves changing colors, remember? And you'd still be close to home." She half laughs, stubbing out her cigarette.

"I don't know, maybe you're right."

"I am?" This startles her even more. She lifts a soft smile, pulls her hair up in a straggly bun on her head and cinches it in place with another pencil.

Her eyes have found that long-lost blue aventurine sparkle again—a stone used to find inner strength, to speak your truth. Something we were always good at together. I know she's searching for the right words here. Like me. I can see it so clearly. We both have so much to say for very different reasons. Turns out, my brain is stuck, trying to unlock this chamber of my heart, the room that lets her in. It's been so long, I can't remember the combination to open the door. Maybe she feels the same.

"It's nice to have you join me," she says finally. She glances down at her crossword, jots another answer on the page. "How's Christopher doing?"

"What? Why?"

"Just asking. Haven't seen him over here in a while. Curious how you two are—"

"We broke up."

She gasps. "Oh, I'm so sorry, honey. I—"

"It's fine."

"You want to talk about it?"

I ran him off, like you did with Dad! Guess it's genetic. That's what I want to say. Instead I say: "No," and I scour the ArtCenter brochure, burning a hole in the pages with my eyes.

"I was thinking," she says. "Tomorrow's Sunday."

"It is." I need water. I teeter over to the sink and fill a glass.

"So maybe a picnic in that park in front of the Beverly Hills Hotel, like old times? We can make up stories about faux-celebrities as they drive by."

"We haven't done that in forever."

"That's the point. Or we could invent our own characters and go house hunting. Remember when we used to do that?"

"Don't you have to write?"

"Been stuck for a while," she says to herself. You don't say.

"Mom, I . . ."

"What is it, honey? Something's on your mind."

How can it be so hard to just say, "Mom, tell me the truth about Dad"? But it is. When something's been locked up inside you for so long, it's downright scary to let it go. I see that now. And maybe this is exactly how Mom feels. Maybe this is what Charlie meant. I take a deep breath. "Mom, I need to know why—"

"Oh, gosh. Hold that thought, sweetie. Before I forget . . ." She rummages through the papers on the table. "Ah. Here we go." She lifts a piece of mail tucked deep in the stack. "Who's Aunt Luna?"

"What?" I jump over, snatching the envelope from her hand.

Mom recoils. "She must be important."

There's a letter inside! With a picture of some sort! I feel like I'm holding the Holy Grail. I'm giggling so hard I don't know what to do.

"Honey, what is it?" Mom. Forgot about her.

"Nothing! Everything! I mean, I don't know!"

"Okay . . ."

I dash by her, quickly peeking down at the puzzle. "*Cipher*," I say.

"What?"

"That one. Six across. 'Words that wear disguises.'"

I hear her scribbling as I bound back up the stairs.

39

Rose Tyler pokes her head out from under my sheets.

I leap on the bed, and she snuggles up next to me. My heart's revving its engine, ready to take off.

I lift the envelope to my nose. Smells like sunshine and suntan lotion. And a curiosity shop filled with incense. Aunt Luna. I can't believe this is happening. How did she know where I lived? That's right. My scrapbook page. I left her my address. *Just in case,* I said. Well, just in case, indeed!

I carefully slip the letter open.

First, a note from her written on flowered stationery, which immediately transports me back to her garden. Listening to Max and her carry on about sacred calculus or some such, lost in the succulents.

> *Sweet One,*
>
> *I've been looking through all my scrapbooks since you left.*
>
> *What a treat to visit old friends, to feel so loved. I'm one lucky old broad.*
>
> *I found this note from 2001, and I somehow remembered this is who you were looking for. Funny how the mind works. Seems Alex was searching like you. Guess we're all here looking for something more, aren't we? And*

usually, it's been right in front of us all along, patiently
waiting for us to see. Maybe this will help open your eyes.

Ever yours,
Aunt Luna

A photo falls to my lap. My hands quiver. There's Dad in full, blazing color, holding Mom. Or maybe it's the other way around, it's hard to tell. Their love is infectious. Mom's younger, her sandy-blond hair billowing out of frame. Her long white dress lifts behind her like angels' wings. I don't think I've ever seen her so happy. But it's undeniable now. Dad, in flouncing white linen, long lemon-yellow curls, the mischievous glint in the eyes lined with black liner—like they know all the secrets of the universe—that blinding smile. They stand together in front of an old château of some sort, pink bougainvillea crawling up the sides. I wonder where this is. When this is.

Left inside the envelope: A folded note. And Dad's unmistakable handwriting. I read.

December 26, 2001

> *This morning, I found the first letter I'd left here in Luna's scrapbook of souls. 1966. I was so young, so lost. Reading it made me realize how I'd sealed up my heart the second I stepped off that Greyhound bus from Oklahoma City. I was so scared of where I came from, where I was going, that I couldn't even begin to see who I actually was.*
>
> *Hard to believe it's been over thirty years since Luna took me in, held my heart. And yet, it's also taken me this long to finally find the real me:*

I AM a transgender woman.

Damn. Feels so good to see it written so clearly, to say it aloud, to keep it safe and sacred in this scrapbook.

You may wonder how it could take me this long to accept who I am, especially after all those years of bleeding and fighting for the community. I suppose when you grow up being told you're wrong for something you know you're innately right for, no matter how hard you fight it, that feeling's embedded in your soul. And that's not something you can easily let go of.

Perhaps it's taken me this time to accept myself as a trans woman, so that I could first find love. Maybe I would've never met the people I've been so fortunate to know along the way. Maybe I would've never met Meredith Griffin. Either way, a soul's voyage is infinite, so in the scheme of things: What really is time and why should it ever matter when?

That said, it's time for me to live the life I was always meant to live. And to do that, I have to forever close this door to who I was. It's the only way I know to move forward.

I'm scared. I don't know what's next. But because my heart tells me this is the way, I follow.

If you open yourself up to it, love will always light your way.

That's what my dear Meredith taught me. She's the reason I'm able to take this leap into the unknown. For that, I am immeasurably grateful.

And so, as Luna instructed, I leave this note and picture of us in her scrapbook: to keep me safe, to keep our hearts protected.

Off I go. To new adventures, to old stories, to this moment right now: on the edge of being. And I can't wait to see how it all turns out.

Now, then, always, and forever,
Alex Stryker

"For a woman, I think a man is always a stranger.
And there's something awful about being
at the mercy of a stranger."
Where I Am Is Where I'll Be. M. G. + A. S. = 4VR

The words have blurred. I only notice I'm trembling when I grab my phone off the bed. It's hard to type.

Hey, I write.

Hi u, Max replies, a few minutes later.

> **Me:** Comin' to work today?
> **Max:** Forgot abt that! Crazy night.
> Will figure out how to sneak away.
> I need this day.
> And I'd love to see you.
> **Me:** Good. Same.
> I have another surprise.
> **Max:** Oooh, lucky me!
> **Me:** Me too, Max.

Me too.

40

"Heya, Fig," Max says.

"Heyheyhey!" I jump up from behind the marbled booth and wave and quickly sit down, then jump up and wave and sit back down again. What the hell is happening to me? I'm malfunctioning. It's been a couple weeks since we've seen each other in person. And it's clear now I'm pumped with adrenaline from Dad's latest letter, something I've been reading and rereading as I've sat behind the Griffith Observatory ticket counter these past few hours. Okay, I stay seated. It's a solid choice!

She laughs, affects some Southern dialect. "I do declah, it's a thousand degrees out there, sugah. Feels good in here, though."

"It's the structure. Made of concrete and marble and . . . yeah."

"Ah." She scans the rotunda, the mythological murals donning the ceiling, mouth agape. "Holy wow. It's been a long time, friend." She fans herself with her faded purple shirt. And her blue hair's tied up on her head but is barely blue anymore, more of an ocean gray. Like she really is a carbon-copy version of herself. Except for her eyes. They look heavier somehow, sadder even. But still, I think they're swathed in mascara, or possibly charged with Tesla coils; this close, they electrocute you if you look too long. Forgot that part.

"Hand me a paper towel," she says. I do, and watch her dab her glistening chest, still wide-eyed and taking it all in.

"Did you walk here?" I ask.

"Mm-hmm."

"From the *Valley*?"

"Up the hill. Which might as well be the Valley. I forgot how high up this place was."

"What happened to your car?"

"Fake Mom impounded it. Don't ask." She wads up the towel and tosses it to me. It smells like I remember her: a Coppertone commercial. "Oh. My. God."

"What?"

"There's a show called *Water Is Life*?"

Oh. She's looking at the show schedule on my desk. "Wanna see it? It's beautiful."

She lifts an eyebrow.

"Right," I say. "You'll love it. Here." I hand her a ticket. "And that's not even the surprise I had for you."

"You said *two* surprises. I'm holding you to it," she says, giggling.

"Don't worry. I won't forget. But go, now. The show starts at three and they're super intense about starting on time."

"Eeeeeeeee," she says, waving the ticket like she's about to enter the Chocolate Factory. "This is the best Saturday of my life. And I am doing everything in my power right now not to flop up on this counter and slop a kiss on your cheek."

"Thanks for restraining," I say, laughing. "The line's out the door."

Her face scrunches. "What about you? You can't join?"

"Not now. I'm stuck here most of the day. Later, though."

She starts to run off, then stops. "It's good to see you again, Fig. I mean, for real this time, not on the phone."

"You too, Max."

She cartwheels off. Basically. Stopping first to take in the swinging pendulum that sways back and forth in front of me all day. ("Ohmygod," she yells to a nearby stranger. "We are literally witnessing the earth rotating right now. Ain't that something else?" They stare back.) And I hear a few more *ohmyholywows* clamor out of her mouth before she disappears.

This goes on all day.

After she returns from the *Water Is Life* film with black streaks running down her cheeks, Max grabs my hands and says, "That was everything for me right now, Fig. Thank you," and disappears down the Observatory halls for another couple hours. Every so often, she blazes by my ticket counter saying, "Fig! I found that awesome periodic element thing you told me about!" and "Holy moly, Fig, I saw the real live sun!" and "Did you see that wall of galaxies?!" Like she really did swallow the Chocolate Factory.

Hours later, I pop outside to join her on the rooftop terrace.

Hazy nights make LA sunsets supernatural. But tonight, it's a revolution. Like some mad painter has stood on the clouds, stomping on paint tubes that squirted out newly invented colors in all directions. It's so raw I lift my hand thinking I might be able to touch it, scrape my fingers through the paints, when Max pulls my hand into hers.

"We're so lucky, Fig," she says.

"Yeah," I say, smiling. "I guess we are."

"I needed today," she says, still looking into the vibrating clouds. "More than you'll ever know. Life's so crazy. Like sometimes it's so dark and depressing you wonder why any of it even matters, or why we even exist. But then you see something like this and, just, *kapow.* You know?"

"Yeah." A tear falls, which she quickly swipes away. "You okay, Max?"

"I'll be fine." She clutches our palms together. "Let's not talk right now."

So we watch the sun slowly disappear into the ocean.

An hour later, after my shift ends, I hand her a ticket to the final showing of *Centered in the Universe* in the Planetarium.

And this is where we sit now.

"Your first surprise," I say.

The lights fade to instant black, not giving your eyes or thoughts time to adjust. And blinking on above us:

One by

one by

one.

A sea of stars: devouring us. Just when you think there couldn't possibly be room for any more to fill the Planetarium sky, a million more stars appear.

It's the literal definition of breathtaking.

Max gasps, grabs my hand. "Fig. I—"

"I know."

"Is this real?"

"Yeah."

"I forgot . . . there's so, so many."

"I know."

Tears kiss the corners of her eyes.

I remember this feeling. First time I saw this show was the first time I ever really saw stars. Mom took me on my seventh birthday. I screamed and cried because it was so vast it scared me. She held my hand and said, "It's okay. You're not alone."

Like I'm doing for Max now.

41

After the show, we stroll outside along the narrow concrete corridor, seemingly on the edge of the world, holding hands. The city lights glitter and wave in the far distance like a mirage. We look up, trying to find the real stars in the real sky. Never works in this town.

I think about the last time I was here. Christopher holding my face in his palms. Us holding the stars in our hearts. It's only been two weeks. Feels like lifetimes.

I say, "Did you know there are more stars in the universe than all the words that have been uttered by every human who has ever lived?"

"Really?"

"Dr. Wheeler told me that. She works over there." I point to the domed chamber that holds the magnificent telescope. It's closed now, but I can't wait to bring Max back to see it.

The thought fills me with light.

Her fingers trail the wall. "You know that stuff they talked about in the movie? The dark matter and dark energy stuff?"

"Yeah?"

She sits on the ledge, her legs swinging. "I've never thought about that before. Like the dark matter that's in between the stars holding up space. What is that?"

"Exactly," I say, scanning the sky. It's anything but dark stuff now. More like orange-glowy stuff.

"Sometimes I feel like the only place I feel safe is in the dark stuff," she whispers.

I watch her, lost in the radioactive sky. Her cheeks are damp. Hard to tell if it's sweat or tears.

That's when I notice her forearms. She's rolled her sleeves up, and most of her cuts are scabbed over, but something's changed. A few markings vibrate. Throb, even. Like they've been drawn over with a pink highlighter. The tangled vines start to twist through me. Tightening my heart.

"You're cutting again," I say faintly. Afraid the city might hear.

Her feet drop. She doesn't answer, doesn't move.

"You said you stopped."

She slowly rolls her sleeves down, not looking at me.

"Max? Why are you cutting again?"

"I don't know, Fig. My fake mom. Dad. My real mom . . . All of it. I go numb sometimes, like I'm a zombie, and it makes me feel again, brings me back to life."

"What about your fake mom and—"

"Told you. Stephen King wrote Carrie's mom after meeting her. Not joking in the slightest. Had to tell her I was going to meet up with friends about church stuff just so I could sneak away."

"She wouldn't let you come *here*?"

"You have no idea, Fig. Look, I don't cut a lot, or even that often, and I'm okay. I promise." She still hasn't moved from that spot, still grips her rolled-down sleeves, like she really is glued in the darkness. And I'm not convinced she's okay.

After a long while, she asks, "Can I tell you a secret?"

"Of course."

"I've never talked about this with anyone, but I've been thinking about it a lot lately." She leans back against the ledge, looking down.

City lights sparkle around her like fireflies. "My real mom? She didn't want me. I don't know why. Dad never talked about it." She slips her hands in her pockets, rolling the soles of her shoes over some loose pebbles. "But that's not something you ever let go of, you know? She left and it was my fault. Because I was born. I guess it's hard to love something you never wanted in the first place."

"Max, that's not your fault. You had no control over her leaving. That's *her* choice, and there's nothing we could've done to—"

I stop myself.

I hold her hand.

We face the glimmering skyline.

Long, skinny palm trees sway in the breeze, dotting the cityscape. Like dandelions you could make thousands of wishes on. So I do. I wish for us to be filled with more joy than can fit in the stars. I wish for us to live inside their wonder.

"I think about fate a lot," she says. "Like how seemingly random events in your life might have been predetermined to bring you here. That's why it's so weird we met. I mean, your dog's name is *Rose Tyler*, which is what Dad used to call me all the time. And, well, he always said to *follow the signs*." (I say this with her; she laughs. Oh, that laugh.) "So, yeah, it felt like that one smacked me right upside my head." She takes a deep breath. For both of us. "Wonder what would've happened if I kept going that day. If I hadn't stopped. You ever think about stuff like that? Like there's a parallel version of us somewhere out there who haven't met—"

"I'm glad you did," I say.

"Me too." She punches my shoulder. "Hey, look at me."

I do.

"I'm okay."

I nod.

She wipes a tear from my cheek, whispers, "You're not like anyone I've ever met before."

"I feel the same about you."

"You have such a big heart, Fig. It's a gift."

"I don't know," I say.

"You do," she says.

We're so close now I can feel her breath on my lips.

Our eyes meet.

I slowly lean in to kiss her—

Her phone buzzes, startling us both.

She lifts it from her back pocket, scowls at the screen. "Fake Mom sure knows how to kill a moment. Come on," she says. "You can show me that spot you wanted to take me to before we go. And don't think I've forgotten about that other surprise you have for me, kiddo." She winks, thrusting her hip against mine.

"Seems so silly now."

"No surprise ever is."

Her arm pendulums between us. I can't decide if she wants to hold hands again, so I let mine dangle, every so often feeling the brush of her skin tickle my palm.

42

Max reads Dad's last letter, her audible gasps the only sound between us. We're leaning against the bronze bust of James Dean that overlooks the other side of the city. The Hollywood sign dots the hill behind him. The deep black ocean melts with the sky in the distance, so you can't tell where one ends and the other begins. My favorite spot.

"I can't believe you've been holding this back from me all freaking day," Max says, shaking the letter, eyes brimming with more tears. "This is beautiful. And this photo!"

"I know. I've read it a thousand times at least."

"Well, they were obviously in love, right?"

"Something. But why run? And where to? And why didn't Mom join? And still, it makes no sense why she would've lied to me about this all those years ago. Look at them in the picture."

"I can't stop."

"Where was that taken, I wonder?"

"I don't know." The adventure happening on her face is the adventure happening inside me. She turns back to the pages, flipping back and forth. "Have you put this letter and picture together with the others and all the research you've done?"

"Not yet. I had to come to work—"

"I feel like if you do—" She lifts her eyes, which are lit like the North Star. "I'm telling you, Fig. You're so close to figuring all this out."

"I hope you're right."

A car honks. Mom's waiting in her litter box, parked under a street-light in the employee parking lot. She waves. We walk toward her through the main lawn.

"We'll take you home," I say.

"Oh no."

"No, we will definitely take you home. Mom won't care and—"

"No, Fig. For real. You're not taking me home!" she yells.

"But—"

"Trust me, okay? It's for the best."

As we approach, Mom cranes her head down, peers at us through the windshield.

"So, what, you're just going to walk home?" I ask. "To the Valley? It's dark. There are mountain lions out there, not to mention muggers and—"

"There are no mountain lions, Fig, but fine, maybe a ride to the Metro. If it's okay with your mom."

It is.

We drive down the hill.

After ten minutes, Mom says, "Wait. You're *the* Max?"

"Oh. What? Who?" she asks from the back seat.

"What are you talking about, Mom?"

"*The* Max. The one from San Francisco."

"Indeed I am, Mrs., Miss . . . Huh. Just now realized I forgot your last name, Fig."

"Griffin," Mom says, staring at Max in the rearview mirror. "Wondering if I'd ever get to meet you."

"Mom. The road?"

"I see it, Isaac." She glances again in the rearview mirror, then looks at me and lifts an eyebrow. I don't know what this means.

"You sure you're okay if we leave you here?" Mom asks, after pulling over in front of Grauman's Chinese Theatre. "I swear that creepy Superman over there has semen stains on his tights."

"*Mom!*"

"Well, honey, he does."

"Ha, wow, okay, yeah," Max says, standing outside the passenger window. "I'm fine. Just running down those stairs to the train. But thank you, you know, for caring."

"Well. Run, then. I'm not convinced he's there to take pictures with tourists. We won't leave until you've made it on the escalator. Not that it's any safer down there. Are you sure we can't—"

"Mom. She's tough. She'll be fine. I mean, you will . . . won't you?"

"Yeah, he's right, Ms. Griffin. I'll be fine. Thanks again." She starts to leap off, then runs back and says, "And thank you for today, Fig." She leans in, kissing my cheek. "See ya!"

I blush, roll up the window.

"I like her energy," Mom says. "Sweet, calming."

"Mm-hmm."

"Seems a little sad, though."

"Mm."

"You sure she's okay? She'll be safe?"

"Yeah." I hope so.

We drive home.

At one point, Mom flips on the radio to Love Songs on KOST. We listen to people dedicate songs to lovers, crying to strangers on the radio.

At another point, when I glance over, Mom's looking ahead at the road, smiling.

43

Day turns to night as Sunday's sun whisks across the sky. But the thickness in the air remains. Not even a slight breeze to waft my thoughts away, which keep circling back to one thing: *Is Max okay?* I'm sure she's fine, but still, something didn't feel right. Still doesn't. I texted a few times, haven't heard back.

I've been trying to piece this puzzle together once and for all. I have everything perfectly scattered on my bed, with its own specific place—and notecards labeled different years—connecting all the printed papers, photos, and notebook pages that seem to fit together. Like a literal puzzle. Except one you buy at a garage sale with missing pieces, because there are still so many holes.

Splayed out in front of me is the missing life of Alex Stryker.

The first love letter to Mom connects to the last letter Dad wrote before leaving their old life behind, and in between, their photo of unquenchable love. Dad ends each letter with a quote; they're both from James Baldwin (I found the second one pretty easily), but I have no idea why.

From there, I've gone back in time, far, far back, to the letter I discovered when Dad first stepped off that Greyhound bus and life would never be the same. I printed two pictures of Esmeralda I'd found online: In one, she stands in front of the El Rosa Hotel. I assume this is where she was deemed the Queen Mother. In the second, she's at some New Year's Eve ball posing next to Dad and a clergyman in full-on collar and cassock. (Pretty spectacular, actually. In 1965, queer and trans folks held a dance at Glide Memorial Church with the local clergy; the ministers wanted to show their support for the community. Police raided, of course. But it caught the attention of media everywhere: People sympathized, police presence decreased, and it ignited sparks for the soon-to-come uprisings.)

Then there's the letter we found in Luna's scrapbook: When Alex Stryker bled through the prison bars and finally felt free, when Dad *fought with the best of them*. Pictures and printouts of Vanguard protests. The Compton's riot. "Gracie and Friends." The names and faces lost in history. Still piecing it together.

I run my fingers through my hair.

And that's when I notice something I hadn't seen before: The date of Dad's first love letter, December 18, 2001, and the last Luna scrapbook note, dated a week later. It takes me a minute to do the math, but . . . I was born June 18, 2002. Which means I was conceived sometime in September the previous year.

And it hits me. Hard. Because I realize it's true then: The minute Mom learned about me, Dad ran and never looked back. Maybe it wasn't Mom's fault after all.

I feel the tears burn my eyes. A rage smoldering inside me. The memories on the bed blur. This is what I feared most.

You needed to find your truth, Alex Stryker? Fine. But what about the people you left behind? How are they supposed to move on? How can they let go?

There's a knock at my door.

"Not now, Mom."

"It's not your mom."

It's also definitely not her voice.

44

Rose Tyler peeks her head up from under the sheets, twists her ears to the door. I jump off the bed, drying my face with a wadded shirt on the floor, try to calm myself. "Who is it?" I ask, knowing full well.

He opens the door before answering.

"What are you doing here?"

"Your mom called me," Christopher says. Rose Tyler blasts off the bed and into his arms in one fell swoop. "Aww, hey, girl."

He leans in the doorway, backlit by the hallway light, so his muscles etch perfectly through his polo shirt and jean shorts, all statuesque.

"She called you? Sorry. God," I say, patting my hair down and trying to smell my breath. "She doesn't know what happened . . . between us, I mean. Sorry."

"Smells like a locker room in here," he says.

"Yeah, sorry." I run to the window, stumbling against my bed, push it open. The sweet air clears my eyes, my thoughts. I stand there, unsure what to do, what to say. "I don't know why she called you. She's been worried about me, I guess. But I'm fine, Christopher. You can go."

He doesn't move.

He kisses Rose Tyler, scruffs her hair. She licks him. All over.

"Think she missed you," I say.

"I missed her," he says. "Seems like ages ago we were running through those cows."

"I know."

We're stuck in place.

"Christopher, really, you don't have to—"

"I wanted to see you," he says, still leaning on the door. "Can I come in?"

"Oh. Of course."

As he walks in, our eyes lock. He looks different now for some reason. Stronger, I don't know. It's hard to concentrate with him standing in my room and the flood of memories that come with him, so I turn to the window. A cloudless night. A nearly full moon hangs over the city. Still no stars.

"Haven't seen you around much," he says.

"I thought you wanted space."

"I did. I came to check in on you and—"

"I said I'm fine."

"And to say thank you."

He stands at the edge of my bed, cloaked in darkness. The moonlight shines on half his face. "For what?"

"I came here to tell you what happened to me, why I've been so lost in my head." He twists the soles of his Vans into the floor. "Damn, I've told my folks and a therapist, but it's still hard to say."

"What is it?"

He looks down. "You know how I went to that screening with my agent after Christmas? He took me out to dinner, wined and dined me, talked me up to all these celebs like I was one myself." He takes a deep breath. "Well, then he took me back to his house and . . ." Another breath. "It's still kind of a blur, but he cornered me on the couch. Pinned me down. I couldn't move. I didn't know what to do. I was so scared, so I just went limp."

"Christopher," I whisper.

He gazes at the stars on my ceiling, a few tears falling. "He was kissing me when you called. You remember that night? You'd just found that letter from your dad. I said it was an emergency and ran out the door before anything else could happen. Before it got too out of control, you know. And I went home that night feeling so sick. And used. And ashamed. I didn't know how to tell anyone. Didn't know who'd believe me anyway."

I want to reach for him, feel his skin kiss mine, his heart beating against my own.

But I just stand there.

"And then when I got home, after that night in San Francisco—" He looks down, making infinity signs with his shoes. "I was so angry. At me. And everything, I guess. And the next day Mom and Dad asked me what was wrong and it's like, I don't know, I cried in their arms like a little baby. I couldn't stop.

"And Dad kept saying, 'What's wrong? What's wrong?' Which only made it worse. It made me cry harder. Feels like a long time since someone asked me that."

I nod, staring at the floor.

"Anyway." He inhales so deep it rattles my heart. "I still couldn't tell them anything. It's like I could feel the words in my throat, but they were trapped. And I wanted so badly to see you, Fig," he says. "To talk to you, to lie here and play games on my phone while you did homework, or to just hold you. Anything but think about it, you know? Anything to forget. But I realized that's part of the problem." His voice wavers. He sniffles. I think he's crying. "I needed space, time alone, away from you and everything. And I started thinking again about Gracie."

I glance up. The moon shines brightly on his face now, clear and confident.

"I was so freaked out by everything she said that day. About fighting for your truth and standing up for yourself and all that, I had to run away. I mean, Jesus, she was, like, showing me everything I didn't want to see."

"I know," I whisper.

"It scared the shit out of me, Fig. I walked through those streets, crying my eyes out. I snuck into a few bars, charmed the pants off the bartenders to give me drinks." He chuckles to himself. "Which they did of course. And, well, the rest you know. Sorry for being such a dick that night." He lifts his shirt, dries his eyes. "But what she said really made me think. Once I actually could. And I'm so glad we met her. She was exactly who I needed to meet in that moment."

"She was?"

"Exactly. That's why I wanted to thank you. If you hadn't called me that night, or we hadn't gone to San Francisco, who knows what would've happened." He sits on the edge of my bed, careful not to touch any papers. Rose Tyler leaps into his lap. "But I was finally quiet with myself for the first time, like, ever, really. No phone or anything. And in that quiet, I heard *me* for the first time. And I knew I couldn't hide it anymore." He kisses the top of Rose Tyler's head. "So the next day, Mom and Dad took me to House of Pies and I told them. Everything."

"What'd they say?"

"They were furious, of course. Never seen either of them so mad before. Dad called the agent while we sat there and said he was fired, went on and on about sending him to prison and— I couldn't really hear, it was all too much."

"Wow."

"Yeah. And I'm seeing a therapist now, which is what all good actors do, I guess." He laughs. "At least it's not chewing at my guts anymore."

"I'm so sorry, Christopher."

We're lost in each other. Charged. But we still don't move.

"I've missed you," I say.

"Me too," he says.

I start toward him, then stop myself.

"But I don't know," he says, standing. "I mean . . . I feel like I'm not all there yet. Like I'm still all messed up in my head, you know?"

"I do."

He focuses on his twisting soles.

"I'm sorry I wasn't there for you," I say.

"I wasn't there for you either," he says. "Maybe the things that hurt us the most can help us the most, you know?" He lifts his eyes to mine. "Look, Fig. Sometimes I think we all need a little push, and I'm telling you this because . . . well, because I love you."

"Tell me what?"

Look at his beautiful, crooked smile. "Don't let yourself get lost in your head like me. You'll never find yourself if you do."

Never has his voice sounded so calm.

"Therapist told me that one," he says.

His face glistens, swathed in tears, but otherwise he's crystal clear. Like a layer was peeled away. Maybe I've only known the carbon copy of Christopher this entire time.

He walks toward the door.

"Christopher?"

He turns back.

"I love you too," I say. "Always will."

He smiles, slaps the wall twice.

And just before he turns to bounce down the stairs, he flips on my light.

45

Without another thought, I climb up to the attic, grab the box tucked deep in the shadows, and crawl back into bed.

Rose Tyler snuggles next to me, her sweet face peering up at mine, her one broken ear flopping down.

I take a deep, pulsating breath. I lift the lid. James Baldwin's tattered book. Green cashmere turtleneck. Black leather jacket. All still folded neatly in place, untouched memories I can always hold.

I slip the gold Gemini pendant around my neck, raise it to the moonlight. Maybe we share the same birthday, the same Gemini qualities. Playful. Curious. Insatiable thirst for knowledge. A dreamer who never stops dreaming. I think we do. I picture us blowing out candles on two different cakes, giving each other our wishes for the year.

Maybe in another time that happened.

But not in this one.

I lift the framed photo and unclasp the fasteners on the back. Slide the picture carefully out from under the glass. I want to be as close to Alex Stryker as possible. To hear her laughter like there's no tomorrow and smell her patchouli fill the room.

I close my eyes and I try.

Nothing happens.

Instead, her frozen smile is all I'll ever know.

And it's time for me to be okay with that.

I reach over to my nightstand, hold the wooden box. My hands tremble, but my heart strangely doesn't.

"Never cruel, nor cowardly. Never give up. Never give in."

I unlock the clasp, remove my lucky talismans, and for the first time since that kindergarten morning, I slowly unfold our crumpled family tree.

The drawing blurs. Tears start to flow but I don't wipe them away this time. Taking me back to that moment I first felt the shame. Of thinking something was wrong with me because I didn't have a dad. Of thinking I wasn't a good enough person. I drew Mom in her favorite yellow sundress she always wore. Me in my turquoise swim shorts I lived in that summer. Holding hands under a weeping willow, smiling under the clear blue sky.

Before I knew anything.

I'd scratched over our faces in angry, jagged markings to erase our joy. Because I didn't feel like I deserved any.

And I cry.

I untwine the stack of unopened letters from the box, letters I'd written to Dad over the years, hoping to one day share them. I open them and read.

Dear Daddy, I lost my first tooth today.
Here's a picture of it.

Daddy, I fell off my bike and skinned my knee real bad
today. I wish you were here to hold me.

Dear Dad, I kissed a boy on the jungle gym today.
Would you like that or be mad at me?

Dad, I had to shave for the first time today.
And learn to tie a tie. My first homecoming.

And on and on. Moments I'd wished I could've shared. Moments I never will. Taking cross-country adventures together, arms in the air, free. Eating endless slices of pizza in different cities. Watching Dad cry as I marry my husband or wife along the cliffs of Big Sur. Us, older, playing together with my children. Us, older still, sitting on a porch swing, gazing out at the sunset. Always holding hands and smiling.

I cry.

Thinking about the moments I'll never have in between. The smiles. The tears. The screams. The heartbreaks. The stomachaches. The late-night talks. The feeling of being infinite, looking at the stars.

But.

That's not what I was given, that's not who I am.

And that's okay.

I cry so hard, Rose Tyler starts licking my tears, whining. I cry so hard, my heart hurts, actually hurts. I cry so hard I feel like the whole world's cracking open.

Because, I realize now, I taught myself all the things I'd hoped a dad could teach me. To ride a bike. To tie shoelaces or a tuxedo bow tie. To believe in myself. To love.

And I think of that little fatherless boy, staring out the window, longing to hold someone I never would.

I grab his hand and say, "I got you. You're not alone. You're going to be okay."

It was never my fault.

I was never alone because I always had me.

And if I never learn another thing about Dad, at least I know this: Her fight for love is why I'm here. And that will last forever.

It feels so good to cry.

46

"Isaac? What is it, honey? What's wrong?" Mom stands over me, holding my hand in hers. I didn't even hear her come in.

I let my tears fall. "It's because of Dad," I say.

Her eyes widen. "What?"

"That's why. I went to San Francisco to find Dad."

"I don't understand."

"Look." I point to Alex Stryker's scattered life on my bed.

"What is all this?" She riffles through the pages and whispers, "Alex?" Tears rush down her cheeks. "This picture . . . where did you— Oh my God." She picks up the letters, starts reading. "Isaac, when did you find— Why didn't you tell me?"

"I tried!" Her eyes flood with confusion. "*It was an unknown donor,* you said. Why didn't you tell me the truth?"

"It's not like that," she says. "You were young, and I didn't—"

"Then at Christmas you got so angry when I asked again."

"I know, honey, I—"

"And I shouldn't have had to ask anything!" I scream. "And ask what?! What color the test tube was? What the freaking handwriting looked like on the paperwork?! You lied to me."

"I didn't mean to." She shakes her head, like she's shaking everything free. "I was going to tell you one day. I swear I was. But when you asked me at Christmas, I froze. It'd been so long I almost convinced myself of another truth." She holds a photograph, still in disbelief. "So long . . ."

I shove my tears aside to see more clearly. "Just tell me. How'd you meet? What happened? Where is Dad? Who is she?"

She inhales deeply, transfixed by the papers on the bed. "I don't know where to start. You've found out so much already. More than I ever . . ."

"I want to know everything."

She turns to me. And for the first time, maybe ever, we see each other. "Okay," she says.

She studies the framed picture I found in the attic, spellbound. "She was the only person in the world . . . I let myself love."

My heart's barreling around inside me.

"My best friend," she continues. "We met in San Francisco. 1995. At this weird little dive bar. I saw Alex and immediately felt safe. It's the only way to describe it." She chuckles to herself, remembering. "Her smile, and those eyes. So full of mirth and mayhem." She looks up, matching my gaze: wild and untethered. "I don't know if you've ever met someone and instantly thought, *I need this person in my life*, but that's how it was when I met her.

"And she was a writer, like me. The most extraordinary writer I'd ever met, Isaac, my mentor. Older than me, which was always our running joke. We became inseparable after that. Both of us struggling in our own ways just . . . latched onto each other." She traces Dad's face on a photograph. "I stupidly fell in love, even though we promised each other we wouldn't, that we were just friends. I was lonely. It's hard to explain."

She wipes her cheek with her sleeve, riffles through more papers. "But I knew she was leaving one day. She told me that night we met.

About her dreams to open a bookstore somewhere in Europe. To start a whole new life. To disappear." Mom's lost in another photo, as if Alex is gazing back at her. They're together, right now. "She was still so scared after all those years—God, this is harder than I . . . I haven't talked about this in so—" She takes another deep inhale.

"She always said she would never be able to fully and completely be herself while she still lived here," she whispers. "That she carried with her too much pain and baggage from the past to fully let go." She's breathing heavy now. "I never meant to fall in love. I knew better. But I held on so tight to what I wanted *us* to be." She lays her palm on the bed, the letters, Alex.

"It wasn't supposed to happen." Our eyes meet again. "You weren't supposed to happen. You weren't a mistake. In fact, I dreamt about you my whole life. But you weren't planned, and certainly not with Alex. My tiny little miracle." She dries my face, kisses the backs of my hands. "Never thought we would ever—it was a crazy night. 9/11 happened one week. The next week we were both deliriously happy, celebrating another book deal for her. I'd sold my first script. And just life, you know, honey . . . *life*."

She picks up the old photo I found in Aunt Luna's scrapbook. "I've never seen this before. Look at her . . .

"So, a few months later, the night I finally felt safe to tell her we were pregnant, Alex came home and said the time had come. She had to go. To finally start her new life after all those years she'd fought for it." She pauses, still lost in the picture. "It's funny, she said it was my love that made her feel like it was finally okay to go. She just never knew *how* much I loved her."

"You never told her?"

"No. And her face," she says. "Oh, her face, Isaac. You should've seen it. So clear, so bright, so . . . free for the first time. She was excited for this adventure. I'll never forget it." Her hand hovers over her chest. "I couldn't take that away from her. Not for me. Not for us.

"So the next day I helped her pack, and that night she was gone."

I swallow, understanding for the first time. "You never told her about me."

She shakes her head. "I thought I was being selfish if I said anything. Maybe she wouldn't have left then. Maybe she wouldn't have allowed herself to finally become the person she always was. Maybe I was being selfish by *not* telling her—I don't know—that's been the question ever since."

Then softly, sounding far away, she says, "Love makes no sense at all."

And maybe that's exactly the point, I think.

"I'm sorry I didn't say anything sooner," she says, straightening up, brushing the tears away from under her glasses. I've never seen her look so vulnerable. Like a little girl lost on the playground. "I wish now I had. And I know that's not going to make it all go away or change anything that happened. But it's all I've got. I never meant to lie or hide this from you."

We sit in silence, studying the scattered pages on the bed, filling in the missing pieces of Alex Stryker's life.

"My God," she says. "Where on earth did you find this picture of us? I'd forgotten all about it."

"Aunt Luna sent it. Alex left it there before she took off to wherever she is. You never tried to find her? She never told you where she went?"

"She didn't want to tell a soul. That was the deal we made when we first met. That was her way of starting over—a clean slate. I just held on to something that wasn't meant to be."

She holds my hand, following the lines in my palm with her fore-finger, something she always used to do. "But after you were born, I did look for her online, called old friends. There were so many places she could've been. I mean, I basically spent a year in a crime scene investigation montage—kind of like this," she says, chuckling, waving her hands over the bed.

Now her fingers trail along the creases of Dad's black leather jacket, the soft sleeve of the cashmere sweater, the Gemini pendant around my neck. Maybe these were her lucky talismans. "I thought I'd give it a couple years, that she'd eventually reach out to me. That I'd finally get to tell her all about you, show her pictures. She never did, and I'm still not sure why. It's been so long now."

"But look at that letter. She wanted you to find *her*." I hand her the first note I discovered, the one that started it all.

"I remember this. Haven't read it since that day she left. It was too hard to—" She peers over her glasses. "You went through my things."

I shrug.

She reads. And through more tears, I see this veil of turmoil slowly lift from her eyes.

"Oh," she says. "Oh!" She clutches the letter. "I don't remember her writing . . . I never understood why she didn't want me to . . . But she did. You're right. She wanted me to find her." A smile stretches across her face, as if the plotline since the moment Alex left was sud-denly rewritten to finally make sense. "That was so her. She loved sending people on quests, writing out riddles."

"Maybe it's not too late," I say.

"Maybe it's not."

Mom's still grinning, entranced by the photo of their insatiable love, realigning the pieces of her own broken-heart map. Out the window, the moon lights a still and starless sky. Orange blossoms waver through the curtains.

"Mom?"

"Yeah, honey?"

"Make a wish," I say.

"What?"

I inhale deeply, breathing in new life, hope. Magic, even.

Her smile is mutinous. "It already came true."

47

Mom's lying in my bed, immersing herself in my search for Alex Stryker. She reads the letters Alex left behind, flips through the photos and articles I printed. I sit, propped against the bed on the floor, with Rose Tyler fast asleep at my feet. The moon's moved farther across the sky now, but its light still glints through the curtains.

And here we are. War-weary and free. Sort of. Something still tugs at my heart. An uncomfortable itch I can't reach. Not sure what it is.

A thought flashes through me: Max and me at the Observatory, lost together in the darkness, on the edge of the world. *You're so close, Fig,* she said. I want to call her, tell her everything I've learned.

"Well, this is *not* how I saw our evening going," Mom says, throwing her glasses down on the bed. She sighs. "That's exactly how you were on the sonogram, by the way."

"How?"

"All rolled up in a ball like that, with your knees tucked into your chest. The doctor said you looked like one of those babies who never wanted to leave the womb."

"Can you blame me?"

"Well, selfishly, I guess, yeah. I wish I could hold you forever. But that's not our job, is it?" She studies their photo of young love again, as if transported. Smelling Dad's patchouli and roses and feeling the fresh sea breeze. "Every day I have to wake up and let you go a little bit more. Tough as shit some days, and I'm admittedly pretty awful at it."

"No kidding."

She slaps my head playfully. "But it's what I have to do. That's the point really." She strokes my hair. "Remember when we painted your ceiling?"

I look up. "Yeah."

"You were so angry because we kept getting the placement of the stars wrong."

"I don't remember that."

"We'd look it up online to see if you were right. Turns out you were. Every single time. Every damn star up there is perfectly placed."

"How could I know that?"

"I still wonder," she says.

We sit some more in quiet as she reads the letters again.

"Did Dad have some kind of pen name?" I ask. "You said she wrote some books and a screenplay, but I never found that in my research."

"Ezzy Taylor," she says. "I think it was because of Elizabeth Taylor, but I never asked."

"No," I say, smiling. "I know exactly why she chose that." And I shuffle through the papers to find Esmeralda's name on the letters. The pictures I'd printed out. The corner of Turk and Taylor, where Compton's Cafeteria once stood.

"Well, I'll be damned." Mom shakes her head, flipping through the photos. "I have copies of her books in my office. I think you'll love them."

"And why did she sign that first note to you as Alex Griffin?"

"She said we would always and forever be spiritual partners. And she used to say this a lot, too: *I can't wait to see how it all turns out.*"

"Why?"

"That was her way of reminding us to live in the question, in the wonder and surprise of what's to come. It's there, she said, the magic lives."

"She sounds a lot like you," I say.

"Oh, we were insep—" She stops herself, examining the notes, then the photo of the two of them again, and back and forth she goes, until I see her eyes widen even more in glee. "Oh, you sneaky little devil, you."

"What?"

"Of course," she says, throwing her head back and cackling. "Of course. Why didn't I think of this before?"

"You know where she is?"

"I think I do."

I sit up to look at the photo. "Where?"

"Well, this letter has that quote from James Baldwin—"

"Right."

"And this last one she wrote, the one Aunt Luna sent you, before she left—"

"That's also a James Baldwin quote."

"Is it? No, I meant this part, where she writes, *Where I Am Is Where I'll Be.*"

"Yeah?"

"This picture of us? It was taken at our favorite spot in the entire world. We took a trip together soon after we first met, traveled all throughout Europe. Come to think of it, maybe she was location scouting. But this was in the South of France. James Baldwin's château."

"It is?"

"Oh, you would love it there, honey. The air is like nothing you've ever breathed before, the flowers like nothing you've ever seen. An

absolute paradise. 'Our very own little Eden,' she used to call it. And,"
Mom whispers to the picture, "the most perfect place to start a new life."

"You think she's there?"

"I don't know, but it would make sense." She shakes her head again,
muttering to herself. "Can't believe I didn't think of that."

We're magnetized to the photo, to that moment in time, to knowing where Alex might live now. And the thoughts swell, one on top of
the other, inflating my heart. That I finally might be able to meet her.
And hug her. And help shelve books in her bookstore or trim roses in
her garden—

"But I searched everywhere online, Mom. I found nothing about
her being in the South of France."

"Maybe she changed her name again."

"To what?"

"I'm not sure." Mom's now carefully turning pages in the tattered
copy of *Giovanni's Room*, the book tucked inside the box from the attic.
"This was her favorite novel. She said it challenged her and scared
her and made her angry . . . that it was the reason she ran away from
home, the reason she knew she had to become a write—"

"What is it?"

"You said that quote from the last letter was also from James Baldwin?"

"Yeah?"

"Do you know where it's from?"

"I can't remember." I grab my laptop from the desk and flip it open.
Then I type in the quote.

She squeezes my arm when we both see it's from *Giovanni's Room*.

"I didn't even put that together . . ." I mumble. "But why—"

"Which of his characters said it?" she asks, bending closer to see
the screen.

I click the first link.

"Her name's Hella," I say. "The only female character in the—"

We look at each other.

"Do you think?" I ask.

"Worth a shot," she says.

I type in "Hella Stryker South of France," and the second I do, we both gasp.

Mom clutches my arm tighter.

We don't move.

"Mom, it's—"

"Alex."

Staring back at us is Dad. Long, yellow hair falling over her shoulders in a soft pink blouse that seems to billow through the screen. Her cheeks flush with joy, her smile as contagious as ever. And there's a softness in her eyes I haven't seen in any other picture of her. A stillness.

Mom covers her mouth, as I try to read the translated piece aloud:

> *Hella Griffin-Stryker, recent owner of the Vanguard Room bookstore, died peacefully in her sleep on Sunday of natural causes. Her friends say it was because her heart was too big for this world. She curated the most valuable books in her tiny bookstore—a place folks would soon call their home away from home—from first editions to collector's items to the largest collection of LGBTQ+ books in the country. Any guest—or "extended family member," as she called you—who entered through the famous red Dutch doors was instantly greeted with a smile and a cup of hot tea, made with fresh peppermint and herbs she grew in her garden behind the brick-covered storefront.*
>
> *Although she lived in Saint-Paul de Vence for only a few years, she made an enormous impact on the community,*

having organized speaker events and safe gatherings for LGBTQ+ youth in the area and surrounding regions, hosting monthly Queer Seniors luncheons at the store, and contributing thousands of euros to local LGBTQ+ centers and high schools to expand their library selections for young people.

When asked where she came from, or any details of her life before moving to Saint-Paul de Vence, her neighbor recalls, "She never talked about the past. She only lived for the moment." And through tears added, "And she was the greatest woman I've ever known."

A memorial is being arranged in her honor for June 18, 2005, at the Vanguard Room bookstore. Community members will come together to have a plaque erected in her name, which will be permanently placed at the store's entrance. A dedication ceremony will take place that evening, when her ashes will be scattered in the garden grounds.

In lieu of flowers, donations can be made to the Hella Griffin-Stryker Vanguard Scholarship Fund, an annual award that will send a trans youth to the college of their choice.

Hella's wish, according to her neighbor, was simple: "For you to love more fiercely today than any of your remaining tomorrows."

We stare at the screen, Mom holding me tight, both of us awash in tears.

"I think she finally found her peace," I say softly, resolutely.

"I had no doubt she did," says Mom.

48

I finally understand the difference between loneliness and being alone.

Loneliness is searching for something that can never be found.

Being alone is sitting in the comfort of knowing it was never lost.

I hold Mom in my arms as she cries.

49

We've been lying here for an hour at least, maybe more. Laughing, crying, reviving lost memories, discovering new ones. Together for the first time.

"Strange how calm I feel," Mom says. "Maybe a part of me already knew, but I wasn't ready to accept it." She combs her fingers through my curls. Like a lullaby. Like she used to do. "Anyway, we were closer than ever after she left."

"How so?" I ask.

"I kept her alive in my heart," she says, laughing to herself. "Forever and always spiritual partners . . . Right again, Hella."

"Maybe we can go there one day," I say. "To the South of France. I'd love to see where she lived, visit her bookstore."

"Oh, we most certainly will," she says, still caressing my head. "I forgot how soft your hair is. Like it's one gigantic fluff ball."

"Or an overgrown shrub," I say.

She laughs. "It does kind of smell like grass."

I lift my head. "Like dirt, you mean?"

"I didn't say that, exactly."

"Mom!"

"Well, when's the last time you washed it?"

"I don't know."

"I mean, I like it," she says. "Reminds me of when you would come back in from playing outside, smelling like sweat and sunshine."

My phone buzzes on the nightstand, surprising us both.

"Goodness. What time is it?" she asks, lifting her head.

"Almost ten," I say, checking my phone. "It's Max! I've been wanting to tell her everything about Dad—she's been helping me with this. Do you mind if I—"

"Answer it, honey."

I click on my speakerphone. "Max! I've been thinking about you. There's so much I have to tell you. I found—"

But I'm interrupted by loud gurgling sounds. Like she's thrown the phone in the toilet and it's drowning. "Max? You okay?"

"What is that?" Mom asks.

"I don't know. Max?" More garbled sounds. This time, it sounds as if she's been caught in a windstorm. Maybe she called me by accident. So I yell her name louder. "Max? Can you hear me? Did you mean to call?" I strain to listen, trying to pierce through the cacophony of noise.

Then, a barely audible whisper shatters through: "Fig?"

"Did you hear that?" I ask Mom.

She nods, her eyes wide and confused. "Is she okay? She sounds hurt."

"I don't know. She's been having a hard time at home and . . . other things—I don't know. Where are you?" I yell to Max.

More loud strangling noises. "Home," she says. Then there's a deafening silence.

"Max? What's wrong?"

This time I hear it crystal clear, and the words thunder through my heart: "Help me, Fig."

Mom and I look at each other, both registering the same dread.

"You know where she lives?" Mom asks.

"Yes."

"Grab the keys."

50

Twenty-seven minutes later, we're parked down the street from Max's house. It's perfectly 1950s Americana, all white-picket-fenced with white shutters. Manicured flower boxes in the windows. Lights shine through doily-laced curtains. I'm half expecting her stepmom to walk out wearing a ruffled apron, whistling with a bluebird on her forefinger.

Mom jumps out of the car, lifting her pink velour hoodie over her head.

"Mom, wait."

"What?" Her eyes look manic.

"Here's the thing: Apparently her mom is super controlling. Like scarily so. No friends are ever allowed to come over. So first, we assess. If Max is sitting on the couch watching TV, we run. If we don't see her, follow my lead. Okay?"

"Done. Now let's go save your girlfriend."

"She's not my—"

But she's already jogging up the street to Max's house.

"Maybe should've worn all black," she says once I reach her. She tiptoes up the sidewalk. "Hot pink is not very subtle."

"Mom, quit acting like a cartoon burglar. You're drawing suspicion." I look around at the neighbors' houses. Clear and unstirring. Perfectly suburbanite. Normal. Except for the two crazy crooks prowling down the street. God.

Rosebushes strangle the picket fence of Max's house.

"Not a good sign," Mom whispers.

"What isn't?"

"This house. Just saying. Too perfect. Exactly how I'd write it in one of my scripts to hide what's really going on inside the home."

"Stop it."

"Well . . ."

We peer into the living room through the lace curtains, shadowed by a few trees blocking the streetlamp. Hard to see inside. Light from the TV flickers in front of a white woman, presumably asleep, on a reclining chair. Must be Max's stepmom. Her hands cross neatly on her lap, her mouth agape, curlers flop in her hair. Is she dead? No, she stirs. Just sleeping.

A lone kitchen light interrogates the room in the far background. Wood-paneled. Flowered curtains. A velvet painting of Jesus. I think he's winking. Or I'm dizzy. I crane my neck but see no one else in the house, no one lurking in the shadows.

"Damn, I don't see her," I say, taking a huge breath. "Let's go in."

We lift the metal handle, creaking open the gate for all the Valley to hear. We stop, not moving a muscle, not even blinking.

"Come on, this is ridiculous," Mom says. "We're just checking in on your girlfriend."

"At 10:20 on a Sunday night? And she's not—"

"We'll make something up. Like we used to do."

"This isn't one of our make-believe adventures, this is real—"

But she doesn't hear. Instead, she sprints up the stone pathway and rings the doorbell.

"Mom, this feels weird."

"Don't worry. We're here to help, remember?"

"But you don't know everything she's been—"

Something grunts through the doorway. We jump. A rustle, like it's charging toward us. A fumble. Another grunt. "Goddamn it!"

I'm clutching Mom's sleeve. She smiles, patiently staring at the door like we're on another house-hunting expedition. She clears her throat.

"Who's there?" a voice shrieks out.

Mom looks at me, waiting. She nods toward the voice.

"Oh—uh—hey—Mrs. Whitaker?" I say. "My name's Isaac. I'm a friend of Max's . . . from school. Sorry to disturb your evening. Is she around?"

Mom winks and nudges and thumbs-ups me.

"Hold on!" She fumbles with a dead bolt and the door creaks open a few inches. My heart fist-bumps my throat. Mrs. Whitaker peeks through a chain, squints. Trying to focus maybe? She smells like a whiskey factory.

I smile. Too extra, I know.

"Who?" she grunts.

Mom wraps her arm around my shoulder, looking like a hot-pink Barbie doll. Seriously wrong choice of wardrobe. "Hello, Mrs. Whitaker, my name's Meredith. I'm Isaac's mother." I smile wider. It hurts. "Isaac and Max are science partners. Maybe she's told you?"

She looks Mom up and down. "What the hell are you?" She doesn't have eyebrows.

"Oh, I'm Isaac's mom and—"

"Whaddya want?" She stumbles into the door for some reason. "Shit."

I clear my throat. "Well, you see, we have this project due tomorrow and I needed to go over a few things with her. Is she here?"

"Yeah. She's here." Progress! And thank God.

But Mrs. Whitaker doesn't move.

"Can we see her?" Mom says finally. "He's been working so hard on this project, you see. It would mean everything to him." She could've stopped there. But she doesn't. "They've been working on this big diorama about photosynthesis. With these gargantuan plants and black lights and plastic dinosaurs I got them from Michaels. How much light, you see, does it take for photosynthesis to occur? Do you have any idea? I sure didn't! I mean, it's genius. Absolutely fascinating."

I want to die.

Mrs. Whitaker burps. "My head hurts," she says, starting to close the door.

"Oh. Uh—" Mom puts her hand up to stop it.

"My grade depends on it," I say. I try peeking through the chain past her in hopes I can see . . . anything. But no. "I can't . . . graduate without her help."

She looks at me. Sort of. She looks at the top of my head where perhaps my face appears to be hovering for her. "Tough titties," she says, pushing the door harder. "I'm not letting no strangers in my house."

"Oh, but I'm not a stranger. I'm Max's friend."

She cackles. "Max doesn't have no friends." She slams the door.

"But I read the Bible with her!" I yell.

Mom flinches back, mouths, *What?*

I whisper, "Max said her mom's a religious nut."

Nothing happens.

Then, a slow squeak of the door opening again.

"We do Bible study together," I say, when I see Mrs. Whitaker's squinting eyes again. "You know, Hail Mary and Joseph and such." I smile. "It's part of the project. She loves it."

"She does?"

"Oh yeah. I let her borrow my rosemary, even."

"Your who?"

"Rosary, honey," Mom says, smiling. "He said rosary. It'll just be a few minutes, Mrs. Whitaker."

She looks at us a little longer, then closes the door.

Our smiles drop.

There's a jiggling of a chain. For too long. And when the door flings open, I should be relieved. I am not. I hold my stomach, more terrified than ever.

"Well, come in," she says.

The fact that we haven't seen or heard from Max still is concerning. Maybe she's locked up in her room?

Mom pulls me forward. Inside, every corner of the house is pristine: a flowered couch, a leather recliner, glass tables that sparkle with a few fanned-out magazines on top like they've never been touched. And there's an overpowering smell of carpet deodorizer filling the air. Mom's right: too perfect.

"Sit on the couch," Mrs. Whitaker says. We do. Some woman on TV who looks like the Joker with a pixie cut talks from behind a podium in one of those wacky megachurches. The volume's turned down so I can't hear what she's saying.

Mrs. Whitaker fumbles against the couch, clinging to it as she moves to her chair. Like she's walking through a haunted house in the dark. Mom's smile vanishes. Perhaps finally realizing the hazardous situation we've entered.

Mrs. Whitaker plops down on the recliner, scratches a curler in her hair. Then: "MAX!"

We jump.

"She never told me she actually liked to read the Bible," she says. I think that's what she said, anyway. Words are muddled coming out of her mouth. She chews ice from her glass; water slops down her chin.

She looks toward the hallway, rubbing her temples. "MAX!" We jump again. "Your friend's here . . . What's your name again?"

"Isaac."

"ISAAC . . . Damn girl can't hear nothing," she mutters.

My body's twisted up so tight right now, I can't think clearly. I also can't breathe. And I can't see down the hallway. There's no movement, no lights, no sound. Nothing.

"That's a beautiful painting," Mom says, pointing to Velvet Jesus in the kitchen.

Mrs. Whitaker flounders in her chair to see. "Oh, isn't it, though? Found it at a garage sale. It's one of those hologram-y things."

"Oh. My. Wow," Mom says. "Can we take a closer look? It's extraordinary."

"Yes, we should. He winks." Mrs. Whitaker rolls out of the recliner and walks toward the painting. Mom follows. As she does, she waves her hands for me to go down the hall.

"Oh, it's just gorgeous," I hear Mom say as I stalk away, disappearing into the darkness.

Okay, I know I don't have long. I have no idea what I'm even doing. I only know I'm still alive because I hear my breath.

There's an open door to my left: a pink-tiled bathroom. A door to my right: I stand on my tiptoes to knock for some reason. No answer. I grab my chest, waiting for someone to come popping out of the shadows. Linen closet. A clock ticks somewhere, taunting me. Another door on my left: A light shines under, splashing over my Vans. I knock. Carefully. Nothing. I slowly inch it open.

"Hello?" I ask so softly even I don't hear it. "Max?" I didn't think about what I'm going to say next. Especially if she's lying in bed, reading. Or God knows what.

She is not.

This is definitely her room, though. The painting above her unmade bed. Soft jazz music playing on her stereo. The room is littered with candy wrappers and cartons of chocolate milk and emptied pudding cups. Sheets and pillows are thrown on the floor, almost as if there was a struggle of some sort.

"Max?" I say a little louder. "I'm so sorry. This is very stalkery, I realize. I thought I heard you say you needed help, so I wanted to check on you. It's me, Fig. You here?" I don't see her. Maybe she ran away, snuck out through that window by her bed without her stepmom knowing. I creep over. It's locked.

There's a closed door by her closet. God, this is so weird. Like walking smack-dab into someone's diary. Still, I knock on it. "You in there?" Nothing. I start to turn the doorknob but stop. I hear a low mumble, like a groaning wind. "Oh! I didn't mean—" I back up, speaking in tongues to the door. "God, sorry. This is your bathroom, isn't it? Wow. This is excruciatingly embarrassing. I thought you called for help. That's what it sounded like when—"

Another low grumble waves through the door. This time, a little louder. "What'd you say?" I bend closer, my ear against the door. "Say again?"

Nothing.

"I'll wait outside. Sorry."

But as I turn, I hear it. A whisper. Like it was my own breath. Choking. "Fig . . . help."

I knock on the door. Louder. "Max? Max, you okay?" Nothing. I slap the door a few times. Try the handle. Locked. "Max? Open up, Max!" I jiggle the handle. Harder.

"Fig . . ." This time, it's louder. Stabbing me. *No. No no no.* I try the door again. Push against it. Again. And again. Shoulders crunch. "MAX!" Hips slam. The door rattles some. "Max, open up!" Hips slam again. Harder. "Fuck!" I lift my foot, kick the door. It splinters at the hinges. I kick again. And again. It smashes open. "Max?! Max?!"

She's curled in a ball.

"Max!"

A puddle of vomit.

An empty bottle of gin.

And trails of blood.

Everywhere. Dripping down her arms, pooling around her chest.

"Max. Jesus Christ. Max. Wake up! Wake up!"

She fumbles around, blinks a few times. "Fig . . . is . . . that . . ." She lifts her bloody arm, slops her hand against my face.

"Don't worry, okay? We're here, Max. You're going to be fine. We'll get you out of here."

"Tired . . . Fig . . ." She closes her eyes.

"MOM," I scream, lifting her under my shoulders. "MOM!" I wrap a towel around her arm, then another to stop the bleeding.

Mom comes charging in. "What is— Oh my God." She helps me lift Max by her other arm. "What happened? What—her arms— Isaac, what's—"

"Should we call an ambulance?" I ask as we stagger down the hallway.

"No time. I'll get us there faster. Hold that towel tight. Get her in the car."

"What about her mom and—"

"Figfigfigfigfig," Max mutters, draped over us, a wilted rose.

"Shhh, it's okay. We got you. You're good now. You're going to be fine."

"What the hell you doing with her?" Mrs. Whitaker screeches when we pierce the darkness. "Shit! She did that damn thing again."

"We're taking her to the hospital," Mom says pointedly, not stopping.

"The hell you are. You aren't taking her anywhere. I'm not paying for no hospital," she yells, sloshing her drink, tripping over the dining room chair. "She always does this shit for attention! Hey! What the hell you do to her, boy?"

"Mrs. Whitaker, you take one step closer to my son and I swear that will be the last thing you do. Isaac, I got her. Go get the car."

I grab the keys from her and run out.

Seconds later, I zip the car in front of their house. Mom wobbles down the path with a broken scarecrow.

We lay Max in the back seat. I strap the seat belt over her and hold her head up, making sure the towels are tightened around her arms.

I kiss her head.

I whisper over and over and over again, "You're going to be fine, you're going to be fine, you're going to be fine."

But all I keep thinking is she's about to die in my arms.

51

"Honey, wake up."

"Huh?" I wipe a stream of drool pooling on Mom's shoulder. "What time is it? Is she okay?"

"You were dreaming," she says. "It's after midnight."

Dr. Andrew steps into the waiting room. We straighten up. Fluorescents shine down on him like he's the archangel Michael. Without the smile.

"How are you, Meredith?" he asks. "Isaac, it's good to see you again. Wish it were under better circumstances."

"How is she?"

He sits, facing us. "Sorry to keep you waiting. We needed to make sure she was safe, lucid, so she could answer some questions. She says you're her guardian?"

"Oh, thank goodness," Mom says. "Yes, I'm her guardian. She's okay, then?"

He nods. His eyebrows furrow together, thick and angry like a Muppet's. "For now," he says. "She's stable. Alcohol poisoning. She's taking fluids, so that's good. And the recent cuts . . . they were pretty deep, but they didn't hit any major arteries. She's a lucky girl."

Mom shakes her head.

"But I am concerned," he says. "Did you know about the cutting?"

"No."

"I did," I say.

Dr. Andrew turns to me. "She wants to see you both. But just for a few minutes. And, Meredith, I'd like to talk to you privately. Ask for me at the nurses' station after your visit, will you?" Mom nods.

A door buzzes open. We follow him down the hall.

Through the small window in another door, we see a version of Max I don't recognize. Lying in bed with a glaring light overhead, her skin's dull and flat, not a glimmer in sight. Her eyes peek half-open at the ceiling. Her arms lie stiff by her sides, strapped down to the bars on the bed.

"Is that necessary?" Mom asks.

"It is, I'm afraid," Dr. Andrew says, opening the door.

Max lifts a small smile when she sees us. Her carbon-copy version. Lifeless. *Like overexposed film,* I think. Even the blue tips of her hair look white, disappearing against the sheets.

"Hi, honey," Mom says. The door clicks shut behind us. "Good to see you awake. And okay."

"Yeah," says Max, like she's talking with a mouthful of rocks. She smells like sick and ocean and freshly ground pepper. She lifts her hands some. "Officially crazy!"

I can't form words. Tubes drip fluids into her veins. Her arms are bandaged so only a few scar-vines peek through.

Mom brushes away a strand of hair plastered to Max's cheek. "Honey—"

"I'm not suicidal, I swear."

"You can trust me, you know."

"I know, Ms. Griffin." She turns to me briefly before peering out the window. "Believe me, I know I can. I'm really not . . . it's . . . a long story."

259

"Okay," Mom says. "Rest now. You're safe. We'll help you figure this out."

"Thank you," says Max. A tear falls. "For everything."

"I'm going to leave you two for a minute," Mom says. "Going to talk more with the doctor. Isaac, come meet me outside when you're ready, okay?" She walks out.

Max doesn't move.

Then she lifts her head some, still not looking at me. "Can you help?"

"Oh. Yeah." I fluff the pillow and push a button so she's sitting up. Her soft hair tickles my hands.

"Thank you," she says. "Your mom's amazing, Fig."

"Yeah, she is."

"I'm sorry you had to . . . for all of this, I mean."

"Why'd you do it, Max?"

"I didn't mean for it to—" She coughs. I lift her head. "Ugh. I feel like Death's asshole. Can you help me sip some of that water?" I grab a cup next to the bed. She slurps from the straw and lies back, scanning the ceiling, as if searching for the right words. Finally: "I felt like I was going nuts. I mean, I was. The fake mom had me on lockdown from life since Dad died, tried to control every little thing I did. I don't know why—she never liked me. That's why I ran away. Didn't really know where I was going but I had to get away from her, from everything."

She shakes her head, looking out the window. Our reflections peer back at us through the mirrored glass. "But I realized I couldn't run away from myself no matter how hard I tried. And when we returned from San Francisco, it got worse. She took my car away. Couldn't drive. Couldn't use my phone without her permission. Couldn't sleep.

She made me pray every day—and, I don't know, everything started spiraling from there. All the stuff I told you about that night at the Observatory."

Her breath quivers. "Then she got drunk again, passed out, so I grabbed a bottle. I just wanted to sleep is all. Have a few drinks and finally rest. I couldn't *feel*, Fig . . . anything . . . and I wanted to feel . . . something. So I cut . . . but . . ." She turns to me. "It started to bleed, and I couldn't stop it this time. I swear I didn't mean to go so deep." I wipe a few more tears on her cheeks. "I swear I didn't." She looks back at the ceiling. "I swear."

I hold her hand. She gently presses her palm into mine.

"Where is she?" she asks. "My stepmom, I mean. I don't remember."

"Not here."

"She knows where I am?"

"Mom called her from your phone. Told her everything. She never showed up. She'll call her again to let her know you're okay."

"I'm not crazy."

"I know."

Our fingers interlace. So tight, it feels like they've been permanently fused. I'm okay with that.

"I don't know what I would've—" She stops herself, closes her eyes. "I can't go back there."

"You don't have to."

Then softly, looking into my eyes, she says, "I need help, Fig."

"Life preserver reporting for duty," I whisper back.

She chuckles to herself. "I can't believe all of this. Dad was right."

"About what?"

"When he died, it felt like all the light went out in my world, you know?"

"I do."

"And he said whenever I missed him to meet him in the Northern Lights, that I'd find the true meaning of life along the way. I thought he was delirious from all the pain meds they had him on. But when I wanted to run, that was the only direction I had to go. And then you—"

Her eyes glaze over, fogged from the pain she's been holding on to all these years. But there's something different in them now, a clearing I've never seen before. Hope. And in them, I see me.

"I don't know what would've happened to me if you weren't here," she says.

"I feel the same about you, Max."

I hold her hand tighter.

"Golden rule number one," she says.

"What?"

"Like seriously, you'll-never-get-a-Wonka-Bar-again rule."

"What?"

"You're not allowed to hang this over me. Like, in forty years if we're fighting, you can't say, 'Hey, Sugar Tits, I saved your life, remember?'"

"Wow. Sugar Tits?"

She shrugs.

"Forty years, huh? Can we at least make it through prom first?"

She blinks dramatically. "Why, Isaac Griffin, are you askin' me to the prom?"

"I mean—no—I mean—"

"This how you always get the girls to say yes? Strapped down and helpless?"

"This is definitely a first on a thousand levels."

"When is it?"

"In a couple weeks, I guess. But I'm only kidding, I—"

"It's a date."

"First, get better. Then, we'll see."

"Good to have something to look forward to," she says. Which seem to be the words that cut through the years of pent-up pain. She begins to sob. "God, I'm sorry, Fig. I'm sorry. So, so sorry. I'm sorry."

"Shh, it's okay. I'm here. I'm here."

I hold her hand and stroke her hair and lay my head on her chest.

And we cry.

Two stars, shimmering.

Glued together.

In the infinite dark.

part four

BEING

52

You are the narrator of your own story.

I wrote that in my journal for inspiration, something I haven't felt in years. Didn't think I would ever feel it again.

After leaving Max, making sure she was settled and safe, Mom said I needed some "quiet time to balance all the recent madness" (I didn't disagree), so she excused me from school that next week. And instead of lying in my bed, lost in my ceiling, I picked up extra shifts at work.

I watched and rewatched the Planetarium shows, picturing Max: Her eyes wide, looking up at the stars. Running through the marbled halls like a seven-year-old who ate too much sugar. Smiling so bright people skip the Tesla coil exhibit just to watch her.

And every night I seeped into the sunsets, each one more an-archic than the next, where I remembered what she'd said: *We're so lucky, Fig.*

Yeah, we really are.

Mom's been going back and forth to the hospital these past couple of weeks: helping Max with paperwork, checking her into a rehab center to help forge her "new chapter." She said Max looked fiercely determined, that Dr. Andrew was helping her find her light again.

"She never lost it," I said.

"True. And neither did you," she said.

Mom has also miraculously been writing again. Seems to have found that Sacred Flame of Inspiration reignited within her, too: a new script based on my quest to find Alex Stryker. She's calling it *In Search of Being*. Which is still ongoing.

I've asked Mom every question about Dad I can possibly think of, questions I've been wanting to know the answers to since that morning in kindergarten: *What was her favorite food?* (Spaghetti with meatballs.) *What was her biggest fear?* (Spiders. And people who refused to change.) *Did she believe in God?* (She believed in love. Especially when it hurts.) Even still, Hella Alex Griffin-Stryker is somewhat of an enigma.

But I no longer let the darkness of the unknown swell within me. Instead, I think of it like that nebula we could almost touch in the sky and sit in its silent wonder.

The following Monday, my first day back to school, I ran into Charlie. Even though we'd talked on the phone (and I assured them I was fine—for real this time—that I wanted to be alone by *choice*), it was the first I'd seen them since everything happened.

They were twirling white Christmas lights around a pole in the Commons, decorating for prom. When they saw me, they nearly fell down the ladder, still wrapped in the lit strands. They stood in front of me and smiled so wide it made the lights twinkle ten times brighter.

Then they hugged me so tight I lifted off the ground.

We held each other until the bell rang.

I saw Christopher a few times. We chit-chatted some, small-talk stuff. He already found a new agent, a woman he feels *so safe with*, he said. And even though he'd been focused on finals to keep his full-ride scholarship to USC, while also juggling therapy and rehearsals and all his feelings in between, he still looked, I don't know, content. A nice change.

When we first ran into each other again, he hugged me. My face buried in his neck. That smell: mint aftershave and fields of lavender. I missed that smell.

"This is nice," he said.

"It really is," I said.

We stood like that in the hallway for I don't know how long. Not talking. Just breathing together. It's hard to explain my feelings in that moment. But honestly, I think that's okay. I realize now that sometimes words can do a severe injustice to what you actually feel.

I told Christopher my plan for a pre-prom night gathering. He's in. I asked if he had a date to bring; he said he did but left it at that. I didn't push.

This brings me to my date.

It's Friday evening, the night before prom. No idea what time. Late-thirty.

I grab an armful of snacks from the kitchen, sneak past Mom's office, where light pours through her opened door. Incessant *tick-tick-ticks* on her computer. She's writing. Whistling, even! Will wonders never cease?

No, they won't.

Because as I step into my doorway, I swear my heart sprouts wings and soars out through the open window.

Mom's sewing machine revs to a slow halt. Max looks up from an ocean of cerulean blue tulle and smiles. Like a weary traveler. "Oh, thank God, I'm *starving!*" she cries.

Rose Tyler growls, tugging at a piece of crinoline. "Rose Tyler, no! Don't rip that!" I snatch it away, and she rolls onto her back, surrendered.

Max laughs, petting her belly. "That crinoline didn't stand a chance, did it, RT."

We plop down in the middle of the fabric sea gathering on the floor. The wind whirls in, rippling blue all around us.

"Butterscotch pudding," Max says, opening a cup.

"Your favorite," I say.

We eat in silence.

"This is really good," I say eventually.

"This stuff is so underrated as you get older."

"Totally. Like rolling down a grassy hill."

"Oh!" She grabs my wrist. "I haven't done that in forever!"

"That's my point."

"We need to do that."

"I know the perfect spot."

"Eeeeee!"

Max's new outfit of the day: sweatpants and a short-sleeved I'M AN OFFICIAL STAR-GAZING GEEK T-shirt from Caltech (long-sleeved shirts, begone!). She's decided to no longer hide her arms, which are currently still bandaged. *War wounds*, she calls them. *I've still got work to do, and I'm not proud of them, but I'm no longer going to live in shame because of them.*

As she finishes her pudding, I munch on some pretzels and left-over jelly beans from Easter. "You seriously got these pudding cups for me?" she asks.

"A few days ago," I say, picking though the beans, pushing the black licorice ones to the side.

"How'd you even know I'd be here?"

"I'd hoped," I say.

She pops the licorice beans in her mouth. "And you're sure you're okay with all this?"

"What?"

"All of *this*," she says. "Me staying here for a couple months, until I can check in to my dorm room at Caltech. That's not weird to you?"

"Why would it be weird? It's just Mom and me in this big house. You have your own room and bathroom. It's meant to be."

"Like us meeting in a cow pasture."

I laugh. "Exactly. So, I've been thinking."

"Not always a good thing."

"In this case it is." I chew a few more beans. "Maybe the ArtCenter would be a good fit for me."

She grabs my hands, her eyes suddenly charged. "In Pasadena, you mean?"

"Mm-hmm."

"Um, that would be a resounding yes. We'd be neighbors!"

A huge smile breaks across my face. "*If* I get in."

"I have no doubt you will."

"We'll see . . ."

Dad once wrote, *Life is a series of choices that can make our hearts sing.* I still don't know what it is I want to do, but for the first time I feel a direction toward *something* that feels good to me. So, I follow my heart.

We hold hands.

"Max, you are just—"

"What?"

Staring into her eyes, feeling lost, but found; found, but lost. I don't know what this is exactly, but I realize now I don't need to. Maybe life is better lived in the question.

"You make me feel like I'm floating and falling all at once," I say. Then I scrunch my face. "Oof. That sounds super corny, doesn't it?"

"Not as corny as me saying you're the gift that keeps on giving."
She leans forward. "Come here."

We kiss.

"Oh, you and your cinnamon lip gloss."

"What can I say? It's a trademark." She leaps up, running back to the sewing machine. "Now, I have a ton of work to do if I'm going to finish this by tomorrow."

"Where'd you learn how to sew like that?"

"My dad was full of surprises," she says as the machine whirs to life. "Damn, it feels good to do something constructive again."

Over the course of the evening, we giggle and gab, in between long moments of contented peace. And a stillness begins to settle inside me, one I haven't felt in a long time: a feeling of well-being.

53

The next chapter of my life starts like this: walking on the edge of the earth, following a lighted path. Max next to me, holding my hand. We stand in the middle of the Observatory gardens for our pre-prom night gathering. Twilight settles over the city, casting purple garnet shadows across the sky.

Mom stands on my left wearing her gold-sequined Oscar de la Renta from the Academy Awards show that year. Rose Tyler snuggles in her arms, smiling at the sky.

Max's face is dusted in brilliant metallic blues and silvers like a morpho butterfly. She looks at me, beaming.

Charlie's the next to arrive.

When they step out of the car, we have to shield our eyes. They're head-to-toe covered in crystals in a skintight pantsuit dotted in every color jewel imaginable, with tiny diamonds diagonal-ing their face.

"Wow," I say.

"Prom night can't even with me," they say. "Hi, Ms. Griffin, good to see you again. You look beautiful." They hug.

"You too, Charlie," Mom says. "Smashing as ever."

Charlie turns to Max, gasps. "And you must be Max. Damn, you're gorgeous."

"The incomparable Charlie," Max says, slapping Charlie's hand down and grabbing them in a hug. "Nice to finally meet you."

"God, the tulle on this dress," they say, "and this crinoline—and the beadwork on this bodice—I can't finish my sentences. This is beyond incredible. Mind if I touch the handiwork?"

"Go ahead," Max says. "I love when strangers feel my boobs."

They laugh.

"Where'd you ever find this?" they ask.

"She made it," I say. "She's been working on it for a few days now."

"No. Fucking. Way. Sorry, you're making me cuss here."

The dress is designed in the shape of two perfectly symmetrical translucent butterfly wings, matching Max's glittering face. *In honor of Hella and Gracie and my dad, who helped transform us,* she said. The tulle stretches out in a whispery train, and the bodice is beaded in every color of blue ever invented—and some I think she created over the past twenty-four hours. She even had time to sew some fiber-optic lights into the tufts of crinoline to spell out *I Am Joy, Compassion, Peace,* and a myriad of other Max affirmations. If you look closely, the wings flap in the light when she moves.

"I'm stunned," Charlie says. "This is me officially speechless for the first time in my life. And you." They turn to me, rubbing their palms on my black velvet tux. "A most excellent choice in fabric. You look like a starry sky."

"That was the point."

"And your tie!" (At the last minute, Max sewed some lights into a piece of leftover fabric to say *I Am Love.*) "And oh my God, Fig, your hair! I didn't even notice in the dark—" They stand back, admiring us like an art exhibit. "How did you—it's so—purple! But like the perfect shade with blues and pinks and sunny blond streaks and— I'm dying. I'm dead. This is me dead. You're actually talking to Charlie's ghost right now."

We laugh.

"So," they say, squeezing between Max and me, "what's the big surprise?"

"Just waiting for Christopher," I say.

"Any idea who his date is?"

"None. But we're about to find out." Because in that moment Christopher's Jetta zips up the hill and into the parking lot. He's parked in the shadows of the streetlights so it's hard to see, but as they walk toward us and eventually step into the light—

No.

No way.

Christopher saunters up to us, grinning, hand-in-hand with his date: Gracie Thompson. Her hair's wild, blown out in long, windy curls, and she's wearing a silver lamé dress that slides through the air like an oil slick.

"*Gracie?*" I say. "How did you—what are you— You look amazing."

"Isaac. Don't you look vibrant." She bends in, kisses my cheeks.

"I tracked her down at the library where she works," Christopher explains. "I needed to tell her how much she meant to me that day."

"And we've been chatting ever since," she says, interlacing their arms. "It's nice to have a new friend. Thought he was joking when he asked me to prom. But how could I resist? I've never been to a prom. I feel like a schoolgirl again."

"You look dazzling," Max says. "It's so good to see you."

"I wanted to surprise you," Christopher says to us.

"Isaac?" Mom steps in. "Who's this?"

"Mom! This is Gracie. She knew Alex! They were friends and—"

"What an honor to meet you!"

"And you!" says Gracie. They immediately hug and begin talking as if they've known each other their whole lives.

"Holy hair, Fig," Christopher says. He looks so dashing and perfect in his simple slim-fitting tux.

"I can't believe you called her," I say.

"It was my therapist's idea. I couldn't stop talking about her. Gracie's really cool. The stories she has—"

"I think it's beautiful," Max says.

Christopher turns to her. "You look . . . wow. It's good to see you again, Max."

"You too, Christopher."

"I'm sorry for what happened in—" She slaps her hand over his mouth and hugs him.

Peering over her shoulder at me, he closes his eyes, smiles.

"I love that Gracie is your date," I say. "Love it."

"Yeah, me too," he says, straightening his tux after he and Max separate. "So, how you feeling, Fig?"

"Fine. I'm fine. For real this time."

"Why are we here?"

They all look at me, gleaming: five fearless constellations dancing through my dark sky.

"Let's go," I say.

✦

The twinkling skyline dotted with palm trees paints the background as we walk into the domed Observatory building where Dr. Wheeler awaits.

"My goodness," she says. "I feel very underdressed for this occasion."

"What's going on, Isaac?" Mom asks.

"Is it ready?" I ask Dr. Wheeler.

"She's all yours," she says.

My heart is buzzing. "Everyone," I say, holding my hand up to the telescope. "I'd like you to meet Hella Alex Griffin-Stryker."

Confusion wavers over their faces, until Christopher says, "You named a star."

"Take a look," I say, lifting a smile.

As they do, one by one, audible gasps fill the room. Then tears. And laughter. And a stillness that only exists in awe.

At one point, I look through the lens with Mom, her hand gripping mine. My dad exists near the constellation Cepheus. She's hidden behind a cluster of stars, fighting to be seen, but resolute in her position. A brilliant shade of amethyst with misty pinks and sapphire clouds emanating from a bright white center. And she is glorious.

No one says a word as we gaze into the sky, and I remember my dream.

If broken hearts are maps to the soul, why do I keep getting lost?

Over time, I thought a part of me would be missing forever. But I was wrong. Because in my quest to find Dad, I found something far greater: That indefinable space between the stars, the thread that holds us together and connects us across time: love. And I found it right here. Feeling magic under orange blossoms with Mom and warm snuggles with Rose Tyler. Finding lost history with Gracie and passionate kisses in the stars with Christopher. Sharing hugs that lift me from the darkness with Charlie and wishes on dandelion palm trees with Max.

And looking up at the sky to know Dad's star lives inside me.

This is my map home now.

And I'll never be lost again.

Author's Note

Is it true that history repeats itself? That historical patterns are societal comfort blankets to make us feel safe? I'd like to think otherwise, but time and time again I'm proven wrong.

As I write this today, trans and queer youth are once again being targeted by hateful, right-wing, misogynistic white cis men and women in power who are so scared of losing control (because they slowly are, and they know it), they'll do anything to retain it. Human rights, trans and queer rights specifically, are once again being challenged. In short, people in power continue to try to erase our existence.

For a while, they were successful. Queer history is an ongoing unfolding mystery because many folks were ignored, shamed, prosecuted, or even killed, simply for choosing to love. So many moments have been lost over time, some we will never know, because those voices were snuffed out by the white patriarchy before they could be heard. The fact that we know any names at all demonstrates the sheer bravery, courage, and fortitude of these folks to stand up against the most impossible of odds.

And since then, many queer historians have tirelessly devoted themselves to uncovering more of these moments. Take Dr. Susan Stryker, as an example. For many years, she worked at the GLBT Historical Society in San Francisco—a place I called home for endless days and countless hours, diving into the archives for my book research and personal inspiration. (If you've never flipped through scrapbooks filled with personal photos from your ancestors or held actual love letters written in secret, I highly recommend you visit your local historical society archives to do just that; it's life-changing.)

Dr. Stryker, while archiving materials, stumbled upon a short blurb hidden deep within the pages of a local San Francisco newspaper—dated August 1966—which mentioned a small riot that unfolded at the Compton's Cafeteria. From there, she dug deeper and discovered a rich and layered tapestry of Black and brown trans folks, lesbians, and gays who had actually sparked the first known riot for trans rights in the United States. Her beautiful documentary *Screaming Queens: The Riot at Compton's Cafeteria* is a viewing must to learn more about this important turning point in the trans and queer movement. But as one participant noted, which I paraphrase here, "We weren't thinking of making change, we were just trying to live."

Such is the case for any moment in queer history. Survival was the impetus behind action. San Francisco's Penal Code 650.5 (which made it a misdemeanor to "personify" someone "other than your-self") was among many other "masquerade" laws in the country that were the eventual sparks to ignite the flames of anger within. One such law, originating in the nineteenth century, was originally meant to stop farmers who had started dressing like Native Americans to stave off tax collectors. At the turn of the twentieth century, it began targeting trans folks, most notably sex workers. If you were caught wearing the clothes opposite of your birth-assigned gender, you were arrested. The discovered loophole? As long you wore at least three articles that matched your ID (socks not included, for some reason?), you were protected. This, of course, didn't stop the police from harassing and entrapping transgender people, and most specifically

Black and brown trans folks, who considered police harassment as commonplace as brushing their teeth.

Inspired by the growing movements of the time, including civil rights, women's lib, antiwar, and the counterculture crusade, trans and queer people began standing up against these ordinances and the often unprovoked and harsh police treatment. Now considered the first gay liberation organization in the country, the youth-led Vanguard was formed to fight these daily discriminations. Consisting of mostly white gay cis men, in July 1966, they organized a "Street Sweep" protest just outside of Compton's Cafeteria in San Francisco's gritty neighborhood the Tenderloin to demonstrate how police not only were ignoring the harrowing plights of the community, but considered those living there to be part of the street's trash. ALL TRASH BEFORE THE BROOMS read one protest sign, meant to represent the queer community uniting under the guise of "Street Power," retaking ownership of the place they called home.

But therein lies the rub, because Black and brown trans folks didn't feel like they could participate in or connect to such a movement; they were, after all, the main ones being targeted by police and often had to hide in the shadows to survive. At night, the street was their safe place, sometimes the only way they could earn a living. When it came to the workforce, they were either "too effeminate to wear boys' clothes" or "too masculine to wear girls' clothes" and were quickly fired from their positions, or simply not hired at all. All that was left for them was the street; take that away, and they had nothing. Their frustrations mounted that scorching summer of 1966, and in August, one (still unknown and unnamed) trans woman had enough. When the police raided Compton's Cafeteria, asking each person to show their ID and prove their gender identity, she promptly threw her scalding coffee in an officer's face. The rest, as they say, is history. And thus, the path was paved for the infamous Stonewall uprising a few years later, birthing the modern-day 2SLGBTQIA+ movement.

But even with the years of progress we've made, the fight continues. Recent bills being passed around the country would prevent teachers from allowing healthy discussions about sexuality and gender in schools—other than that which fits into the conservative, binary, and heteronormative mold—and trans youth are being told they simply don't exist. This ignorant and archaic sensibility is not only disturbing, to say the least, but obviously damaging to a young person's psyche. Just because we can't talk about something doesn't make it go away; in fact, it only makes a person seek other outlets for acceptance. And sometimes those outlets can be harmful, if not fatal.

Growing up in the eighties in St. Louis—in a Catholic, conservative home—being gay was not a real possibility for me. In fact, I didn't even know a healthy homosexual existed; I was only told it made you sick (not just mentally, but quite literally, since it was during the AIDS epidemic) and that it was an unforgivable sin. I didn't recognize myself as feeling "different"; I only felt like I never belonged. My peers were having feelings I didn't feel or understand, my teachers were teaching about sexuality that felt foreign to me, and in turn, I became withdrawn, isolated even from myself. The irreparable damage the lack of healthy dialogue and constructive counseling seeded in me during those formative years of my life is something I still work through.

But over the years, my white privilege has afforded me more opportunities for self-healing and growth. And that is why I immersed myself in our queer history: I wanted to find a sense of rootedness in this world through my queer ancestors, I wanted to know the folks who allowed me *to be* today, and I wanted to honor them in my life's work. *The Edge of Being* is a product of that research, a love letter to the trans people who fought for me.

Although Gracie Thompson is a fictional woman, she represents many trans voices of the time. "Those with the least to lose are the first to raise a fist," she says. Black and brown trans folks have been at the center, if not the very crux, of the queer movement since its inception. It is on their shoulders we, as a community, now thrive. And it is because of their fearless actions throughout history we are able to stand together, out from the shadowed darkness and into the light of hope.

Shame is a powerful white patriarchal tool that's been used for centuries to control others. And it's being used again today. Perhaps I'm too optimistic, but I choose to believe *we* are the ones we've been waiting for. And for our Black and brown trans family, we should do everything in our power to help change the system once and for all. We can't do it alone. We must come together. And I believe, through Love, we will.

Keep reading for more
from James Brandon

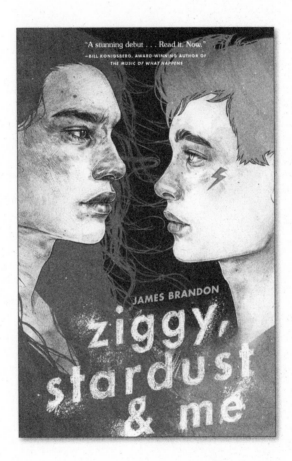

1.

—

Saturday, May 19, 1973

IT STARTS HERE: The day my world begins falling, we're sitting in Starla's bedroom watching *Soul Train*. On the surface, it's a typical Saturday morning—I mean, everything *appears* normal. Should've known better. I'm the master of that game . . .

After our usual pancake breakfast, we slink into our spots: Starla sits cross-legged on her ruby-red shag, gluing silver rhinestones to a pair of Levi's for some design contest she's entering. I bob up and down on her waterbed, flipping through the new *Interview* magazine she could hardly wait to give me.

We're quiet, lost in our own worlds, waiting for church to start on TV—well, our version of church anyway: *Soul Train*. It started last year after Starla snuck me downtown to my first-ever Ziggy Stardust concert, and let's just say, whoa: He blew my brains to smithereens. Maybe literally. He wore this skintight, leopard-print leotard and huge platform shoes so he towered over us, and his face was dusted in white powder and glittery makeup and his hair was fire-engine red, and whambamthankyouma'am I was *reborn*.

At one point, he shielded his eyes, scanned the audience, and sang "Starman" pointing directly at me. I swear his voice shattered my soul, and in that moment, the Holy Spirit boogied in me. Afterward, Starla said, *"Jesus works His miracles in mysterious ways. He reveals Himself in everything, if you're looking. Maybe Ziggy's your Messiah,"* and she wiped the tears from my eyes.

Since then, she's decided music's my religion. So every Saturday morning we hang out in her bedroom to watch *Soul Train*. (Finally, a church I can get behind.) And it's about to start in T-minus ten minutes . . .

The TV sits in the corner on a rolling cart. A commercial for kids' cereal crackles through.

Her window's propped open and a sticky breeze left over from the three-minute downpour wafts in. Typical St. Louis spring. The wind crinkles the collage of faces plastered on her walls, making them sing and laugh and chatter up a storm of politics. Cutouts of The Jackson 5 and Jesus and Coco Chanel and "Power to the People" signs, and every female hero of hers since the Birth of Man—from Joan of Arc to Joan Baez to Angela Davis to Twiggy. Oh, and framed pictures of her secret crush, Donny Osmond. Yes, really.

Roberta Flack drips honey on the record player. And Starla . . . sings. *"Killing me softlyyy . . ."* She's in her church's choir, but well—hmm, not exactly the voice of an angel. Bless her. Starla. My best friend of forever. People think we go together; I let them. It's safer that way . . .

And yes, Starla's her real name. Well, sort of real name. The name she was born with was DeeDee Lucinda Jackson, but she told me one night when she was five years old she had a dream, and in that dream Jesus came to her and said, *"You are from the stars and you came here to heal the world,"* so she made her mom and dad change her name to Starla. I think it's cosmically perfect, like her, and kind of fitting because her face is covered in a galaxy of freckles. And man, without her I would've been obliterated into Jonathan bits long ago.

"Force fields come in many forms." That's what Dr. Evelyn told me a few years ago after I told her Starla was like mine.

"With his song . . . ooh . . . oohh . . . oohhh . . ." she sings.

Ohhohohohoh. Bless her, Father, she knows not what she does. She is cute, though. Her hair's slicked down under a swirly orange headscarf. Tongue's curled to the corner of her tangerine-glossed lips. She looks like a sunset.

Back to *Interview* magazine. I flip through page after page of weird indecipherable conversations, some new Andy Warhol painting of Mao Tse-tung, far-out pictures of half-naked women colored in neon finger paints, and then

Oh.

Three bold words punch me in the face:

"GAY IS GOOD!"

Alongside a handful of hairy muscled men dancing together.

Oh.

Really.

What parallel universe are these furry dopes trippin' in? Not in this one. Not in Missouri. Not in this broken little town of Creve Coeur. Nope, these guys would go to jail here. Or get thrown in the loony bin. Or worse. Believe me, I know—

But boy, are they dancing. And kissing! And smiling so hard it torpedoes through the page, knocking me out cold, and

I sink into the picture . . .

Music thumps. "Hey hey hey, Jonny Collins, glad you finally came out to play, play, play." His mustache tickles my cheek. "Sorry it took so long, my main squeeze," I say. "So many parties, so little time, you dig?" His arms engulf me. Sweat slides down his chest, gluing us together. His lips devour me, like we can't get enough, like there's never enough—

"Hey! You hear me?" It's Starla.

3

I thrash the magazine closed; our world thunders back. "What?"

"You spaced out again."

"No."

"Yeah, you did. You okay?" Her eyes narrow, scanning me. They're this crazy green that look like two pieces of uranium glass under a black light.

"I'm fine."

"You hear what I said?"

"Nothing. No, I mean. What?" Happens a lot. The *space-out* thing. Aunt Luna once told me, *"Your imagination is your safe space, an escape pod to another dimension where you're free to be."* And she said mine's the wildest one she's ever seen. She's also a wackadoo hippie, so I don't know. But she's right, I guess, and it works, I guess, because I'm traveling through my imagination all the time. Where I'm most safe. Anything to escape this reality.

"Come down here. Next to me," Starla says, back to her glue gun. "I wanna talk to you."

"One sec." Because I can't move. Yeah. My hard-on is supernatural. Dammit. Also, it's sizzling. Like a downed electrical line. (Everlasting side effects from Dr. Evelyn's treatments. More on that soon.) But the two combined: definitely not good.

Starla doesn't notice, lost in her rhinestones. I roll the magazine up and stuff it in my back pocket. I'll stash it in my closet later so those guys are lost under my stack of *National Geographic*s for good. That's where they belong: tucked away. Where no one can find them.

I *carefully* adjust, wiggle off the bed, grab a pencil and some nearby paper, and start drawing to distract myself. *Did Starla know that article was in there? Is that why she was so hell-bent on giving it to me? No. She knows how I feel about that sick stuff.*

"Why do you like to draw my freckles?" she asks.

"What? Oh. Because they're amazing."

"I hate them. I feel like a spotted leper. *Ohhohooohooohooh . . .*" she sings.

"Are you kidding? They're your greatest feature. You're like a walking, breathing nighttime sky."

"You're incorrigible." She glues another rhinestone, which is now clearly part of a peace sign on the back left pocket.

I find a spot, trace a new constellation on her cheek. "See, I just found the Teeny-Weeny Dipper."

"Oh, Jonny Jonny Jonny . . ."

"Oh, Starla Starla Starla . . ."

"What am I going to do without you?"

"Huh?" I stop drawing.

She doesn't answer. Just drops the jeans and replaces the needle on the record. Roberta Flack drips again.

"Starla?"

She turns to the TV; *Soul Train*'s started.

"What do you mean, 'without you'?" I ask, grabbing her hand. It's sticky from the glue.

"I'm just . . . I don't know . . . I'm going to miss you, is all."

"I'm not going anywhere," I say.

"No," she says, turning to me. "I am."

All the pictures on the wall gasp. "What? Where?"

"For the summer. To D.C. Momma got some job teaching and Poppa wants me to, you know, learn more about the movement and all that jazz. I've been meaning to tell you, but—"

"Oh . . ." I don't know what else to say, so all I say is, "Oh . . ." again.

"I know."

"Really?"

"Yeah."

"Oh."

No. This cannot be happening. I haven't spent a summer without Starla since IT happened. I'm getting dizzy. The world tornadoes around us while we sit with our hands glued together in the middle. I close my eyes.

"You okay?" she asks, wiping my tears. Didn't even know I was crying.

"Of course," I say, mustering the fakest smile I can. I will not let her see. "I'm happy for you. Just gonna . . . miss you . . . you know . . ."

She lifts my chin. "Look, I know it's crazy, but I talked it over with my parents, and Momma says you could come with us if you want— wouldn't that just be everything?"

"Oh . . . yeah . . ."

"We're leaving the day after school gets out. That way, we're always together, and you'll be so sick of me by the end of summer you'll be *dying* to get back here." We laugh. Sort of. "Anyway, it would do you good to get out of this square little town, Jonny . . . see new things . . . meet new people . . . you know . . ."

"Mm-hmm . . ." I know she's still talking, but I can't hear. My brain's paralyzed. *She's right. I've never left the confines of Creve Coeur, but I've always dreamed of it: hitching a ride to California to be a rock-n-roll star. But I can't. Not now. Not until I'm forever fixed. How am I going to do this without her?*

". . . and we can camp out at the National Mall with all those Vietnam protesters. Maybe actually do something about that stupid, good-for-nothing war, you know? Come on, I don't want to do it alone. We'd have so much fun. Please say yes." She smiles: a tug-of-war smile. Because she knows.

"My dad would never let me, Starla. I'm only sixteen and—"

"You'll be seventeen in a few weeks! Poppa said he'd talk to him if you—"

"And I still have my treatments."

"Oh . . . right . . ." she whispers.

"You know I can't miss those." She shrugs. "I'm going to be fine, okay? Like you said, it's just a couple months. And anyway, you *have* to go so you can finally scream at Nixon like you've been wanting to. For both of us." I blot her tears. "Don't worry, okay?" I say this more to myself than her. I have one more set of treatments left, but I've never survived them without Starla around . . . I've never survived *anything* without Starla around . . .

"Yeah, okay," she says.

We sit in silence. It sounds like the world's crackling to pieces, falling down all around me, until I realize the record's ended and the needle's skipping.

"Come on," I say. "Let's go to church." I click the player off and turn the volume up on the TV.

We watch the *Soul Train* line.

Bobby Womack sings some funky version of "Fly Me to the Moon."

We hold hands the entire time.

I can't decide which one of us is afraid to let go.

That night, I'm in bed. Can't sleep. The full moon ripples through the cottonwood tree outside my window, casting little disco ball dots on my walls.

The flip clock on my nightstand says 3:13.

My body trembles. Like it's sinking in a bath filled with ice, but every nerve's afire. Radioactive. Had that dream again: Dr. Evelyn's whistling Bowie's "Life on Mars?" Smiling. Painted just like him, with that aquamarine eye shadow and thick pink slabs of chalk on her cheeks. I sit, propped up in a wooden chair. She straps me down. Wraps leather cuffs around my wrists. Buckles them. Tight. Then my thighs. Electric wires, coiled to a machine on the table in front of me, squirm out of each cuff.

She smiles, still whistling.

Cushioned headphones sink over my ears, muting the world. I see her lips move, but hear nothing. She walks out, taking the light with her. I'm sailing through space. Alone. Waiting. The slide projector finally buzzes on. Blinding me. Pictures begin whirling by, until—

An electric volt swims through the wires, singeing my thighs, my wrists, my heart. Round and round the projector goes. Frying my thoughts to oblivion—

That's when I wake up.

Except, I don't. Not really.

Dr. Evelyn says, *"Secrets feed the sickness,"* and I'm not supposed to keep them anymore to help me with mine, so . . . *DUN DUN DUNNNN* . . . First Secret: I am sick, those are my treatments, and this is how I'm being fixed.

So far, I think it's working. I really do. It better be. Or I'll end up like my uncle, in one of those padded rooms in the nuthouse, lost forever . . .

I grab the *Aladdin Sane* album from my desk—Ziggy's latest, the white one with a fire-red flash zapping his face. The *Mona Lisa* of rock. Iconic.

"You around?" I whisper.

He lifts his eyes, smiles. "Hey, my little Starman," he says. "Look at you, you beautiful boy, my super-duper rock-n-roll alligator."

"I'm scared," I say. "I can't do it, Zig. I can't do this alone . . ."

"Hey now, hey now . . . You're going to be okay. You just gotta see beyond all this here, believe in who you really are out there in the stars. I do, baby."

I nod, wipe the tears stinging my eyes.

"Come on," he says. *"Let's boogie . . ."*

And for the first time in a long time,

I pray.

Acknowledgments

This book is about finding the courage to allow your true being to shine, even among the most impossible of odds. And this story would have never found its North Star without these fearless constellations to light my way:

To Barbara Poelle, agent and bestie, for *never giving up and never giving in* on me. And to Stacey Barney, an editor I feel so lucky to call friend, who continues to see the truth in my storytelling (and me) even when I can't. Thank you both for your wisdom, patience, and compassion. This book would literally not exist without these two beautiful beings in my life.

To Stephanie Dees for her infinite encouragement (and copious notes, both for the story and my soul), to Steve Susoyev for inspiring the narrative's origin and for the sea of research books he delivered to my doorstep during the pandemic when going to the library was impossible, and to Lawrence Kulig for sharing his wisdom and heart-felt stories from his "fabulously gay" life spanning five decades in San Francisco, thank you. To the GLBT Historical Society in San Francisco for allowing me to spend endless hours digging through the archives to find this story, and to Isaac Fellman in particular (who it seems may be the subconscious inspiration behind the naming of Fig's character!) for his patience in helping me along the way. To Mey Rude for authenticity reading and her kind—and deeply thoughtful—affirmation, as well as Charley Miller for her beautiful and informative podcast, *Changes in Latitudes*. And to Susan Stryker for her fortitude, for unearthing this book's explored moment in history, and for helping me cross the finish line with her further books and personal outreach.

To the Penguin family, who once again championed every aspect of this book: Theresa Evangelista, the brilliant art director for the cover, who never ceases to amaze, as well as Tomasz Mro for once again creating the stunning cover artwork. To Diane João, Bethany Bryan, and Cindy Howle for their careful copyediting and Caitlin Tutterow for her tireless commitment to us all. To Lizzie Goodell for being the publicist extraordinaire. And to the many names and faces I'll never know behind the scenes who make it all look so easy, I thank you.

To my mom and dad for their unmatchable kindness and wisdom, and for never allowing me to say no to myself.

To my biological father, who shall always remain a mystery to me, thank you for being my greatest teacher. To Ernie for embodying the purest essence of unconditional love to me.

And to you, dear reader, for inspiring me to keep going. Since *Ziggy, Stardust & Me* debuted in 2019, I've had the great privilege to hear from some of the most amazing humans across the planet. Thank you for sharing your stories, your truths, your heartaches and joys, and most of all your passions, compassion, and love with me. You give me hope. You are the reason I continue to write. You are the reason I've been able to step deeper into my own being. Thank you.